THE BEAUTIFUL MADDENING

Also by Shea Ernshaw

The Wicked Deep
Winterwood
A Wilderness of Stars

THE BEAUTIFUL MADDENING

SHEA ERNSHAW

SIMON & SCHUSTER BFYR

NEW YORK   AMSTERDAM/ANTWERP   LONDON
TORONTO   SYDNEY/MELBOURNE   NEW DELHI

SIMON & SCHUSTER BFYR

An imprint of Simon & Schuster Children's Publishing Division
1230 Avenue of the Americas, New York, New York 10020
For more than 100 years, Simon & Schuster has championed authors and the stories they create. By respecting the copyright of an author's intellectual property, you enable Simon & Schuster and the author to continue publishing exceptional books for years to come. We thank you for supporting the author's copyright by purchasing an authorized edition of this book.
No amount of this book may be reproduced or stored in any format, nor may it be uploaded to any website, database, language-learning model, or other repository, retrieval, or artificial intelligence system without express permission. All rights reserved. Inquiries may be directed to Simon & Schuster, 1230 Avenue of the Americas, New York, NY 10020 or permissions@simonandschuster.com.
This book is a work of fiction. Any references to historical events, real people, or real places are used fictitiously. Other names, characters, places, and events are products of the author's imagination, and any resemblance to actual events or places or persons, living or dead, is entirely coincidental.
Text © 2025 by Shea Ernshaw
Jacket illustration © 2025 by Jim Tierney
Jacket design by Sarah Creech
All rights reserved, including the right of reproduction in whole or in part in any form.
SIMON & SCHUSTER BOOKS FOR YOUNG READERS
and related marks are trademarks of Simon & Schuster, LLC.
For information about special discounts for bulk purchases, please contact Simon & Schuster Special Sales at 1-866-506-1949 or business@simonandschuster.com.
Simon & Schuster strongly believes in freedom of expression and stands against censorship in all its forms. For more information, visit BooksBelong.com.
The Simon & Schuster Speakers Bureau can bring authors to your live event. For more information or to book an event, contact the Simon & Schuster Speakers Bureau at 1-866-248-3049 or visit our website at www.simonspeakers.com.
Interior design by Hilary Zarycky
The text for this book was set in Adobe Garamond.
Manufactured in the United States of America
First Edition
2 4 6 8 10 9 7 5 3 1
Library of Congress Cataloging-in-Publication Data
Names: Ernshaw, Shea, author.
Title: The beautiful maddening / Shea Ernshaw.
Description: New York : S&S Books for Young Readers, 2025. |
Audience term: Teenagers | Audience: Ages 14+ |
Summary: Seventeen-year-old Lark lives in a decaying family home where white petals cause the locals to fall in love with anyone who bears the Goode last name, but when she meets a boy who seems unaffected by the family curse, she finds herself falling into a feeling she has spent her life trying to avoid.
Identifiers: LCCN 2024031519 | ISBN 9781665900270 (hardcover) | ISBN 9781665900294 (ebook)
Subjects: CYAC: Fantasy. | Love—Fiction. | Magic—Fiction. | Blessing and cursing—Fiction. | LCGFT: Fantasy fiction. | Novels.
Classification: LCC PZ7.1.E755 Be 2025 | DDC [Fic]—dc23
LC record available at https://lccn.loc.gov/2024031519

For my grandmothers

PROLOGUE

Locals say the dirt in Cutwater isn't good for farming. Too swampy, too clotted with clay, too much rain in the fall and not enough in the spring. But behind our house the tulips break through the mud, fearless, staking their claim in the terrible soil.

They are night bloomers.

Tiny green sprouts twirling upward in wild, broken rows beneath a star-crusted sky. Full of promise.

But after a time, when the smooth, silky heads begin to unfurl under the dusky light of a spring moon, the blooms reveal their truest, darkest nature.

The white petals are marred.

Imperfect.

Cut through as if by a villain's bone-sharpened blade.

Crimson streaks run down each delicate, buttery petal, as dark and gruesome as blood freshly broken from young veins.

Mrs. Thierry, who lives half a mile down the dusty, rutted lane, calls it a curse. Some peculiar poison in the land. Others say it's a result of the graveyard whose headstones once dotted the meadow behind our house, bodies rotting beneath the earth, ancient blood leaching up into the tulips. A reminder of what lies below.

Whatever the cause, these rare tulips have darkened my family for generations. For it's not only the tulips that others find strange. . . . It's *us*.

The Goodes are a family to be avoided. The odd and unordinary. The ones who speak in riddles before we can even walk, who prefer night over day, who drink sunrises and sleep in a drafty, cobwebbed attic. Or so the locals like to say. Most of it isn't true.

Far from it.

But still, they steer clear of us, of the teetering house where we live, built—foolishly—over Forsaken Creek. Glacier water rushes beneath the floorboards at all hours, even while we sleep—our dreams are saturated with the sound of it—the current threatening to carry the old, rotted house away into the elm woods, into the soft, grassy valleys at the lower end of the state. *Good riddance,* most would say. Because the Goode family is anything but *good*.

When I was young, I used to believe it was the creek that split us apart, made our family wild and feral and heedless. But it's the tulips that make us go mad.

The tulips . . . that will destroy us all in the end.

ONE

Their eyes stab my flesh, the back of my skull, watching as I rise from my seat at the front of the bus and escape out into the cool spring air, drawing it into my lungs.

They fear me. *They should.*

I don't turn. I don't glance back at the faces of my Cutwater High classmates, gaping out at me through the dirty square windows of the school bus, relief in their eyes, glad to be rid of me. *Poor Lark Goode,* they think, eyes skipping past me to the awful, slack-roofed little house at the end of the driveway. The only house on this sad stretch of backwoods road that sits half-perched on wooden stilts to keep the wet, swampy ground from swallowing it up. To keep the creek from spilling through the floorboards. *Poor cursed Lark, who has to wake up in that shithole house each morning and return to it every day after school.* With no way out. No other option. A life handed to her by fate—cruel and snickering, with fingers crossed behind a back.

The bus spews out black smoke, sputtering on up the road—taking their awful glaring eyes with it. I know their pity is fleeting, because it's mostly fear that occupies their small minds. A wariness of getting too close. *Lark Goode will snatch out your heart and bury it in the garden behind her house.* If only that were true. If only I could.

I slide the headphones down around my neck, pressing stop on the ancient Walkman—Cyndi Lauper's "All through the Night" ceasing to vibrate in my ears. The Walkman belonged to my mom when she was a teenager. The stack of cassette tapes beside my bed was hers too. But the clunky Walkman isn't a token of my retro coolness, it's just the only option I have. It's one of the few things Mom left behind the day she dragged her suitcase out the front door, the broken wheels thumping down each step, while the early-morning sun speared through the elm trees beside the driveway, making her dark hair glisten like raven feathers.

She never looked back.

Not once.

I yank open the tiny metal door of the mailbox—overstuffed, *always*—letters spilling out. Lipstick marks crisscross the envelopes, pastel hearts sketched with marker and eye pencil beside the address, 114 Swamp Wells Road, followed by tiny sunflowers and daisies trailing up from the *o*'s and the *s*'s. As if these symbols were a part of our address—the post office unable to deliver our mail unless these hieroglyphs of love have been properly accounted for. *Unable to deliver as addressed; more hearts required.*

I scoop up the fallen letters, irritated—Archer didn't even bother to get the mail—and I make the long march up our driveway, stepping wide over the cold creek that cuts in front of our slanted porch. I wrestle with the front door—always stuck, always hanging wrongly from its hinges—and finally push inside. "You got more letters," I shout to Archer, tossing the envelopes onto the kitchen table, knowing tomorrow there'll be even more. And more the day after that,

The Beautiful Maddening

jammed into our mailbox until the postman has to leave a stack in the dirt, neatly tied with string.

Archer is perched against the kitchen counter, spooning a mouthful of sugared cereal into his mouth. He smiles crookedly, impishly. "It'll only get worse," he answers, still chewing. "Did you see the garden?"

Dropping my canvas bag onto the wood floor—damp from the creek roaring below, moisture stuck to everything—I move past him to the sink, fill a glass with cold water, then down the whole thing. The bus ride home is always too warm, humid and thick, the windows all stuck shut, so we sweat and breathe in fumes and one another's teenage stench, arriving home like animals sent to market. "Haven't noticed," I lie, because in truth, I can see the whole god-awful garden from my back bedroom window. I wake to it each morning, the sea of green stalks teetering in the sharp morning air. Taunting me, cloying and malevolent.

Archer chews loudly, noisily—on purpose, just to annoy me—then drops his empty bowl into the sink, spoon clanking against the drain. Our kitchen cupboards are poorly stocked with boxed cereal, dried rice, canned beans, and a few jars of peanut butter. A sad assortment. Dad sends us grocery money from time to time, he pays the utility bills online—thankfully—but it rarely seems like enough. If it weren't for Archer's flirting, for the jars of homemade jam, baked strawberry pies, dusted sugar cookies, and casseroles that adoring girls leave on our front porch for him, we'd never have a proper meal.

"End of May, just like clockwork," he adds, walking to the screen door at the back of the house and resting a hand against the doorframe, the wind stirring his black T-shirt and his dark hair.

My twin is comfortable in his own skin, cool and calm, a sanguine ease in every move he makes—a nonchalance that came easy to him right after birth. While I have tiptoed carefully around in my skin, certain I was born in the wrong house, in the wrong town, in a place meant for someone else.

My self-assured brother has never once stumbled, never woken with hair that wasn't perfectly tousled or with clothes that were damp and wrinkled. He strides through town with his wicked, cloying smile that can charm the skirt off any girl or boy who has the unfortunate luck to happen across his path, never again able to look away. He is a twin that casts a shadow, long and lean, a shadow that's nearly impossible to crawl out from under.

But to be honest, I like it in the dark. In the shade of invisibility.

Because I've felt the opposite: the madness that comes from standing in the light. The way others contort themselves to be closer to a Goode. Then run screaming when the seasons change.

It's safer in the dark. And that's where I'll stay.

"You missed school again," I point out, uncoiling my hair from its braid, letting the auburn waves spill down my shoulders and using my fingers to work out the spiderweb knots.

"Like I said"—he nods through the screen door at the garden beyond—"they're almost in bloom."

I stand beside my brother, gazing out at the acre of dark, ruddy soil. He's right: the tall green shoots—wide leaves peeled open, with closed buds shaped like teardrops—will soon crack apart and reveal their strange, unnatural petals to the sky. Scarlet and vermilion, like dark red wine. Like blood. Like a sacrifice.

This season's crop . . . is about to bloom.

The Beautiful Maddening

"You should stay home too," he adds, gray eyes cutting over me as he pulls the blue guitar pick from his pocket and flips it easily through his fingers. He claims that it's his lucky guitar pick. But luck in this family doesn't come from guitar picks. Our fate is determined by that acre of flowers. "No point going to school now. You'll only make it harder on yourself."

My throat tightens. The afternoon breeze rolls throughs the garden of tulips, their weighted heads like babies unable to hold up their own skulls, as if they're a little drunk—chugged too many beers at one of Roy Potts's infamous lakefront-cabin parties during midsummer. "There's only a week left," I answer, holding strong to the promise I make to myself every year: *Stick it out, suffer through these last few days before summer break.* Finish school, graduate this year, because even if I can't afford college, at least I'll have something. A high school diploma. At least I won't repeat the same mistakes my mother made: dropping out when she was only seventeen. Pregnant and alone.

Archer shrugs, raising a perfectly framed eyebrow, then walks to the kitchen table to rip open one of the letters. "Soon enough you'll be getting as much mail as me."

"I don't encourage it like you do."

He flashes me a smug look, the guitar pick now perched between his lips. "It's more fun this way. Might as well use our fate for something."

I feel my teeth clamp together, hating the self-satisfied way he brushes everything off like it's nothing at all, like our lives aren't some cruel, inescapable joke. In a few days' time, late one night, the tulips will break open, unfurling their rare, curse-ridden petals toward the stars. But Archer's never cared what any of it means, he only cares what it *does*—the side effect bestowed on him.

On both of us.

Because when the tulips finally bloom, love and madness knot themselves together, and *your* heart is no longer your own. It belongs to us. To the Goode family.

The sun rises into a gray, rain-weighted sky—the tulips still not yet bloomed—and I board the bus to Cutwater High while Archer sleeps in. He's no longer interested in attending the last week of our senior year.

I sit at the back of the bus, headphones on, listening to the Counting Crows *August and Everything After* album, imagining Mom playing this same cassette, on this same ride to the same awful school. Lives repeated.

Inescapable.

Destined.

I feel the eyes of Abby Reece, seated across the aisle, skip over me once, twice, until the bus stops to pick up Mia Churchill, and Abby bolts from her seat and moves three seats away, unwilling to take the risk any longer.

To live in the town of Cutwater is to know countless stories about the Goodes—fables of heartbreak and madness and desire.

But to understand the truth of our past, one must go back to the middle. Because the beginning is too far away and too troublesome, wrought with lies and riddles that I've still never quite picked apart. Lies are that way: sticky, honeylike, melted into the truth until it's impossible to know the sweet from the sour.

The Beautiful Maddening

Our birth—Archer's and mine—was an inconsequential one. Trivial, at least according to our father, who paced the tulip rows unfettered by the event, while our mother bent her face to her chest with the pain of labor yet never made a sound—according to the two attending midwives whose names have never been told to us. What was also never told to us was the timing of our births: who was born first, Archer or me. We were told only that we came into that damp, rotted house sometime after midnight but before the sun rose. And that in the custom of all Goode family births, it happened in spring, just as the tulips began to bloom. As though the awakening of the blossoms had stirred our mother's womb, calling us out. *A curse awaits you, it's time to be born.*

But a curse is only known as such depending on the affliction. And to some, what we suffer might be seen as a gift, handed up from the soil each spring. A birthday always marked the same way: warm easterly winds through the elm trees and a tide of sweet floral scents carried through the windows.

At the onset of tulip season, when the garden breaks open with their snow-white blooms—a slash of color through each petal—desire and desperation, love and lust, are not far behind.

The bus idles to a stop in front of the school, and I find myself striding down the hall to first period, my classmates parting around me as if I were a death ship sailing through a black sea. They press themselves up against their lockers and duck into bathrooms. They know madness season is close. But some watch me with renewed, even if hesitant, curiosity. They look at me as if I were a flower breaking through my old skin.

A girl who they suddenly can't turn their eyes away from—for reasons they don't entirely understand.

Shea Ernshaw

By lunchtime, spring rain gives way to opal-blue skies, and I sit alone—far away from the others—in the grass near the high school parking lot, under one of the sagging elm trees, listening to "Love-fool," by the Cardigans—a silly bubblegum song about a girl begging a boy to "leave me, leave me, just say that you need me." I let it play while I eat my flattened peanut-butter-and-grape-jelly sandwich. Wiping the crumbs from my lap, I flip open my notebook and press the sharpened pencil to a fresh, blank page.

I scan the lawn, dotted with my classmates, their faces bent toward cell phones while their mouths lazily chew their food, most looking a little frayed—that anxious excitement layered with exhaustion from a school year that's almost over. Only four days left until summer break. And you can feel the cracking edges, the parts of us that are ready to break.

Across the newly cut grass, Jude—a short, bony kid with coils of light blond hair and pale, close-set eyes—wanders through the sea of Cutwater High students. In his left hand he holds a chatterbox: a paper origami fortune teller, folded at the corners. He makes a new one every morning in first period, doodling on the outer corners in elaborate floral patterns with black ink. On the inside he sketches either numbers or words, like "ochre," "azure," "periwinkle." And beneath the corner flaps are hidden fortunes. Little glimpses into your future that Jude writes himself.

Fate revealed on lined notebook paper.

I watch as he kneels down beside a group of freckle-faced girls from band class, flutes and harmonicas and trombones resting in their shiny black cases beside them. A girl named Clementine hands Jude something, and he takes it in his palm before sliding it into his

The Beautiful Maddening

pocket. He dispenses fortunes only in *trade* for something—they are never free. A stick of gum, a pretty piece of agate, a ride home after school, a song played on a guitar. I can't see what Clementine gave him, but he never takes money, only a trade. "The barter system was the fairest form of economy," he once proclaimed in fourth-period history class. He holds out the paper chatterbox for Clementine to select a number or word, then he opens and closes the origami to reveal her fortune.

Her cheeks turn pink, eyes watery and bright as she listens to him recite her fate. I can't hear a word of it over the Cardigans singing in my ears. So I drop my eyes back to the notebook, my pencil carving out the slope of his cheekbones and a flat, pinched mouth. I wasn't sure who I'd sketch today, but the coils of hair begin to form from the scalp, and I see Jude take shape from the end of my pencil, small eyes set into his soft face. As I shade in his hands, the chatterbox held delicately in his fingertips, my eyes lift to see that Jude has stood up from the group of girls. His gaze sways over the front lawn of Cutwater High, seeking the next person in need of a fortune, but when his eyes catch on mine—only briefly—he snaps his head away and starts toward the small, grassy hill at the east edge of the school. He's never read my fortune. It's not worth the risk. Like everyone else at school, he keeps his distance.

No eye contact, no straying looks.

I'm too dangerous.

But I keep my distance from them, too. When you risk madness laced in love every spring, you can't risk friends. The few friendships I've made never lasted: a girl in fourth grade with black hair and clear-framed glasses who always chewed gum when she talked. We'd spend weekends at my house and mornings chatting on the bus, until the spring of fifth grade, when she began looking at me as if I were air itself. As if she wouldn't survive if I didn't love her back. Freshman year, I shared a locker in the south hall with a boy in my biology class who seemed unaffected by the pollen scent of my skin. For a time, I thought we'd stay friends until we graduated. But then three days before summer break, we stood at our locker and he lifted a finger, tracing a line of yellow sunlight—from a nearby window—across my cheekbone down to my chin. And I could see it in his swimming eyes, in the curious, soft flutter of his bottom lip—I knew it even before he did. He had fallen in love, just like that, snap your fingers and it's tulip season.

Blink your eyes and love has knitted beneath the bones.

"Love finds the Goode twins," I hear them hissing in the halls. Even when they don't understand why, even when they swear it won't happen to them—because what is there to love about two half-orphaned misfits whose house is sinking into the wet, swampy soil? Two twins who, without logic or reason, smell like the wind, like a perfume spun from ancient magic.

So most stay away . . . from *me*, anyway. I sit at the far back of every class, near a window, where the fresh air dulls the heady scent of spring flowers on my skin. I sit alone outside at lunch. I keep myself separate. Unlike Archer, who strolls through town when he should be at school, wandering into the small music shop on the corner of Willow Street and Goose Neck Drive—the only intersection with a blinking light—where he thrums through the wall of guitars, playing a few chords. And by some lost, spell-spun magic, the girls walking by outside pause to press their fingertips to the glass win-

The Beautiful Maddening

dows, then shuffle inside the shop to watch him play. He's not even that good—he could never play in a band—but it doesn't matter. It's him they're after.

He just has to be a Goode. A boy born into a family where love comes easy.

And easy it does come. For all of us.

But it's much harder to keep it away. To rid it from the skin once someone has clawed their nails into you.

I fold my notebook closed—a notebook filled with sketches of almost everyone at school. If I can't get near them, at least I can draw them onto paper, feel some closeness in the gray lines that shade their eyes and chins and somber mouths. It's a notebook filled with the people of this town, a collection of lives pressed flat onto paper.

The Cardigans' cloying love song ends, and the next track begins: "The Great Divide."

The irony is not lost on me. So I hit the fast-forward button—the sound of the spinning cassette tape shrieking against my ears.

A few yards away, Olive Montagu blows bubbles from a blue plastic wand she holds in front of her glossy pink lips, adorning her circle of friends with delicate, floating bubbles that break against their smiling, impossibly porcelain faces. Occasionally Olive glances my way, a touch of curiosity in her blue eyes, before blowing another wave of bubbles toward Lulu Yen's phone, pointed in her direction. Olive's group of five friends take countless photos of themselves throughout the day: a camera lens documenting every application of eyeliner in the bathroom mirror, every outfit planned and choreographed so they're all color-coordinated as they stride into first period, talking to the camera as if they were talking to an audience—a delicate facade captured for the world to see. Every moment posted mere seconds after it happens. As if they're afraid of being forgotten.

But unlike Olive and her friends, I want nothing more than to be *forgotten*. A girl lost to memory. Olive blows another wave of bubbles through the tiny wand, and they're caught by the wind, spiraling through the warm air in my direction, but before the little orbs can reach me, I notice something from the corner of my vision.

I hit stop on the Walkman.

Across the grass, Tobias Huaman, who was seated on the concrete steps near the main doors, stands up suddenly, blinking away the brilliant midday sun. He is tall, muscled, with dark skin and dark, striking eyes, and I watch as he begins moving toward me, a smile taking shape along his arched lips—that terrible, familiar expression.

Shit.

The tulips aren't yet in bloom, but the air that hovers around me has shifted—the promise of what's to come—and the faintest hint of tulip pollen is already dusting my flesh.

His white sneakers start to carry him across the lawn, his green raincoat unzipped—a coat he wears because Jude once told him to beware of rainy days. And at Cutwater High we believe in fate and fortunes and bad luck. But before Tobias has taken even five steps, a hand grabs his shoulder, firm and abrupt, yanking him back. His best friend, Mac Williams—all full lips and football shoulders and midnight skin—stops Tobias from going any farther.

From getting any closer to me.

The Beautiful Maddening

Several others on the lawn have paused to watch Tobias, breaths held in throats, a weighted silence suspended in the spring air.

Mac wheels Tobias around so he can no longer see me, then forces him to sit back down, crouching beside him and saying words I can't make out—as if they're in a halftime huddle and Mac is giving him an impromptu pep talk. *Get a grip, bro,* I imagine Mac muttering. *Don't be an idiot, she'll have you following her around like a puppy by the end of the day.*

And I could, if I wanted.

I could control every last one of them. I could be voted queen at prom, ice princess at winter formal, have my locker overstuffed with love notes on Valentine's Day, be swooned over and pawed at and adored like royalty. They wouldn't stand a chance.

I could have any boy or girl I wanted, just like Archer.

But instead I only want one thing: to get out of here.

I want freedom from this town and everyone in it.

Across the lawn, voices resume their muttering, a few side-glances are shot my way—but quickly; they never allow their eyes to linger for too long. For fear I'll ensnare them. I'll bewitch them like poor Tobias Huaman, who nearly stumbled closer, compelled by a feeling he didn't understand.

The bell rings, lunchtime over—third period about to start— and the horde of students begins the slow, reluctant shuffle back toward the double doors of Cutwater High.

I stuff my notebook into my backpack, then brush away the grass clippings from my pale, bare legs and the blue summer dress embroidered with forget-me-not flowers that was once my mother's—one of the few things she left behind in her closet.

15

Shea Ernshaw

She must have thought she wouldn't need it. Or it wasn't good enough to take.

Left behind: worthless and meaningless.

Just like *me*.

Just like the name she gave us: Goode. *Her* family name. Not our father's.

But I wear her things because I long for her in a marrow-deep, aching part of my chest that I wish I could scrape away. I wish I didn't miss her. I wish I didn't think of her every day.

I wish I could just fucking forget her.

I stand up, sling my bag over my shoulder, but I wait before heading toward the school. I'll be the last one to step through the doors—the last one to pass down the nearly empty halls, where only a few stragglers retrieve textbooks from lockers or hustle from bathrooms—then I'll slip into my economics class just before the final bell tolls, skirting down the edge of the room to the back, eyes on the floor, careful not to look at anyone. This is how I get through the day.

But as the last of the students swing through the doors, the noise of footsteps and murmuring voices fading into the walls of the brick building, I notice something.

Some*one* who wasn't there a moment ago.

Out in the school parking lot.

I pull my headphones off, slinging them around my neck, and blink through the midday sunlight—eyes narrowing on a boy standing in the shade of a crooked elm, long branches tilting in the breeze, not far from the weedy, overgrown soccer field. One hand is slid into his jeans pocket, the other holds a paperback book. His eyes are lidded and soft, settled on the pages like he hasn't heard the bell at all.

16

The Beautiful Maddening

I watch him a moment too long—and his eyes tip upward, finding mine. A cool, clement green. Or maybe blue. It's hard to tell at this distance. But they reflect the sunlight strangely, beautifully, as if he were some rare creature awoken from a storybook, whose eyes are meant to be seen only by the one who finds him, rescues him, who digs him up from some underground catacomb. But I don't know who he is: I've never shared a class with him or seen him in the halls or at assembly or crowding out of school at the end of the day.

Either he's new, a transplant from some faraway city, or he's a boy who doesn't go to Cutwater High.

I blink again, knowing I need to look away—if I stare too long, he'll find himself shuffling closer, pulled by some strange thread in his chest, a *need* he didn't know he had until this moment, as if caught by some indefinable longing. But before I can cast my eyes away, he turns suddenly—unaffected, *unfazed*—and strides casually out across the parking lot toward the street, the paperback book now slid into the back pocket of his jeans.

He walks away.

Away.

As if he felt no pull toward me, no sickening, undeniable enchantment swirling in his gut, no thread of need in the center of his chest. He looked Lark Goode dead in the eyes, met her stare, then walked away. As if, *as though*, he felt nothing.

An impossibility.

I swallow, feeling strangely unsteady, like my knees want to hinge, sink down to the dirt.

But the boy is already gone. A phantom, a chimera, slipped from the shadows back into the daylight.

I can hear the sounds of lovesickness as soon as I drop my bag onto the couch: the rustling fingertips, the laughter that is more *desperation* and *need* than the ease of real love. Through the back screen door I see Archer out at the edge of the garden, at the border of the woods—where he's pressed a girl up against a swaying birch tree, her hair knitted between his fingertips, kissing her neck while she giggles uncontrollably, teeth smiling up at the cloudless afternoon sky. Tulip season is almost here, and the girls are already fretting over him, besotted, bending themselves closer, hoping they catch the light, catch a Goode in the palm of their hand. Although I've always thought they'd love him even if he weren't a Goode. Even if he were a boy by another name, they'd spill into his arms like milk down a drain.

It makes me cringe, a bitter prick along my spine—that love can be so foolhardy and false, contorted by old, misunderstood magic. By a garden of tulips.

Love, I've always known, cannot be trusted.

Finally Archer slips away from the girl, flushed cheeks and lips, fingertips lingering against hers, arms reaching long, before at last they release each other, and Archer strides idly through the tulip garden toward the house, the girl following, brushing her palms down her cheeks as if she could wipe clean the dizzying lust she feels when she's near him.

She doesn't know that the garden of flowers where she walks is partly to blame for the desire she feels for my brother.

But Archer doesn't bring her up to the back porch—he knows better. Knows I'm tired of the nameless girls he brings home, then

The Beautiful Maddening

never sees again. Knows it'll start an argument between us—and starting a fight with your twin is like fighting with yourself. No one wins. Instead he walks her to the side of the house, where I can just see a sunshine-yellow bicycle leaning against the toolshed. He kisses her one last time before she pedals away up the driveway, then turns toward town. Five miles. Uphill. All to spend a few moments pressed against Archer.

I push open the screen door, and the air has that dreamy summer feel: bees humming, a woodpecker thumping against the trunk of a tree somewhere in the woods, searching for insects. The season is changing.

Archer perches himself against the porch railing, the sun in his eyes, and runs a hand through his hair. "How miserable was school?" he asks, looking lazy, casual, like James Dean in an old film poster.

But I ignore his question because I'm thinking of something else: the boy I saw at school. The one I didn't recognize but who seemed completely unaffected by me—Lark Goode, who can ensnare another with just a glance.

And yet the Goode curse is *not* a witch's spell. It doesn't force a person to love another. It's merely a little *enchantment*, a glimmer in the eyes, a hint of seduction in the lips. My classmates still have control of their own minds, their own actions. They decide what to do with the desire they feel. But most are weak, unable to resist the magnetism that stirs inside them whenever they're near a Goode.

Still, somehow, the boy at school seemed to feel none of it.

Not even a hint of fascination when he looked at me.

I shut my eyes, pushing away the memory, savoring the soft spring breeze against my cheeks.

"What will you do when we graduate?" I ask Archer, lifting my eyelids.

He stares down at the creek rushing below the house, tracking the path it makes through the center of the tulip garden before it disappears into the woods beyond, eventually joining with Rabbit Cross River and running all the way to the sea. "Doubt I'll graduate," he answers bluntly, elbows pressed against the railing. "I've missed too many classes."

"Then why bother staying in town at all?" My brother has always behaved as if his own life bored him, as if he were indifferent to the outcome. As if life weren't unfurling rapidly before us—and if we don't grab ahold of it, if we don't alter its course, we'll be doomed to the fate of every Goode who came before.

My brother grins, cheeks still flushed from the girl. "Why would I leave? I can do whatever I want in Cutwater."

He's never felt a lump-in-the-throat desperation to escape this town like I have. He'll probably live in this sorrowful, old house for the rest of his life. Maybe he'll even marry a local girl, have babies—children who will be just as ill-fated by the Goode name as we are now. Somehow he'll be satisfied to never see what waits beyond this shithole town.

I feel Archer looking at me. "You really think you're getting out of here, don't you?" he asks. I shrug, refusing to meet his eyes, and he snorts, lips curled down, holding back a laugh. "How? You don't even have money for bus fare."

I dig my thumbnail into one of the porch posts—the soft wood starting to rot, like everything else, the creek slowly taking back the house and the land.

The Beautiful Maddening

"It's not like you can get a job," he adds. "You can't scoop ice cream at the Tasty Swirl, or shelve books at the Cutwater Library, or run the cash register at Al's Hardware. All the customers will fall in love with you."

I dig my nail in deeper, making a half-moon shape in the wood, a marker that I was here—*Lark Goode lived in this awful house*. But he's right. Any job won't last. I've seen how quickly love can spiral into devotion and then obsession: I've seen the girls at school tattoo Archer's name onto their forearms and wrists; and the boy who once sang a song to Archer during an assembly our freshman year, belting out "I Will Always Love You" in front of the whole school. But no one laughed, no one snickered at how lovesick and foolish it was. Because they all felt it too—a strange yearning to be near Archer. *To me.*

"If you just used our talent, instead of hiding from it, you'd have everything you want."

"It's stealing," I say, dropping my hand from the post.

"It's not stealing when they hand it over."

"They don't realize what they're doing. They're delirious." I raise my eyebrows at him. "Remember Maisie Lee?"

Archer smiles so wide, his eyes gleam, the memory flicking through him. "She was a *little* delirious," he admits. "But I only winked at her."

"During tulip season," I point out.

Maisie Lee *used* to work at the Square Mart gas station. Her father owned it—owns it still—but last summer Archer convinced her to sell him a six-pack of beer, and instead of making him pay for it, she gave him all the cash in the register. Over $400. All because he winked at her. The next day her father stomped up to our front porch in his muddy rain boots, arms crossed, hair oily and slicked back as if he'd just been crouched beneath a car engine in the repair shop beside the gas station, and demanded all the money back. Archer handed it over, with his apologies, but swore he hadn't "stolen" it. Thankfully, Maisie's father didn't go to the local police. But Archer still manages to come home with cash in his pockets, an extra twenty-dollar bill handed back to him at the movie theater up in Favorville when he paid with a ten. Free ice cream at the Tasty Swirl by the baseball field, free soda and fries at Maple's Burger Stop. He never pays for anything.

I suspect he could even get a free bus ride out of here if he tried.

But he *wants* to stay. This small, backwoods town gives him everything he needs. He stays because of the tulips, because if he left, his charm, his magnetism, might wear off. He needs the tulips.

But our mother managed to leave—without a word, without an explanation. She slipped out the front door and strode down the driveway as if she had already forgotten about the children she was leaving behind. And after three years she hasn't so much as sent a postcard. She's good and gone. *Long gone.* Never even glances over her shoulder, gone.

"You might as well stay," Archer says, turning toward the screen door. "Nothing for us outside of Cutwater. Better just to get used to the place." He steps back into the house, screen door slamming shut, and the thud is like a brick cracking against the hope growing inside me. *Better just to get used to the place.* But I have no intention of sticking it out here.

The Beautiful Maddening

In a few days I'll graduate, and I won't die here, old and bitter beside that god-awful cursed garden of tulips.

Archer doesn't know it yet, doesn't know the plans I'm already making.

But I'm getting out of this town.

And I'm never coming back.

TWO

Headphones on—the Smashing Pumpkins howling in my ears—I stretch out on my stomach, drawing the outline of his face, the curve of his jaw, his translucent eyes like fresh grass or a blue pond. It feels like tipping into a fairy tale, losing myself in the image taking shape at the end of my pencil, as the soft evening wind carries scents of earth and faraway rain in through my open bedroom window.

Usually, I sketch only faces, but I wasn't close enough to see the small details (a freckle here, a stray hair across an eyebrow there), so I draw his shoulders, his torso, the paperback book in his hands. He leans against the elm tree, the afternoon sun speckled through the branches, slightly kissing his cheekbone, while his eyes are just barely lifted . . . meeting mine. Yet . . . he walked away after his eyes strayed over me. Grazed my flesh.

As if he felt nothing at all.

My head thumps, a tiny insect scratch at my skull. *How could he so easily turn away?* I draw him in my notebook to make sense of him. To fill in the parts I don't understand. *The boy has no name.* A stranger. And in a town this small, you know when someone new moves in. You know the names of everyone, you know how long

The Beautiful Maddening

they've lived in Cutwater and the reasons they've never left.

But this boy . . . is something new.

I pull the headphones off, needing the silence to try and bring him to mind, capture some detail I missed. But he's already starting to fade from my memory, the shadowed parts of his cheekbones becoming less distinct. The sound of the creek fills my ears—cold glacier water twisting its way down from the Middle Fork Mountains, then cutting south across Winterset Valley before turning into the lowlands and running straight under the Goode family home. But it's not the creek's fault it found itself here—caught up in the folklore and long-ago curses that haunt this house—it was my great-great-grandfather Fern Goode who built the house over the creek, who deemed it a reasonable place to make a homestead, in the lowest, swampiest soil in town.

A fool's undertaking.

But over the gurgle and rush of the creek, I hear another sound. . . .

The wind has died down, the woods fallen still, but the noise echoes softly through my bedroom window: a breaking open, like tissue paper. Like eyelashes on the surface of tepid bathwater. So gentle and quiet, it's hardly there at all.

I sit up, knowing the sound as clearly as if it were a scream from fearful lungs. I've heard it season after season, since the spring I was born. I leave the Walkman on my bed, move to the back door, and step out into the night. It's late, near midnight. But the noise is unmistakable—the heavy teardrop heads of the tulips are beginning their slow unfurling. Petals peeling open, tufts of silklike layers bending themselves back to peer up at the clear, moonless sky.

25

The tulips are finally blooming.

An effort that happens only at night, only in the dark, as if they don't want to be seen. A secretive, seductive unveiling. Like ladies peeling away their robes. Showing their pale skin to the stars.

With my heart thudding in my ears, I move down the back steps, over the churning creek, and into the garden. The wind stirs, changing direction—it begins blowing from the east. An omen. A portent. I hold in my breath, witnessing the awakening of a plague.

In this dull light, the soft blooms with their snow-white petals and garish red streaks seem innocent enough—a garden of flowers to mark the changing season. But they are not harmless. They are responsible for every bad thing that's ever happened in this family. I reach out a hand, running my fingertip over one of the newly opened petals. The stalks are unusually, *unnaturally* tall, the swaying heads of each flower grazing my shoulders—a crop that reaches the height of cornstalks some years. I draw the air tight into my lungs, each particle heavy with an intoxicating sweetness, making me dizzy, and I know what will come.

Tulip season has begun.

Madness season, most call it.

Because the locals in town don't know that the tulips are to blame. They don't know that these blooms are the source of their twisted-up desire each spring.

But from this moment on—until the tulips wilt back into the soil—locals will feel themselves inextricably, irresistibly drawn to the Goodes, to Archer and me. They will feel a nudge in our direction, a prick at the base of their necks that is nearly impossible to ignore.

The Beautiful Maddening

When the flowers crack open to reveal their inner petals, the *need* others feel for us becomes something abnormal.

A hunger.

A feral wildness that is sometimes dangerous.

A love that becomes greed.

Standing in the garden, the spring air filled with the soft perfume of their petals, I think again of my great-great-grandfather—a man who sailed across the Atlantic from the Netherlands with a small linen pouch tucked into his waistband, a dozen tulip bulbs hidden inside. *Secreted away.* He claimed they were the rarest of bulbs—heirlooms saved from the infamous tulip madness that ravaged Holland in the 1630s. But when Mom told the story, she said he likely stole the tulips, killed a man—a royal gardener—who kept the bulbs in a dark, dry basement. Stolen or bartered, the bulbs contained a madness that made people crave them—*a delirium of love and devotion.* And when he planted the bulbs into this swampy soil, he hoped to make his fortune: he would sell the flowers, be adored and revered, admired from one county line to the other. But instead locals in Cutwater feared my great-great-grandfather. They thought it ill-conceived to build a house over Forsaken Creek, in the marshy lowlands. "No rational person would build their home so carelessly," they whispered. And that first spring, when the tulips bloomed, showing their lurid white petals cut through with scarlet veins, the locals called it a curse and refused to buy a single bloom.

In time the tulips spread, the small garden became a sea of blooms, and some in town found themselves drawn to Fern Goode for reasons they couldn't make sense of—they fell in love with him every spring, like clockwork. And when he had three sons—who grew to be as tall and broad as Norwegian spruce trees—love befell them just as easily. A wild, feverish kind of love. And with each generation, with each Goode who was born into the house, the madness-invoked love became more deeply woven, more troublesome, the blooms braiding themselves into the blood and bones of every Goode.

Inescapable.

I drop my hand from the petal and turn on my heel.

When I was younger, I thought the tulips beautiful, enchanted, but now I hate them. Now I wish I were a girl with a different last name. Any name that wasn't Goode.

Inside the house, I close my bedroom window—so the scent of flowers won't saturate my room—then I sink beneath the sheets, pulling a pillow over my head. I don't want to hear the soft splitting-open of tulips.

I don't want the reminder of who I am. The fate I can't escape.

Tomorrow madness season begins.

The morning sun bursts into the sky above the treetops, and the air inside the bus is already stifling, boxed in. I can feel the eyes of everyone watching me as I walk down the aisle to the last row of bench seats—a strained stillness in the air, breaths held tightly in lungs, the heartbeats of my classmates racing a little too quickly in their chests. I turn the volume up on my Walkman, Lauryn Hill vibrating through my eardrums.

Still, those seated nearest me can't help but flick their eyes in my direction, once, twice, too many times. They feel a longing for anyone with the Goode last name, more persistent than it was yesterday.

The Beautiful Maddening

Lark Goode smells different today, I imagine them thinking, a notion they try to shake but can't. *She looks more . . . like a girl I could fall in love with.*

The microscopic pheromones contained in each bloom are now saturating my skin. Caught in my lungs. Leaving a cloud in my wake.

Like bloodthirsty dogs, they sense it.

Predatory and lovesick.

When the bus finally shrieks to a stop in front of the school, I can't exit fast enough, scrambling down the steps and nearly tripping over my own feet. I glance to the tall elm tree beside the parking lot, looking for the boy. I need to see him one more time, capture the last details of his face so I can finish the sketch. But it's more than that: there is also a curiosity inside me—I want to *know*, to see—can he look at me again and feel nothing, no strained urge to move closer? What if I walk toward him, will he still be able to turn his head and stride away so easily?

I doubt it. Not with the tulips now in bloom.

But across the parking lot there is no boy beneath the elm tree.

No sign of him.

I keep my head down, moving across the lawn, through the school doors, until I reach my locker in B hall—near the gymnasium, the stench of sweat and sneakers and Clorox clinging to the walls. I shove my bag into the metal rectangle, then grab my *History of the World* textbook for first period.

I turn the volume up on my Walkman, Lauryn Hill singing about the nature of all things: "Everything is everything; what is meant to be, will be." My eyes are on the linoleum floor when I round the corner into the main hall, and I'm stopped short.

Shea Ernshaw

A crowd has gathered outside the doors into the lunchroom, near the drinking fountain that no longer works and the hand-drawn poster for Astronomy Club—WHO NEEDS MATH WHEN YOU CAN COUNT THE STARS, it reads in chunky black Sharpie.

I can't make out who's at the center of the crowd, or what's happening, but I can hear the hum of activity through my headphones. Someone shouts, followed by a rush of voices, and I slip my headphones down around my neck, inching closer to the commotion—careful not to touch anyone, to meet anyone's eyes. I slide along the row of metal lockers until I can finally stand on tiptoes, peering between two freshmen, to see Tobias Huaman—tall, broad-shouldered—facing his best friend, Mac Williams. Yesterday Mac stopped Tobias from moving toward me during lunch, from getting pulled in by the fabled Goode enchantment, but now they look like they're about to fight—fists clenching, chests puffed, eyes willful and angry and narrowed.

"You already have a girlfriend!" Mac spits, lifting his chin.

"So do you," Tobias barks back, taking a large step closer to Mac.

The crowd seems to press in around them, trying to get a better view before the first punch is thrown—a stupor of nervous excitement in the air. They love a good fight, especially between two of the most well-known guys in school, who only yesterday were best friends.

But clearly something has changed.

"You've always been an asshole," Mac counters, and he shoves a hand against Tobias's sturdy chest.

Someone makes a soft squeal, a tiny shriek, and my eyes swivel—finding the source of the sound. Clementine Morris, who yesterday

The Beautiful Maddening

had her fortune read by Jude on the front lawn. Now she stands with her black flute case in her left hand, only a couple of feet away from the two boys about to tackle each other. Her dull brown hair drapes long and flat over her shoulders, a few knots visible at the front, and her soft hazel eyes possess a curious glint. I think of how pretty she is—the kind of girl who will probably thrive in the outside world, in the *real* world. She'll become a famous musician or invent a cure for an old disease. And everyone who attended Cutwater High the year she graduated will try to remember who she was but won't be able to. Because right now, in the social ladder of high school, only the loud and glittery survive. Here she is unmemorable.

I scan the crowd, trying to understand what's happening.

Tobias tries to take a step around Mac, a step toward . . . Clementine?

She looks briefly stunned, a little unsteady on her feet, but also . . . something else. A subtle twitch of delight pulls at her upper lip.

I feel my mouth tug down, and I catch the faces of those nearest me contorting in the same confused way. Tobias lifts his arm, but not toward Mac, not in a gesture of anger; he lifts it toward Clementine. He reaches for her—softly, caringly—and she touches his hand in return, a coy smile arching her pinked lips, freckled cheeks blushing instantly.

She's enjoying this.

I hear a gasp from the crowd. The air sucked out of the crammed hallway all at once. I swing my gaze again, as does everyone else—as if we're watching some Shakespearean play unfold before us, and each new development is more unbelievable than the last—and we find

Shea Ernshaw

Olive Montagu with a hand to her mouth, eyes wide and stunned, like a fish left to die on the shore. I can see her throat trembling, soft blond hair tucked back behind her ears, blue eyes welling quickly with tears.

Olive is Tobias's girlfriend.

Since freshman year.

And now she watches as he folds his fingers through the hand of another girl: Clementine Morris . . . who is surely the last person Olive would have imagined stealing her high school boyfriend. Shy, demure, unassuming Clementine has never been a threat.

Until today.

But Tobias touches Clementine only for a moment before Mac barrels into him, slamming his chest with both hands and shoving him back. The crowd gasps, and someone yells—I think it's Olive. And in an instant Tobias and Mac are in a full brawl. A punch is thrown, countered by another. Tobias knocks Mac to the ground and kicks him in the gut. But then Mac is up, ramming him into a row of lockers with a loud, vibrating thud. The crowd moves back, away, not wanting to get caught in the tussle. But before Tobias can land another blow against Mac's ribs, there is a loud, commanding shout from down the hall, then another. Coach Lopez shoves his way through the crowd and yanks Mac away from Tobias, bracing him around the chest to keep him from lunging forward again.

Principal Lee appears, eyeglasses slid down his narrow nose, and he grabs Tobias. "Get to class!" he shouts as he ushers Tobias toward the admin office.

Coach Lopez is already pulling Mac away, up the hall and out through the double doors to the football field. Separating him from Tobias.

"I want you all in first period," Principal Lee adds. But when no one moves, he yells, "Now!"

The crowd drifts apart, scattering to their lockers and classrooms, murmuring, whispering about what just happened, and why the hell it *happened at all*. But I stay pressed to a locker that isn't mine, my thoughts shuttling back and forth.

The door into my first-period class hasn't closed yet—students are still meandering inside—and I slip through unnoticed, pass down the outer edge of the room, and sink into a seat near the back window.

But it doesn't make a difference.

My classmates murmur to one another, pass notes scribbled hastily onto torn pages of their notebooks, then glance over their shoulders to stare at me—but they don't snicker; they don't make jokes at my expense. It's another thing entirely in their expression.

Their eyes give them away, the soft lift of their mouths, the rose-stained tint of their cheeks. They're falling in love.

"Renna!" Mr. Loon barks. "Hand it over."

My gaze lifts briefly to see Mr. Loon marching down the row of desks, stopping beside Renna McPhee's chair and holding out his hand.

"Now," he instructs.

Renna rolls her eyes and places a small piece of paper in Mr. Loon's hand. But when Mr. Loon walks back to the front of the room, I can tell that the thing in his hand has more weight and substance, not paper at all, but I can't make it out. Not fully.

He opens a drawer in his desk and drops the thing inside: just one of many worthless items he confiscates throughout the day. But before he pushes the drawer closed, his eyes stall a moment, staring down into the drawer, and a strange expression curls at the edge of his mouth—disgust, maybe? Something else? Eyes watering.

Someone giggles from the front row, the whole class watching him, and his eyes snap back up as he shuts the drawer quickly. Clearing his throat, he begins his lesson on the fall of Rome, and I keep my head down until the bell finally rings. I bolt up from my chair, desperate to be free of this room, and dart for the door.

But Titha Roberts is there, holding the door open for me, her lovely black hair braided perfectly across her scalp, draped over one shoulder, full lips parted into a gentle, one-sided smile. "You look pretty today, Lark," she says, peering at me with her deep brown eyes. Titha Roberts is one of the elite at Cutwater High—she's captain of varsity volleyball, she's dated every quarterback on our football team, and she's president of the school's Theater Club. And *I* am not someone she'd normally hold a door for. Or waste her time talking to—during any other season.

I slip through the doorway into the hall without meeting her eyes, without saying a word. Because I know she doesn't mean it: I know it's the scent of fresh flowers on my skin that confuses her thoughts, beckons her close.

In the hall, Randy Ashspring is waiting a few paces ahead of me, and he holds a hand toward me. "I can carry your books for you, if you want?" His eyes are all doughy and strange, and I shake my head

The Beautiful Maddening

at him, turning sharply toward the bathrooms located on the far side of the hallway.

"Hey, Lark!" a voice says to my left. I barely glance in its direction and see Cole Campbell smiling at me, his charming soccer-star grin enough to make me slow my pace. Cole plays on a state team—since Cutwater High doesn't have a soccer club—and his shaggy blond hair sways into his eyes as he moves toward me. "I was wondering if you're doing anything after school?" The left side of his mouth lifts, the freckles puckering along his cheeks. "I could pick you up. We could drive to Favorville, see a movie, maybe?" He pauses, like he can't believe his own words, like he can't believe he's asking Lark Goode out on a date. But still, he continues. "Or just watch the sunset from Cutwater Ridge." His eyes sway over me, lost in a dream, a heady, lovesick reverie, but I snap my gaze away—severing his stare before it gets any worse.

"Sorry, Cole," I answer quickly. "I can't." And I slip into the bathroom.

I should have told him, *Hell no*. Told him to *fuck off*. I've found that it's better to be blunt, to the point. The hard edge of rejection sometimes breaks the stupor of infatuation. Even if they still feel overcome by a dreadful sense of longing—a lovelorn sickness festering in their chest—their need to avoid embarrassment can sometimes override any future confessions of their feelings for me.

But right now I feel bad for them—I always do in the beginning—I know it's not their fault, I know their feelings aren't their own.

I lock myself in the far stall, listening to the sound of girls entering the bathroom, lingering a little too long at the sinks, their heads dizzy with a feeling they can't explain—a spirituous scent that causes a prick at the back of the neck, a desire they can't pinpoint—before finally retreating out into the halls. The bell rings for second period, but I stay right where I am.

The echo of footsteps and voices in the hall slowly fades, then falls quiet. My heart settles in my chest, a dulled, temporary feeling of calm.

My second-period class is American Lit, and I know Mrs. Garrison plans to have us sit in groups and discuss our favorite writers from the nineteenth century—Whitman and Poe, Emerson and Thoreau, John Muir and Ida B. Wells. A way to sum up our last year of studies. But I can't possibly sit in a tiny circle of my classmates, their thoughts unable to focus, their eyes unblinking.

I consider leaving the bathroom, grabbing my bag from my locker, and running home. This is exactly why Archer stays away from school once the tulips have bloomed, because it's almost unbearable. But last week Principal Lee made an announcement over the loudspeaker, warning us that anyone who missed a single day of our last week of school wouldn't graduate.

So I stay put.

I'll wait out second period, until lunch.

Headphones on, I mute the world beyond my safe hiding place and slide out my notebook from beneath my textbook, then press it against the wall of the bathroom stall. I open to the last page—*the boy*. I run my finger across his forehead, the stray pieces of his dark hair. I glide my pencil along his temple, shading in his earlobe, then falling to his chin, his mouth . . . but I don't know the exact shape of his lips. I wish I could see him again, up close, get a better sense

The Beautiful Maddening

of his eye color, the shadows made by his eyelashes, the slope of his jawline—before I lose the memory of him completely.

But I haven't seen him in the halls. He wasn't in the crowd before the bell rang—I would have noticed him. But if he doesn't go to Cutwater High, then who is he? And why was he in the parking lot yesterday, reading a book against a tree?

I fill in the parts of him I *can* remember: the broad angle of his shoulders, the paperback book in his hands, the easy way he perched against the tree trunk as if he were a million miles away, lost to the story unfolding in the pages before him. Time slinks away from me, until the bell chimes in the halls again, second period over.

I listen to the rush of students slamming their locker doors as they head for the cafeteria or the front lawn, footsteps echoing off the brick walls. When only a few voices remain, I slip silently from the bathroom and reach my locker without anyone spotting me. I retrieve my bag and push through the double doors, breathing in the crisp spring air—grateful to be free of the school.

There are fewer students scattered across the lawn than there were yesterday. Perhaps the rest have chosen to spend their lunch hour in the foul-smelling, dimly lit cafeteria—*away from me.*

But I don't make it more than a step toward the lawn before I feel a hand on my shoulder. I flinch away, my heart instantly a piston, but the figure moves even closer, forcing me back against the brick wall of the school. I blink, trying to refocus, but a face—Gabby Pines's—is suddenly right in front of me. Like she can't get close enough. Her strawberry hair is pulled up into a bun, and a piece of some unknown candy is pressed against the inside of her left cheek. "Do you have more?" she asks, tone hushed, secretive, her breath smelling of mint and watermelon.

"What?"

I'm shocked that she's this close to me. Surprised she would risk it.

"The tulips," she presses, more insistent now, eyelashes no longer blinking over her glassy blue eyes. "The ones you grow behind your house."

I take a step to my right, but she mirrors my movement, the side of her lip twitching as she shifts the candy from one cheek to the other. "They say it was the flowers all along—they're the reason people fall in love with you each spring." Her nostrils swell, like she's uncovered all my secrets—like she sees what I really am.

My heart starts thudding against my eardrums. Panic claws at my thoughts, causing everything to blur—even Gabby's face.

Locals in Cutwater have always known there is something *odd* about the Goodes. Witches or demons or monsters. But they've never understood why they fall madly in love with us as the season melts from spring into summer. They feel the enchantment to be near us, but they don't understand its origin. Its source.

But now . . . I can see the look in Gabby's eyes. Like she's figured it all out. And my head begins to pound, my fingers shaking at my sides.

"People like to tell stories . . . but it's not true," I say, but my voice is weak, unconvincing. *Shit.* I just need to get away from her, away from the others who have slowed as they walk by, eyes watching me, straining to hear Gabby's words.

"I'll buy one from you," Gabby adds, voice low as her eyes dart to the left like a bird watching for scavengers. "I have cash."

I shake my head at her, my breathing starting to tighten in my lungs. I feel caged in. Trapped.

The Beautiful Maddening

"Please . . . ," she hisses. And in her eyes I see something else, a shift: she's too close to me. She's starting to lose control of her own heart—her eyelashes flit, her mouth parts just a little—and I can see the lovesickness taking shape in the features of her face, in the strange rhythm of her breathing.

I swallow, the cold brick wall of the school against my back, and I know I need to get out of here. I turn before she can tip any closer, breaking away from her stare, and scramble down the front steps of the school.

I start across the lawn, but my eyes catch sight of something.

Some . . . *thing*.

Snow-white blooms.

White and fearful.

Awful red streaks burned across each petal, winking luridly beneath the midday sun.

I squint, certain I'm mistaken.

But the green stem is held in the hands of Mac Williams—one of the boys from the fight this morning. I'm surprised he wasn't sent home, suspended for the last few days of school. But his best friend, Tobias Huaman, is nowhere in sight.

The group of friends surrounding Mac stare down at the delicate flower, talking as if it were some rare artifact, discussing its worth, its intended use, like thickskulled anthropologists.

And I know. . . . It's undeniable.

Mac holds an infamous, whispered-about-but-never-seen-up-close *Goode* tulip.

My heart slams into my stomach. Fear roils up into my chest, like I'm going to be sick.

39

Shea Ernshaw

One of the Goode tulips is no longer safely contained within the garden.

It's here, at school, in the hands of someone who *isn't a Goode*.

The group shifts closer to the bloom, gaping down at it, huddling like they're at one of their Wednesday-night games. Blood roars against my eardrums, making all the voices around me turn watery and thick.

I start toward them, the feeling inside me burning like an electrical wire running down my spine. Mac notices me first, and he takes a quick step back, away from the circle. He's afraid of me—a girl made of rumors and fables knotted throughout my family history, a girl who might as well be death itself. When I'm close enough, I reach out and yank the tulip from his hands, sharp and swift, my eyes burning into his. And he doesn't try to stop me. He doesn't even blink, shoulders pulled back, mouth open slightly like he's afraid to speak.

"How did you get this?" I demand, my voice stronger than I expected, gripping the tulip stem in my fist. "Tell me how you got it."

He shakes his head, but no words come out.

"Did you go into our garden?"

His lower lip falls open. "I, uh—uh . . . I . . . um, it's not . . . I—" He can't find the words, confusion cut across his features—like he doesn't remember how to access his own mind. Like being this close to Lark Goode has rendered him utterly speechless.

I shake my head at him, irritated, angry, and when my eyes swing to his group of friends, they all stagger back, toward the school, as if my stare were cutting them wide open.

"If you trespass on our property again, you'll regret it," I tell him,

40

The Beautiful Maddening

the words sounding like a hex, a malediction, my eyes meeting his one last time. It's an empty threat, but he doesn't know that. And his chin nods swiftly, like *this* he understands, his brown eyes as big as a terrified puppy's.

I shove the tulip into my bag, then march across the lawn. I don't look back, but I know they're watching me, I can feel their eyes, feel the breath held in their tight throats.

And when I reach the far lawn, I don't walk to the elm tree where I normally eat my lunch. I keep going. Past the football field, through the parking lot, and out to the road.

I run all the way home.

THREE

"What the hell happened?" Archer asks as I climb the porch steps. He's seated on the porch swing, strumming our father's old guitar—the strings frayed at the ends, the wood worn thin in places. "You ditching class?"

My tongue feels heavy in my mouth. "There was a fight at school. . . ."

Archer frowns, dark hair sliding over his eyes.

"I think . . ." I suck in a breath, my heart slowing its rhythm. "It had something to do with the tulips."

He lowers the guitar in his lap. "What do you mean?"

But I move past him into the house, dropping my bag to the floor beside the kitchen table, then throw open the back door. As I stand on the porch, the tulips appear motionless, harmless, like children sitting perfectly still in an attempt to appear as if they've done nothing wrong—cookie crumbs on their cheeks and beneath their fingernails.

But I find what's wrong.

Along the east edge of the garden, a swath of white-and-bloodred blooms . . . is *gone*.

The Beautiful Maddening

A good thirty—no, forty—tulips have been snipped clean off from their stems. The green stalks now standing like tombstones, headless, lifeless.

Stolen.

A spike of fear drops into my gut.

In the dirt a few feet from the ravaged blooms sits a pair of shears—I recognize them from the toolshed. Sometime before the sun cracked above the horizon, a thief crept into the garden, yanked the shears from the nail where they usually hang against the slatted wall of the shed, and hacked away at a few dozen Goode tulips.

My temples throb.

A buzzing twists its way up from my stomach.

"Shit," Archer murmurs, standing a few paces behind me, hands on the back of his head.

We've never worried about thieves sneaking into the garden. Locals fear us—the stories of how we practice black magic, how we slice out the eyes and pull out the bones of anyone who steps foot on our land—it's enough to keep them away. Only Archer's love interests dare to visit the Goode family home and only because they are entranced by Archer's whispered words against their throats.

We've never needed a fence or a sign that reads KEEP OUT! We've never fretted about burglars or nosy neighbors wandering through the garden, plucking tulips from the soil. The legend of the Goode family has always been enough.

I move down the steps, running my fingers along several headless stalks, the delicate blooms gone. I hate the tulips, *hate* the garden, but this . . . *this* feels like a violation—like someone has cut out my own flesh.

43

"Who the hell would do this?" Archer asks.

"I think Mac . . . and probably his friends."

Archer makes a face. "Those guys couldn't tiptoe through the garden quietly if their football scholarships depended on it. You sure it was them?"

I lift a shoulder. "Mac had one at school. But I took it from him." The bloom now stuffed into my bag.

"Shit," Archer repeats. "We need to get the rest back."

The sun flashes through the clouds, making me feel dizzy. "I think it's too late for that." I remember the desperate look in Gabby Pines's eyes, begging me for a tulip. But another memory blinks into focus: Mr. Loon confiscating something in class. I wasn't sure what it was exactly—it was hidden in his palm—but now I start to wonder. The way he looked at it, the way he paused, mesmerized. And the fight in the hall, between Tobias and Mac, Clementine watching with satisfaction in her eyes. Did it all have something to do with the tulips?

And now they've surely been traded and passed around school many times. Impossible to find, to recover them all.

Archer rubs a hand across his neck. "This isn't good, Lark."

He pulls the guitar pick from his pocket and starts scraping it against the side of his jeans. A habit to calm his thoughts. "No one except a Goode has ever possessed a tulip before."

"I know."

"And we haven't even cut one from the garden in generations."

"I know," I repeat.

"We don't know what will happen."

I nod, dropping my hand from the decapitated stem.

"We should put up a fence," he says, but I'm not listening. I'm

The Beautiful Maddening

thinking of Mom, and in this moment I wish she were here. She would tell us not to worry in her cool, unaffected way. She'd breeze through the house, calm and halcyon, humming to herself—she crafted an air of ease, which Archer inherited. It's also why it was so easy for her to abandon us; her mind was always set adrift, she went where the wind tossed her. And the stolen tulips would be something she'd ignore, in hopes that the problem would solve itself.

But problems in my mom's orbit rarely solved themselves. They usually grew larger until they destroyed everyone around her.

The night before Mom left, she and I sat on the roof of the house, making wishes on falling stars. I remember the lilac smell of her skin, her hands tapping against the roof, a song always in her head, trying to get out. "I'm looking for a sign, Lark," I remember her saying. She was hoping to find something in the formation of stars, a clue about her life, her fate, her future. She was like that. Mercurial, enigmatic. The kind of woman who people had a hard time looking away from. She was a Goode, after all. Archer got all her charm. I got none.

"There's a wind in my heart," she liked to say, holding a hand to her chest. "I can hear it, whispering to me, telling me there's something better waiting beyond this town." She talked about leaving Cutwater, she talked about escaping.

This part of her, I did inherit.

The desire to get as far from this town as fate and luck would allow.

By the next morning she was gone.

I woke just in time to see her striding down the driveway, pulling the suitcase behind her.

And I haven't been on the roof again since that night. It's a reminder of her, of when I might have been able to hang on to her, keep her from leaving. But I wasn't able to.

Now I lie in bed, unable to sleep.

An owl lands on the highest point of the house, hooting into the dark, and I hear Archer bolt from his bed and slam out through the back door—certain someone is in the garden. He does this a dozen times more during the night. At every sound, every shift of the house, he's up, ready to catch a thief. But he always finds the garden empty.

And the tulips just as they were a few hours before.

After sunup I make myself a cup of tea, heft my bag over my shoulder, and walk down the driveway to wait for the bus. Every part of me is screaming that I should go back to bed. I have no idea what awaits me at school.

But I just want to get this week over with. I ditched the second half of classes yesterday, and I hope that no one noticed—and that they'll still let me graduate.

Beside the driveway, Forsaken Creek is full and rushing, the spring thaw sending snowmelt down from the Middle Fork Mountains. The soft morning quiet is broken by the sound of the school bus roaring up Swamp Wells Road. I draw in a breath, bracing myself for what's to come. But it's not the yellow bus that comes into view. It's a truck—veering off onto the side of the road, kicking up a cloud of gritty road dust, and skidding to a stop in front of me.

I scramble back, nearly slipping into the creek, coughing as the dust settles around me. I squint, recognizing the sun-faded green Ford—it belongs to Talon McDonald, who graduated last year, but

The Beautiful Maddening

like everyone else in this town, he never left Cutwater. He'll rot here.

Wary, I take another step away, the sketchbook gripped under my arm, but I'm afraid to turn my back on the truck—Talon can be a real asshole. But it's also tulip season, so he'll either say some shit-head thing, then peel away, or he'll confess his love for me.

In the passenger seat sits another boy—long dusty-blond hair sticking out beneath a baseball hat and the beginnings of a pale, wispy mustache on his upper lip. I think his name is Raif, a kid who graduated two years ago but has nothing better to do and nowhere to go. In the bed of the truck are two younger boys slumped against the side, staring out at me. One is shirtless, his dark hair windblown and greasy. The other wears a black T-shirt and sips on a can of soda. I think they're Talon's younger brothers. One of them will probably be a freshman at Cutwater High next year.

"You hitchhiking?" Raif calls out through the open passenger-side window, his upper lip curled.

I glance up at the house, gauging how quickly I could run the distance—but they could drive it much faster, and maybe even beat me on foot.

"We'll give ya a ride," he offers, tapping his fingers against the truck door. His face is sunburned, the sleeves of his sailor-blue flannel shirt rolled up to his elbows.

I blink, keeping my mouth shut.

"She's that witch-girl, you dipshit," one of the boys in the back of the truck says. "Didn't you hear what happened at the high school yesterday? Tobias Huaman has a busted rib. They're sayin' it's because of those flowers she grows behind her house." The boy shoots me a look, his pale eyes like a bird gaping at an insect.

Shea Ernshaw

The morning air suddenly feels unbearably hot against my skin. The sun blinding through the trees, and I just want to sprint up the driveway and duck into the shade and safety of the house.

"She looks harmless enough," Raif comments, his eyes lidded away from the sun.

"Careful . . . ," Talon remarks from the driver's seat, nodding at Raif. "Don't look her straight in the eye, or you won't be able to think of anyone else but her."

I wonder why they've stopped at my driveway. Just to be assholes? Just because they're bored and they saw a girl to harass? Or because they want a tulip.

Both of the boys in the back of the truck quickly shift their gazes away. But Raif keeps his focus on me, elbow resting in the open window, forehead already glistening from the morning heat. A second later I watch his expression change: mouth parting just a little, doughy and soft, as he leans farther out the window.

I force my eyes down to my feet, feeling the shift in his stare, knowing it's already happening. Some are more susceptible than others—easily caught by the Goode snare.

I hear the metal truck door creak open, and Raif steps out onto the gravel driveway. His footsteps are heavy and lumbering, and I lift my eyes when he's only a couple of paces away. His eyes begin to water at the corners, like he's seized by something—his heart caught in a vise. "I'll buy a tulip from you. Ten of them." He nods to the house, his tone suddenly serious and unnerving. The blooms, the enchantment, are already beneath his skin.

"You don't have any money, you moron," Talon shouts through the open window.

The Beautiful Maddening

But Raif reaches for the wallet in his back pocket, thumbs through the bills, then holds out everything inside. Four one-dollar bills.

"They're not for sale," I tell him, a sturdiness in my voice that makes my jaw contract, clenching on the words. Biting them until they break.

But Raif isn't looking at me, he's staring up the long driveway at the house, and I know what he's thinking.

"Get back in the truck!" Talon shouts, revving the engine. "You shouldn't be that close to her." But Raif isn't listening, he doesn't hear a thing. He takes a step past me, starting up the driveway. He's going to rip the tulips from the soil, beckoned closer by their hypnotizing scent wafting through the spring air. He's feeling bold, overcome, and maybe it's because of me. The scent is on my skin, too, and being this close to me, near the garden of tulips, it's more than his small mind can manage.

"Be right back," he mumbles, though it's too quiet for Talon to hear. He takes another step, but I swivel around and reach out for him.

"I said no!" I snap, grabbing his arm. He jerks back, his cheeks red, sweat beading down his temple. "They're not for sale." And for a second he looks like he's going to lunge at me, but instead his shoulders drop and his eyes sink low, settling on mine.

"Raif, what the hell!" Talon barks, impatient now.

But Raif lifts his hand, the movement slow, like he's half-asleep, and I can tell he's going to run his fingertips down my cheekbone, caress my skin, while his dark, close-set eyes pinwheel deeper into mine.

"Don't touch me," I snarl, shoving his hand away. His expression tightens with anger, with confusion—his emotions a riot inside his head. He both loves me *and* loathes me right now, and he can't decide which feeling makes sense. But without warning, his features change, turn hard and mean all at once, and he clamps a hand around my forearm, like he's going to drag me with him.

Love has a different effect on everyone. Some want to cherish the ones they love, caress them and care for them and plant delicate kisses across their lips. While others want to control the ones they love, lock them up and keep them "safe" so no one else can have them.

Raif is the latter sort.

"Stop!" I shout, dropping my bag and notebook in the dirt, then shoving my hands against his chest, trying to push him back. But he's too strong, yanking me toward the truck.

I hear the groan of another truck door opening, and Talon steps out. "What the hell are you doing, man?" he says to Raif. But Raif has lost all sense of himself, and I can see the single-minded determination on his face, cut into his sunburned forehead. He's not about to let me slip from his grasp. Not for anything.

"Let me go!" I yell, digging my fingernails into his jaw, his throat, making claw marks down his flesh. He doesn't even flinch.

Time seems to careen forward as he drags me to the truck, the sun wheeling hotly overhead. My mind screams, *No, no, no.* My body pulls fiercely away, without success.

But behind me I hear the screen door of the house slap open and the steady thud of footsteps on the front stairs. "Fuck off, Raif!" Archer shouts.

Raif stops, swings his gaze over my shoulder. And in the next blink I launch my leg forward, kicking him hard in the shin with a

The Beautiful Maddening

loud crack. He cries out, wincing, then buckles over just before he releases my arm.

I nearly drop to the ground but manage to stagger back, thumping against the mailbox.

"Get the fuck out of here, Talon!" Archer yells, striding down the driveway toward us, the anger hot across his face.

I draw in a breath, my heart biting against my ribs, and when I look up, both Talon and Raif are back inside the truck, doors slammed shut, and the truck is screeching away, rear tires kicking up dust. One of the younger boys in the back tosses out his can of orange soda, and it hits the ground at my feet, splashing sticky soda onto my bare shins, before the truck speeds up the road and vanishes around a bend.

In the dirt lies my notebook—pages fanned open, covered in gravel.

I touch my arm where Raif's fingers dug into my flesh, the skin tender but unbroken. Archer stops at the end of the driveway and glares up the road, where gray exhaust clouds the air.

Nearly everyone in town *loves* Archer—whether they want to admit it or not—but some of them also fear him. He's been in enough fights, usually over a lost love or a stolen love or an unrequited love: often a jealous boyfriend picking a fight with Archer after his girlfriend was seen lurking around the Goode house. "You only have to win a few fights before the reputation sticks," he told me once.

"Idiots," he says now, exhaling through his nostrils, then swings his focus back to me. "You okay?"

I nod.

Archer bends down and picks up my notebook from the driveway, brushing away the dirt to reveal the sketch of the unknown boy.

He stares down at it, and for a moment I think he might recognize the face. But then he asks, "Who's this?"

I step forward and grab the notebook from his hands. "No one."

He shoots me a suspicious look. "You only sketch real people, so he must be *someone*. New kid at school? Paperboy? What is it?"

I don't answer him, tucking the book back under my arm, my cheeks still hot from the fight with Raif. Shins sticky, my heart only beginning to slow.

But Archer smirks. "Lark Goode . . . my little sister, keeping secrets." His face brightens, amused, and he starts to move toward me, like he's going to rip the notebook from my arms.

"I'm not your *little* sister," I counter.

He lifts an eyebrow, like he finds this funny. "I guess we'll never know for sure. But it's obvious I was born first: I'm stronger, taller, and more handsome."

I swing the notebook behind my back. Out of reach.

But our attention is pulled away by the sound of another car approaching up the road. This time the school bus comes into view, sputtering and lumbering toward us.

Archer turns back to me, suddenly looking serious. "Maybe today is not the day to go to school."

I brush my hair behind my ears, letting out a breath. I won't let Raif and Talon scare me. And with only two more days of school, I'm so close to being done with this town forever.

"Lark . . . ," Archer says, lifting both eyebrows. "I know I give you shit about going to school. But this is different. Those stolen tulips are in the hands of strangers now—we don't know what this means, what will happen."

The Beautiful Maddening

The bus rattles to a stop along the shoulder of the road, doors folding open, and I look at my brother. "Exactly, we don't know. . . . Maybe the worst of it is already over."

Archer shakes his head but doesn't seem to know what else to say.

"I'll be fine," I assure him, forcing a smile. But my brother doesn't look relieved. Not even a little. He watches as I step up into the bus—my heart banging against my eardrums—and I find a seat near the front of the bus so I can exit faster when we reach the school. I gaze out the window at my brother, standing at the end of the driveway, hands in the pockets of his jeans, our shithole house sinking into the wet soil behind him.

And I'm certain that by the end of the school day, I'll know just how bad of an idea this is.

FOUR

The tulips split us apart, make us a myth—people to be feared and loved and hated. We are a paradox, a puzzle, we are the old wives' tale that locals like our neighbor down the road, Mrs. Thierry, talk about during bingo and brunch club. *The Goodes can't go out after dark,* someone will say. *No, they* only *go out after dark,* another will interject. *They bury their kin beneath the house; they let them float away on the creek; they never die.*

This is the problem with rumors. It's rare to find a kernel of truth within the tangled yarn of tall tales. Too many muddy, mucky lies.

It's impossible to see what's real.

Morning sunlight spears over the treetops, ricocheting through the bus windows. The brown bench seat is cracked along the edge, digging into the backs of my legs, and the air smells like waffles and maple syrup. Tim Zhang's mom makes him waffles every morning before school, and this morning he still had a waffle in his hand when he boarded the bus; now he sits chewing the last of it from the seat in front of me.

I don't mind—perhaps the sugary scent of batter, butter, and syrup will mask the covetous scent of tulips on my skin. I even man-

The Beautiful Maddening

age to get my bus window open just a crack, the fresh air whirling over me.

Still, anxiety clatters along my thoughts.

Get through class, finish out the week, and then I'll be free.

And not just free for the summer.

Free for the rest of my life.

I'll graduate, get my diploma, and then I'm leaving this town.

For good.

In my lap the notebook is spread open, and I shade in *the boy's* hands, his knuckles, imagining the parts I didn't get close enough to see. It's pure curiosity that keeps me coming back to this sketch, a need to finish it.

The bus thumps over a pothole, someone shrieks from the front of the bus, startled, but I lose myself in the rhythm of the pencil scratching against the paper, the side of my hand smearing the edges. I lose myself in his face, the slope of his eyes—how they stared back at me, reckless, unafraid. Sunlight sparking off his lashes. I could have moved closer, I could have asked him his name before he strode away. I should have held on to the moment, squeezed it in my fist until it was burned onto my flesh.

The.

Boy.

I close my eyes, trying to conjure the memory, but the boy is slipping away like a dream at first light.

The bus finally turns into the Cutwater High parking lot and lumbers to a stop. The school looks like a brick prison as I exit the bus, making my way down the metal steps. Only two more days. Two days of suffering, two days of enduring my classmates' covetous stares. But it's more than that now. I don't know how many tulips have been passed and traded in secret; I don't know who possesses them. And I don't know what will happen to those who do.

Sliding my headphones over my ears, hitting play on Oasis's "Wonderwall," I make my way across the lawn—my eyes lowered, the front doors into the school only a few paces away.

But I never reach them.

Chloe Perez—a sophomore who last year had a locker next to mine—appears from behind one of the craggy oak trees bordering the lawn, as if summoned by the shadows. She calls out to me, her eyes watery like she's been crying, but I only make out a few of the words. I let my headphones slide down to my neck—the song still playing from the tiny speakers like a faint insect hum—and she marches up to me, stopping much too close.

"I thought you'd never get here," she repeats, her face a galaxy of freckles, dark hair curled around her small ears, but her features tug strangely to one side, and there's a sharpness in her butterscotch eyes that frightens me. "They were right," she continues, nodding. "There's something inside them, the devil's perfume or . . . or real magic, or the flesh of the dead, I don't care what it is. I need more." She looks like she hasn't slept, but has instead been pacing the lawn in front of the school all night, her cheeks hollow, her lips dry and colorless.

"What?" I say, my voice cracking, as I take a step back.

"The rumors . . ." Her eyes widen like I should know what she's thinking. The air hisses from her lungs, and she lets out a short, uneasy laugh. "It was *always* the tulips that made everyone love you . . . *the Goodes*." She nods again, more manic this time. "It was those flowers. All along. And they've just been growing behind your

56

The Beautiful Maddening

house, sprouting right up from the ground. For free." She laughs, and her eyelashes flutter like the whole world has suddenly come into focus—like she's finally seeing clearly.

She shifts on her feet, then begins rummaging in the pocket of her blue corduroy skirt, before holding something up for me to see: a single cursed tulip.

A Goode tulip.

The petals are still intact, the crimson streaks visible across the soft white flesh, but it's wilted, losing its color—turning pale and lifeless. It should be in a vase of water, but it looks as though she's been clenching it in her fist for at least twenty-four hours, unable to part with it. Let it out of her grasp.

"Where did you get that?" I lean closer to her, wanting to snatch it from her hand.

"Took it out of Connor's backpack at lunch yesterday when he wasn't looking." Her eyes are wild and treacherous—she is pleased with herself, with the heist she managed to pull off. But her words make me feel sick. The tulips have changed hands so many times, there's no hope of ever getting them all back.

She smiles, almost laughs again, her eyes bright and unblinking. "And right after, Archie Green offered to carry my bag. Then Billy Ruthers said he'd give me a ride home today so I don't have to take the bus. *Billy Ruthers . . . ,*" she says again for emphasis, both eyebrows peaked into her forehead like she still can't believe it—Billy Ruthers, who drives an old, restored black Chevelle and parks it in the teachers' parking lot. They just let him do it. Like even the teachers know he's better than this place. *Untouchable.* But yesterday . . . *he* noticed Chloe Perez.

"Please," she hisses, tilting her chin closer to me, unafraid. "I need another one, before this one dies." Her teeth are mashed together, her fingers gripping the tulip stem so tightly, I think it's going to snap.

"I don't have any. . . ." I shake my head at her, "Wonderwall" still playing from the headphones around my neck. "I'm sorry, but—"

She reaches out with her free hand and grabs my forearm, holding tight. "I can't lose this feeling, the scent of it. . . ." Her eyes flutter closed, before she snaps them open again. "Is this how it feels all the time for you, living in that house? Is this how you feel right now? Like your skin is tingling? Like you're sleepwalking but you never want to wake?"

I take a step back, but she follows me, her eyes wetting at the corners. "I don't know what you're talking about," I say, trying to shake her off.

Chloe tightens her grip on the fabled tulip, and her bottom lip trembles, as if she's going to cry. "It's like . . ." She breathes. "Like . . . warm sunlight on my skin . . . like something is shifting my cells, something strange and wonderful. Almost . . ." A laugh bubbles up from her throat. "Like I'm drunk, but only a little. . . . You know what I mean?"

I swallow tightly, not answering.

"I feel"—she leans in close, her voice thin and haunted—"like I'm falling in love." But then her eyes turn serious. "No, that's not it. . . . It's like falling in love for the *very first time*." She nods at me, looking for me to agree, to verify what she's saying. She really does look intoxicated, dizzy, as if the tulip in her hand is coaxing her under a spell so deep and treacherous that she might never find her way out of it.

The Beautiful Maddening

"Is it how you feel?" she presses. "Like your bones are drenched in it, like you could fall in love with the next person you see, or touch? Like the air in your lungs tastes like a summer sunset, a first kiss with someone whose lips you've dreamed of touching for years, like a whisper in your ear, so soft and perfect that you never want to hear anyone else's voice ever again?"

I yank my arm free. "No," I tell her, an uneasy twisting in my gut.

Now I see, I understand: this is what it feels like for everyone else; this is what the tulips are doing to anyone who isn't a Goode. They conjure feelings of delirious love. *False love.* And she's already addicted to it—the tulip makes her feel this way just by holding it. And those around her feel it too—drawn in, pulled by the same sensation. Once you possess a tulip, *you* become the focus of desire. Just like with Billy Ruthers, who suddenly felt pulled into Chloe's orbit.

"I need more," she says, tapping her teeth together, her eyes shuddering, looking at me like I can save her. "I'll pay whatever you want."

I shake my head, backing away. "No."

"Please, you have a whole garden, you don't need them all." Her voice is sugary and plying, odd. *Unnatural.*

The air grows stiff and rancid in my lungs.

"Don't be selfish," she spits, all the sweetness suddenly gone— just like that—her mouth contorting into a venomous grin, baring her perfect row of teeth as she moves toward me.

I eye the front doors of the school across the lawn, *safety*, but before I can even turn, someone else touches my arm. *Grabs it.* "I'll buy one." Titha Roberts, who yesterday said I looked pretty after history class, is now standing to my left, looking edgy, impatient.

I shake my head. "I don't have any." I flash a look behind me to

Shea Ernshaw

the parking lot and the road beyond. The school no longer feels like a haven. I never should have come today. It was stupid to think I could make it to the end of the year.

Titha frowns, like she doesn't believe me, and I backstep through the wet, uncut grass, my sandals catching briefly, my heart starting to race. Both Titha and Chloe follow, matching my steps, looking irritated, desperate, like they're not about to let me leave the school grounds, not for anything.

It's stirring up something inside them. Something hostile. Something dangerous.

But another voice pitches over the morning wind.

"I'll buy all of them!" It's Olive Montagu—who was blowing bubbles over her flock of friends during lunch, who *was* the girlfriend of Tobias Huaman until yesterday, when Tobias seemed more concerned with Clementine Morris during his fight with Mac. Now Olive is striding toward me, hands planted on her hips, fingernails painted a loud shade of bubblegum pink. "I don't care the price," she shrieks, edging past Titha and Chloe, producing a folded wad of twenties from a pocket in her white skirt, then shoving them toward me.

I'm about to tell her that I don't have any, when she abruptly reaches out and yanks my book bag from my hands.

"Hey!" Titha barks, scowling at her. "I was here first."

"Tough shit, I need them more than you," Olive barks, shoving her hand down inside the bag. And to my shock, she extracts a single tulip, crumpled and sad, several of the petals torn away. It's the tulip I took from Mac on the front lawn yesterday—*I never removed it from my bag.* And now Olive clenches it in her trembling fingers, blinking

60

The Beautiful Maddening

down at the unusual bloom as if it held all of life's cosmic secrets and unsolvable mysteries within its white, streaked petals. "Wow," she remarks under her breath. She drops the bag to the ground, bringing the tulip to her face to breathe in its hypnotizing scent. "I know he can't really love that awful Clementine," she mutters, before her soft blue eyes scrape up to mine. "And now he'll love *me* again."

I forgot about the tulip in my bag, and I realize maybe this is why Raif came after me this morning at the end of the driveway. Stupidly, I had a tulip stashed in my bag, the perilous scent scorching the air.

To my left, Chloe's eyes go wide, and she lunges at Olive, ripping the bloom from her hand in one swift motion, then clutches it to her chest. But instead of darting away with it, she brings it to her nose, breathing deeply, entranced by its sickly sweet scent.

"Wait!" someone else cries. Olive's best friend, Lulu Yen, jogs across the lawn, and suddenly the commotion has drawn the attention of others—those who were walking across the parking lot toward school—and they start moving closer, crowding toward me, pressing in, eyes locked on the single tulip. "I'll pay you fifty dollars for one," Lulu says, her voice cracked, jittery.

Olive shoots her a look, one best friend to another. "Screw off, it's mine," she declares, and she snatches it back from Chloe's hands before Chloe can react.

But Lulu's expression changes, the *need* taking shape in her striking chestnut eyes. She leaps at Olive, clawing at the flower, and the tulip petals begin pinwheeling down to the grass like spent autumn leaves.

In an instant, everything changes.

Olive shrieks, reaching out for Lulu with a wildness cut into her usually composed, porcelain features, while her bright pink fingernails flash through the air. Scratching, *tearing*. Titha and Chloe drop to the ground, gathering petals, but there are others pressed in around us now, and when they see the bits of tulip littering the grass, they fall to their knees and begin grabbing for the torn remains, shoving them into their pockets. As if they were a prize, a gift from cruel, spiteful gods.

The air is quickly filled with a familiar, intoxicating scent: the fate-laced aroma of Goode tulips.

Someone screams to my left, their hand crushed by someone else standing above. Billy Ruthers shoves Abby Edwards in the face to steal the crushed tulip petal in her fist, but she bites his hand, drawing blood—*actually bites him*. Someone else shoves half a tulip petal into their mouth, then crawls away from the clot of students mashed together on the ground. I see Dale Dawson stand up, part of a tulip stem in his hand, and he darts toward the parking lot, as if a broken piece of stem were more valuable than anything he's ever held in his life. I spot Olive slinking away too, at least three tulip petals in her hand, and she heads around the back of the school, maybe to hide them, maybe to find a way home, where no one will spot her.

After a half second I, too, drop to the ground, but not to retrieve tulip petals—I'm searching for my bag. I scan the trampled grass and see that someone else has found it, and they're digging around inside, pulling free a few petals—ones that likely fell off when the tulip was still inside. A second later they abandon the bag, but someone above steps on it, leaving a dirty shoe print. I push against their leg and manage to yank it free. But when I try to scramble back, the

The Beautiful Maddening

crush of people tightens around me. Someone yells, a cry of pain or greed, it's hard to tell, then another person slams into my shoulder— they're fighting over the last remaining scraps, any remnant they can find in the damp grass. The wind stirs through the mob, becoming spirited and strange, as if a dark storm has settled over us. A boy—Randy Ashspring—has the last part of the tulip stem gripped between his teeth, and he's trying to army-crawl out of the crowd but gets punched in the face, the stem ripped from his mouth. Someone curses beside me—a girl whose face is beet red, her eyes dripping with tears, looking terrified—and then there is weight on top of me, crushing me.

I feel the air tighten in my lungs, the struggle to draw in a breath—pain working its way down my chest.

I need to get out of here.

I try again to shimmy back, to work my way free, but I'm met with more bodies pressed together. Hands clawing at the ground, faces marred by rage and desperation. The feeling of claustrophobia starts setting in, becoming *panic*.

I try to look up, toward the sky, toward fresh air, just as someone falls against me, knocking me flat against the ground.

My face presses to the wet grass. I choke on it. *Breathe, breathe*—I tell myself to draw in air, but it smells like damp soil and fear, and my lungs are tightening in my chest. The weight is too heavy. *Not enough air.* My head swirls, I lose track of the sky, up from down.

I make a sound, a desperate little cry, but no one hears me—and there is a hand on my arm. I try to shake it free, but it grips even tighter. I try to yell, but only air comes out, and then the hand is pulling me back, opening a space behind me. Whoever has ahold of my forearm is shoving people away, making room, and in one sudden movement I'm yanked free of the crowd.

I buckle over, coughing, hands on my knees, sucking in the clear morning air. A few tears drip from my eyes. But I don't wipe them away. Because the pain in my chest is only starting to loosen, and I pull in a deep lungful of air.

But the relief doesn't last.

"She's right there!" someone shouts. I glance up to see Lulu Yen pointing a long finger at me.

Several faces snap my way, eyes feral and enraged like those of animals who haven't fed in days. The crowd starts to slither apart, their heads lifted in my direction, hands pushing their bodies up.

I draw in a shaky breath. . . .

As if I've found myself in some awful black-and-white horror film—*zombies reborn, bloodthirsty and crazed*—the crowd begins coming toward me.

I stagger a moment, still unbalanced, out of breath, but a hand folds through mine. Strong, warm.

For the first time, I turn, looking at the person beside me—the person who saved me. . . .

Him.

The boy.

He doesn't speak, but squeezes my palm, his eyes swaying from me to the crowd.

I suck in a quick, stunned gulp of air, and he pulls me away from the mob, away from the lawn, from Cutwater High. And we run.

The Beautiful Maddening

The morning air whips past my face, cooling the sweat on my skin, my heart still a roar in my ears.

A half mile up the road we cut into the trees—to a path known only by locals, that winds through the woods along Rabbit Cross River. At last, when the sound of voices behind us fades—the crowd given up, probably gone back to the school to sweep up any last tulip fragments from the grass—the boy and I slow to a stop.

My lungs heave, adrenaline still thumping through my veins, and when I finally lift my eyes, it feels like shivering awake from a strange dream. The same boy I saw days ago in the school parking lot—whose sketch has been slowly coming to life in my notebook, who started to feel like a false memory, a shadow I conjured in my mind—is now standing in front of me.

I didn't simply imagine him.

He is tall, with dark eyelashes and green, *green* eyes—the same hue as the trees behind him—and skin that reminds me of the sky when it rains. Dusky and beautiful. The air gets caught in my throat, before I swallow it down. He is different up close, bewildering and . . . *beautiful.* Wild and civilized all at once, like a sunlit afternoon and the dark, impossible sky. Like he's holding a thousand little secrets beneath his flesh.

He breathes deeply, shifts his weight, then looks up the path from where we've come. For a moment I think he's going to speak, but then his eyes settle on me and his mouth falls still. I should tell him not to get any closer, but my voice feels like mud, and my eyes follow every tick of his movements as he lifts an arm . . . reaching out for me.

My heart scrapes against my windpipe.

65

He's going to touch me, my mind yells.

No, no, *no.*

But his fingers only graze my hair, *just barely*, like the tiniest whisper, the smallest breath, and when I blink, I see that he's holding a single tulip petal between his fingers. It was tangled in my hair, after being crushed by the crowd.

But this one escaped.

Quickly I pluck it from his fingers, not wanting him to hold it too long—or risk madness seeping into his skin—and I press it into the pocket of my shorts. Out of sight.

"Thank you," I gasp, trying to slow my breathing, trying to appear steadier than I feel—staring at the *boy I'd made into a myth.*

He nods, and the curves of his mouth pinch closed. I want to peer inside him, gather up the details of who he is before this moment is lost: a boy with a freckle beside his upper lip, hair that curls slightly around his ears, sweatshirt sleeves pushed up to his elbows, dark jeans faded, well-worn. They've seen miles of walking, of climbing trees, maybe, of being tossed onto a bedroom floor and forgotten for days at a time. Softened by years of wear. I force my eyes away, but they slide back, as if pulled in by gravity, skipping across the sturdy outline of his shoulders, and I'm certain you don't get that strong from only reading paperback books. He is a boy of another breed. Not the kind you find in Cutwater. He is careful, quiet, and I want to tiptoe into his head and unearth all his thoughts. I want to remember him so I can sketch every part of him later, every missed detail.

"Did you just move to town?" My voice breaks the silence, but I'm holding back a tide of questions wanting to spill out all at once.

His bottle-green eyes flash to the trees. "No."

The Beautiful Maddening

"Do you go to Cutwater High?" I'm certain he doesn't, but it feels like the right thing to ask, the acceptable string of questions.

"I go to school in Favorville." I can hear the wariness in his voice, like he's already given too much away. Like he's looking for an escape out of these woods.

Favorville sits just across the county line, only a few miles from Cutwater. But they have a real indoor movie theater and a small local museum and a large public library. Students at Favorville High don't venture into Cutwater—there's nothing here. No reason to waste their time.

A new idea begins to form inside me: a theory, a notion that makes my heart begin to beat nervously again. I harden my jaw. "Someone broke into our garden two nights ago. . . ."

His pupils are flat, emotionless.

"They stole my family's tulips, cut them from the ground."

He frowns back at me, but in an indifferent way. "Are you asking if it was me?"

My eyes feel like they're vibrating, watching him, looking for any hint of a lie. *Someone stole the flowers.* And this boy is a stranger. Maybe it's why he's been lurking around the school—he heard the rumors about my family. Even in Favorville. And now he's been selling the flowers he stole.

A heaviness sinks into my chest, like concrete being poured into my rib cage.

But he exhales. "I don't want your flowers," he answers, staring back at me, like he's daring me to find even a molecule of mistruth in his words. But there is something else in his eyes, or a *lack* of something.

I see no lost, swimming look in the center of his pupils. No dizzying desire. No craving, no twitch of need or longing taking shape in his stare. He seems unaffected by me. By being this close to a Goode. To anyone else, his gaze might feel cold, unsettling, but to me it feels oddly comfortable. *Easy.* Safe in a way I'm not accustomed to.

He is a boy whose face reminds me of a midsummer lightning storm—flashes of light and long, thundering darkness. I am wholly perplexed by him.

But I also believe him.

He seems like a boy who couldn't care less about tulips or a Goode family curse. But this creates more riddles than it solves.

"Are you safe to walk home from here?" he asks bluntly, his eyes steady and unflinching.

I glance up the path, a route I've walked countless times. "Yes."

His feet shift in the dirt, and he seems uncomfortable, as if the moment has been stretched out too long, standing here in the trees with me.

He takes a couple of steps back.

"Wait," I say, moving toward him. "What's your name?"

The muscles in his shoulders draw down, like he might not say it, like he might turn and vanish into the forest and I will never know. But he drags his eyes back to me, swallows. "Holden," he says. "But everyone calls me Oak." He sounds earnest, but there is something else in his tone, like maybe this isn't the whole truth, or maybe he thinks he's just given up a part of himself, like he's worried what this knowledge will mean now that he's said it aloud.

Oak—a tree that grows roots deep in the soil. A tree that's good

The Beautiful Maddening

for rope swings and forts and climbing. A tree that stakes its claim in a bit of dirt and never loosens its hold.

"I'm Lark," I offer, and it occurs to me that I've never needed to introduce myself to anyone. Lark Goode is a name that's known before I even walk into a room.

But this boy from Favorville only blinks.

A second passes, then another, before at last he says, "I know."

And as swift as the creek below the house, he turns away before I can reply, starting up the path toward town—a paperback book still in the back pocket of his jeans.

FIVE

Few people have ever left Cutwater. Those who did never returned. Including our mother, Alice Goode.

In those first few months, I waited for letters to come, a postcard from somewhere beautiful: Mykonos, the south of France, Australia, or maybe a tiny island in the Atlantic. I pictured her skin sunned and salty, spending her days drifting in turquoise waters. I waited for her to write and ask us to come, giving instructions on how to find her. I imagined her setting up a life somewhere, getting it just right, before she sent for us.

I imagined a fairy tale.

One that never came true.

Because in three years there have been no postcards. No word.

She might as well be dead.

And it makes me hate the tulips even more—because whatever the reason for her leaving, the tulips are certainly to blame. One way or another.

I move quickly down the driveway, over the creek, and I find my brother in the kitchen when I step through the front door.

He spins around, and there's something in his hand—but he

The Beautiful Maddening

quickly tucks it away into his pocket. Out of sight. My eyes narrow, a twinge of curiosity about what he's hiding, but not enough to ask. In fact, I probably don't want to know—it's likely something he stole, even though he'll deny it and insist it was given to him by someone who couldn't resist his charm. Or maybe it's one of the love letters that have begun to pile up on the kitchen table—too many to count.

"The school called," he says, turning to the refrigerator and pulling out the carton of orange juice. I wince, certain it's bad news— they're not going to let me graduate, not after what happened on the front lawn. But Archer raises an eyebrow at me. "They said classes are canceled tomorrow," he continues, shooting me a look. "It's the end of the year. No more school . . . ever. We're done with that place." His mouth edges into a smile as he fills a coffee mug with juice, then stares down at it like he's changed his mind. "And since you're home before first period has even begun, I'm guessing something happened."

I sink into one of the kitchen chairs, a sudden relief spilling through me: No more classes. No more awful stares as I make my way down the halls of Cutwater High.

I'm really done. *I'm free.*

"It was the tulips," I answer. "Everyone at school was . . ." How do I explain? "They wanted a Goode tulip, they were begging for them."

Archer stares down at his mug, then asks, "Did you find out who stole them?"

I lift a shoulder, uncertain. "No, but I think they'll *all* be trying to sneak into the garden now. It's like . . ." My eyes click to the front window, the gray floral curtains pulled back, and I stare down the driveway. "Like they're addicted to them."

71

Shea Ernshaw

Archer leaves the mug on the counter and walks to the kitchen table. "Like they're in love?" he asks pointedly, sinking into the chair opposite me and leaning back. "Dale Dawson said that someone was in the alley behind the school last night charging five dollars to hold one of the tulips for a single minute. Dale paid it, and said it was the most *enchanting* minute of his life. 'Like falling in love with a god.' But Dale can be dramatic."

I push aside a stack of love letters on the table, making room to rest my elbows. Mom always said the tulips contain the highest concentration of pheromones of any flower that's ever existed. She claimed that those pheromones could command armies, control worlds if someone wanted. And we, the Goodes, grow them in the garden behind our house. We sleep beside them, live our lives only a few feet from where they sprout from the soil; we're born when the tulips bloom.

I push myself up from the table, the chair scraping against the floor, and walk to the back door. I look out at the uneven rows of tulips: our entire life, our whole fate, tangled up in those flowers.

"There's some old barbed wire in the shed," Archer says. "I'm going to string it up around the garden. I don't know if it'll stop them, but it might slow them down, at least until tulip season ends."

I don't answer. My mind is divided: I hate the idea of others slinking into the garden, ripping flowers from the ground. But I also feel myself letting go of this place. School is done. In a few days I should have my diploma, and then I'll be gone. And I'll no longer care what happens to the tulips, to this house, to the garden. A part of me is already miles away from here.

"Do you think Mom was running away from this house or from

The Beautiful Maddening

us?" I ask, a thought that has lived inside me since the day she left, but I've never said out loud.

Archer exhales behind me. "I think she wanted to be someone else."

I hate this description—because it sounds like what *I* want too. To bury my last name in the swampy dirt and never speak it again. The only thing I don't want to leave behind is my brother. "This whole place feels damned," I mutter.

"No shit." Archer stands up, crosses the living room to stand beside me, then pulls out the guitar pick from his pocket, turns it through his fingers, an unconscious habit.

The sound of the creek fills the quiet between us, and I imagine myself drifting away on its surface, letting it carry me out through the garden and into the forest beyond, a hundred miles to the ocean, where I'll spill into the sea and be set adrift on the Pacific. "Remember when we used to make paper boats?" I say, glancing at Archer.

The features of his face sometimes remind me of our father's—gentle and quiet, unflinching.

"We'd drop the boats into the creek at the front porch, then run through the house, chasing them, and when they appeared from under the back porch, we'd follow them out into the garden."

"You said we should write wishes on our boats," he adds, a smile barely touching his eyes.

I forgot about this, how we'd write our wishes in crayon on the side of our flimsy paper boats, then let them be carried away, hoping they'd come true.

They never did.

Archer sighs, sliding the guitar pick back into his pocket, like he feels it too—that no matter how much we might wish for a different life, wishing won't make it happen.

The notebook lies open in my lap, the sketch of the boy staring back—Oak.

Not the name of a boy, but of a fairy tale, a dream I must not have woken from yet.

I run my thumb along his jaw, and my thoughts tumble back: to the feeling of his hand on mine, pulling me free of the mob. Warm and real and alive—not a dream at all. I can still feel the wind against my cheeks as we ran up the road, our feet smacking against the pavement, and then the coolness of the trees as we ducked down the path, out of sight. In the shadow of the forest I tried to study every feature of his face, gather every detail so I could recall it later. It's been only two days since I stood on that path, staring up at him, and yet I'm already struggling to recall the way his hair swept across his forehead, or the slant of his eyebrows. Did he have freckles? Were his ears level with his eyes? I was distracted, tangled up in a feeling that's hard to describe, but it was more than that. . . . It was the *way* he looked at me. Passively, indifferently. Like he felt no madness-laced desire coiling upward into his throat, felt no need to tip closer to me. Just like the day I first saw him at school.

As if he felt nothing at all.

Yet when he turned away, a flicker of something caught in his eyes: a nervousness, an edge, a hesitation in each blink of his eyelids. But I can't be sure what it was. Not exactly.

Archer steps through the front door, a stack of mail in his hands,

The Beautiful Maddening

and I lift my thumb from the sketch—not wanting my brother to see the concentration in my eyes, the confusion.

He crosses the living room to where I'm seated on the couch, and he drops a large envelope into my lap, covering Oak's image. I frown, but Archer is already striding into the kitchen, thumbing through the rest of the mail.

The envelope is from Cutwater High. I tear it open, and inside I find two stiff pieces of paper.

Our diplomas.

One for Archer, one for me.

Paper-clipped onto the front is a note from Principal Lee: *After this week's events at school, we think it best that you do not attend the graduation ceremony on Sunday. Congratulations on receiving your diplomas.*

"What is it?" Archer asks. When I don't reply, he comes back into the living room and peers down at the two rectangles of paper. "Shit!" he says, yanking his diploma from my hands. "They let me graduate!"

"They probably didn't want you returning for another senior year. Easier to just shove you out into the world, let someone else deal with you."

He laughs. "Works for me." He holds up his diploma in the light, marveling at his achievement. My brother missed at least half a year of classes, nowhere near the attendance required to graduate. But Cutwater High would likely prefer not to have a Goode in their classrooms next year.

I slide my fingers over the heavy card stock, feeling relief, but also a twinge of something I can't pinpoint. I'm grateful we won't need to attend a graduation ceremony—I won't have to face my classmates again—but it also feels lacking somehow, to receive our diplomas this way. In the mail, shoved into an envelope.

"Should we burn them?" Archer asks, raising both his eyebrows, looking impish and full of bad ideas.

My eyes skim the name printed in black ink: *Lark Goode*. And I know . . . this paper is my permission. My freedom. I've graduated, and now I can finally leave this town.

"You can do whatever you want with yours," I say. "But you're not touching mine." I stand up, sliding my diploma back into the envelope.

Archer shrugs, tossing his diploma onto the couch, already disinterested in it, then grabs his jean jacket from the hook beside the front door—the one he found in the alleyway behind Maple's Burger Stop last summer, the one I swear still smells like french fries. But he loves it.

"Where you going?"

"Huck's Drive-In. It's the end-of-the-year party."

"You're not serious."

His hands sink into his coat pockets. "I told Willa I'd meet her there."

"Willa Howard?"

He lifts a shoulder. Willa graduated last year and is entirely out of his league, even for him. *Even for a Goode.*

"You should come," he offers.

"No thanks, I barely escaped a mob at school two days ago. And what if someone comes to the house, tries to steal more flowers? You've barely slept the last few nights, and now you're just going to leave?"

The Beautiful Maddening

His eyebrows cinch together, wrinkling the small scar he's had since we were kids and we both got chicken pox. I managed to avoid scratching, but Archer had no self-control. Now he has a tiny, round mark beside his right eyebrow. "I put up barbed wire yesterday," he answers, as if this has solved all our problems. I walk to the back window and look out at the garden, where a row of wire has been strung around the perimeter. But it's haphazard, sagging in places, having been nailed to a dozen bent and rotted posts he's shoved into the dirt.

It couldn't keep out a toddler, let alone a determined, lovesick teenager. I lift an eyebrow at him.

"I doubt anyone will come here tonight anyway," he adds with a smirk, trying to convince me. "They'll all be at the drive-in."

I want to argue, but I also know my brother will always do whatever he wants. Whether I agree or not. Whether I think it's a bad idea or not.

Archer breathes, then nods down at the envelope in my hand. "Now that you have your diploma, what's your plan?"

We've never really talked about this, not seriously, anyway. Maybe he didn't truly believe I'd do it: leave Cutwater. But now he looks at me with the smallest hint of sadness in his eyes.

"There's a town on the coast, I, uh—I figure I'll start there. Train can get me there in a day."

His face goes slack, eyes falling to the floor briefly before he looks back up. "You don't have any money."

"I have enough . . . enough for a ticket, anyway. I'll find a job when I get there."

"Where will you stay?"

"Not sure yet. Hoping to rent a room somewhere."

He touches the front door handle, then smirks. "You'd really leave all this behind, huh?"

"Because this place is so great?"

"Anywhere can be great if you let it."

A soft exhale leaves my lips. "This place will never be great. As long as our last name is Goode, it will torture us. The only way to become someone new is to leave this town behind."

My brother nods, like he understands. "When you leaving?"

"A day or two. Just need to pack, buy a train ticket. Now that I have this"—I hold up the envelope with my diploma inside—"I don't have a reason to stay."

I realize too late that this sounds harsh—because Archer is a reason to stay. He's the only thing I love about this place.

But he nods, unfazed by my words, and flashes his eyes to the door. "Well . . . we might as well go break some hearts tonight while we have the chance." He winks, and I know: his nonattachment, his recklessness, is how he survives.

Without it, he'd be the one left heartbroken over and over.

"Come on, you're leaving this town anyway. You'll never see these people again. You have nothing to lose. Think of it as your send-off party. One last night out with your charming brother. How can you say no to that?"

I'm about to shake my head, tell him no—I have no interest in repeating what happened on the front lawn at school—when another thought tiptoes through my mind:

Maybe *he'll* be there. At the drive-in.

The boy named after a tree.

If I could see him one more time, I could finish the sketch.

The Beautiful Maddening

One last time . . . would be enough.

It's a simple curiosity, I tell myself. That keeps my thoughts returning to him. Nothing more. He is a boy I don't understand. A boy whose unfinished sketch haunts me whenever I turn the page.

And maybe my brother is right: if I'm finally leaving . . . maybe I have nothing to lose.

"Okay," I say.

Archer's eyes widen, and his mouth falls open.

"Don't make a big deal of it or I'll change my mind."

His jaw snaps shut. "Fine, understood."

Huck's Drive-In used to be called Lost Lane Drive-In, before it shut down back in the early nineties. Mom would tell stories about watching films like *The Outsiders* and *The Princess Bride*, but I think she spent more time in the back seat of local boys' cars than actually watching films.

Now, every summer, Huck Sanchez sets up his dad's projector and plays old black-and-white films that I'm sure nearly everyone at Cutwater High has never heard of. But just like Mom, they only come to drink and make out and do whatever they want without a single adult in sight. All of this I've been told by Archer—since I've never actually seen one of Huck's films. Until tonight.

Moonlight shivers against the trees, laying its pale weight over everything, and we pass a small building—a ticket booth, the rectangular window shattered, graffiti marring the exterior walls. And beyond it, a larger building with a wooden deck built onto the front, the railing now sagging and broken. The sign above reads CONCESSIONS.

A place where you could once buy soda in paper cups, boxed candy, and buttered popcorn. But now the whole place is abandoned, gone back to the forest and the kids who've broken in over the years.

Ahead of us, a half-moon-shaped field fans out around a wooden theater screen, and a sea of Cutwater High students fill the overgrown grass. Some have parked their cars facing the screen and now sit reclined on hoods or perched on roofs, while others are strewn across beach blankets and towels, faces to the sky, smoking, drinking beers, kissing beneath the stars, while they wait for the film to start playing on the massive screen.

Only a few yards away my eyes find Clementine Morris—shy, quiet Clementine—seated on the hood of Tobias Huaman's silver Audi. I squint, certain I'm wrong, but her head is resting on Tobias's shoulder while he plays with her long, unruly hair, coiling it through his fingers like he is completely and deliriously lovestruck. I recall the fight that happened in the hall at school, Tobias and Mac facing off, while Clementine stood nearby, lips curled secretively. Now I'm starting to understand. . . . Clementine must have possessed a tulip, concealed out of sight, and the tiny bloodred bloom ensnared the attention of *both* Tobias and Mac.

And tonight she has found herself in the arms of Tobias.

But that's not the only peculiarity. Two other boys stand nearby, their arms crossed, as if waiting for their chance to confess their love to Clementine as soon as Tobias looks the other way. I wonder how many tulip petals she has hidden in her pockets, in the folds of her skirt. Maybe she's even been bathing in them, letting the perfume soak her skin.

Several cars away, Tobias's girlfriend—or likely ex-girlfriend

The Beautiful Maddening

now—Olive Montagu, leans against the tailgate of a black truck, three boys gathered around her, which isn't that unusual for Olive. Except when another girl approaches—Titha—and the boys snap their eyes to her as if suddenly confused as to who they love more: which girl has more stolen tulips stashed in her pockets. Two of the boys stagger after Titha, their eyes like pools of desire, a pathetic slant cut across their mouths as they call after her, begging her to let them hold her hand.

As my eyes sway over the crowd, I find more evidence of the same awful affliction. At the border of trees, two girls are tugging on the arms of a boy who looks like Dale Dawson, and they shriek at each other, shouting for the other to let go, but Dale just grins. He must have a tulip hidden somewhere, or maybe he swallowed it like several others did on the lawn outside of school.

They're falling in love with one another, desperate and unnatural.

And suddenly I'm reminded why this was a bad idea.

Too many people fill the lawn, and when they notice us, they'll clamor toward the Goode twins, begging for more tulips. *Pleading.*

"We shouldn't be here," I mutter to Archer.

But he claps me on the shoulder. "Let's go stir up some mischief," he answers, and he starts toward the crowd.

"Archer!" I bark.

He turns back, raising an eyebrow at me. "I'm going to find Willa. You coming or not?"

My feet shift in the overgrown grass, and I clench my jaw, wishing I'd never come in the first place. Archer might love the attention, but I never have. This was a terrible idea.

I shake my head, and he sighs. "Fine. I'll see you at home."

Shea Ernshaw

He turns away, and I watch my brother weave through the crowd as people lift their eyes in his direction, whisper words to one another, a few even standing up to follow after him. Archer Goode will indeed stir up mischief tonight. But I want no part of it.

Before anyone can recognize me, I tip my chin to the ground and start back up the dirt road. Away from the theater screen.

When a voice behind me says, "Did you find your thief?"

I stop, taking in a breath. I should keep going, not look back, get away from here before more people spot me. But I risk a glance over my shoulder, and my eyes find the deep green of his.

He's standing beside the ticket booth, one shoulder leaning against the wood clapboards, like a boy from one of his books, from one of Huck's films, not a boy from the real world. Certainly not from Cutwater.

My throat struggles to find its footing. "What?"

"Your thief," he repeats. "Did you find out who it was?"

"Not yet."

"So I'm still a suspect?" His tone is light, but his features are cold, stiff, giving nothing away. He's wearing the same gray sweat-shirt from two days ago, but my eyes trip over the outline of his shoulders, his arms, his cheekbones, instilling them into my memory this time. Determined not to forget. And out of some dangerous reflex, I step toward him, a gravity I can't explain.

"Everyone's a suspect," I answer, surprised at the playful tone of my voice.

His upper lip twitches, nearly becomes a smile. But never completely forms. "I'll have to be careful, then. Until I can clear my name."

The Beautiful Maddening

I can't help it, my own mouth pulls into a grin, then I drop my eyes to the ground, careful not to let our stares linger for too long. But just like before—he seems unflustered by the scent of my skin, the lingering sway of my gaze. His hands are sunk into his jean pockets, his shoulders drawn down. No part of him is beckoned closer to me. No nagging in his chest, no flicker in his eyes reworking itself into desire. He stays right where he is.

"I wasn't sure . . ." I pause. Now that I'm here, this doesn't seem like the kind of place where he would spend his time. A noisy, crowded drive-in. "You came all the way here from Favorville?"

He straightens up from the corner of the ticket booth, and I flinch, ready to back away if he starts moving closer.

"It wasn't far," he answers vaguely. "I came to watch a movie."

"No one comes here to see the movie."

"Then why do they come?"

I flash a look to the crowd; the reasons are obvious: to press themselves close to the one they desire, to do whatever they want without any rules.

"How did you even hear about it?" I try. "No one outside of Cutwater knows about this place."

He lifts a shoulder. "Word gets around."

I can tell he's hiding something—an icy, indescribable edge to each word.

A cheer erupts from the crowd—applause and hoots of excitement. Across the lawn, the old, weathered theater screen is flickering with an image, black-and-white lettering flaring across the screen: CASABLANCA. More shouts of excitement, then a speaker perched on the roof of a blue Honda near the front of the lawn belts out the opening music for the movie, the volume turned up too loud, rattling the speakers. Someone shouts to turn it down, but no one does, and the movie now shows an image of a crowded marketplace. I cringe at the tinny, crackling audio and realize that Oak is now standing closer to me, looking up at the theater screen.

Secretly, I try to capture every curve and slope of his face—the tension along his jaw, the sturdiness of his features, the river-dark hair. Gazing at his eyes, I notice a fleck of brown, an imperfection in his left eye. A notch of hazel in the rim of green. A boy whose eyes are unlike any I've ever drawn before.

I should pull my gaze away, not let my eyes sink into his, not risk letting his heart begin to pump too quickly, his mind turning soft with thoughts of me. But I can't. My eyes want only to peer into him, absorb every outline and shape. Possess it, coil it around my fingertips so I can sketch it later from my pencil onto paper. *This boy I want to remember.*

"Do they always play black-and-white films?" he asks, all soft, languid vowels tangled up in a cool winter breeze.

It occurs to me how strange it is to stand this close to him—to have a conversation that is so ordinary and commonplace, a thing I've rarely experienced—and it makes my chest feel like bubble gum, light and airy, about to pop. "Always," I answer, my traitorous voice a little breathless.

He keeps his gaze on the film as it sputters to life across the oversized screen.

"At least, that's what I've heard," I add. "I've never actually seen a film here."

He shifts his weight, settles a little on his right foot, and his skin

The Beautiful Maddening

seems darker than I remember: amber and tree bark, skin that is pulled from the page of a fable, a boy whose origin is unknown, descended from old gothic tales, from mystery novels. I imagine a past for him that is part fiction and part truth. A boy who has surely seen the world beyond our county line. "Then why'd you come tonight?" he asks.

I flick my eyes away, unsure what to say. "My birthday," I answer. This isn't a lie—Archer and I will be eighteen tomorrow. But it's not a day we normally celebrate. It sits on the calendar as a reminder of the day we were forced into this cursed life. I don't know why I reveal this to Oak, why these words fell from my lips.

"Happy birthday," he says, his bottle-green eyes dipping into my skin. "And . . ." His gaze sweeps over the crowd, the theater screen showing a commotion in the marketplace, music screeching from the speakers. "You're here with friends?"

A short, uncomfortable laugh escapes my throat. "No." *I don't have any friends; no one would dare spend longer than a few minutes with me.*

His shoulders settle, or maybe they tense, and the light that was in his eyes dims just a little. A distance spreading between us that can't be measured in feet, but in breaths held in tight lungs.

I feel a strange, dagger-sharp prick inside me.

The thudding of something that has no name. Indefinable.

His eyes flick away, blunt and quick, as if he's suddenly uncomfortable. He's been here too long. Stood too close to Lark Goode—although he shows no signs of lovesickness taking root in his veins. And this *indifference* only makes me want to edge closer to him—perplexed, fascinated—wanting to know what thoughts are resting behind his impossible eyes.

Shea Ernshaw

I want to speak, to ask him the truth about who he is, but the air in my throat feels like feathers tangled together, like I've swallowed a bird.

I peer at him, beneath the moonlight, sensing a storm of thoughts thundering across the unknowable landscape of his mind.

A few yards away someone shrieks—a girl with blond cascades of hair who's seated on a blanket at the edge of the lawn, two other girls beside her. She jumps up, a beer spilled down her T-shirt, and she stomps away as one of the other girls, with cotton candy–pink lipstick, runs after her.

I swallow, pulling my focus back to Oak. . . .

But he's *gone*.

I spin around. Confused. Head thumping.

And up the dirt road I can see his shadow, hands still in his pockets, striding away—melting into the dark and the trees.

He walked away and never even said goodbye.

Never said a word.

If he felt the luring pull of the Goode curse, he showed no signs of it. Somehow he felt nothing.

I close my eyes, letting the image of him sink into my memory like bare feet in April mud. I need to memorize him, hold on to every detail so I can sketch him later—shade in the unfinished parts of his face, the tensed angle of his neck, the soft arch of his lips when they nearly edged into a smile.

"Hello?" a voice says a few yards away, so small I barely register it.

My eyes flip open, and for a heart-stuttering second I think maybe Oak has returned, circled through the trees and come back. But when I blink through the dark, it's a different boy standing before me.

The Beautiful Maddening

Jude is only a few paces away, holding the paper origami chatterbox in his left hand, his pale blue eyes blinking rapidly as if he's struggling to keep himself calm in the presence of Lark Goode—local oddity, the girl you might tumble heedlessly into love with if you're not careful.

He rubs his free hand down his mustard-gray cardigan, then shuffles in his brown loafers that look to be a full size too big, as if they were borrowed from his dad or pilfered from the local thrift store.

"Do you want your fortune read?" he asks quickly, a nervous twitch fluttering his upper lip.

He's never asked me this before, never dared to get this close, but I shake my head at him. "I don't have anything to trade." I know the rules, but my pockets are empty. I have nothing he needs.

"This one's free," he answers, and there is something in his voice, a slippery tone, like he's wanted to read my fortune for some time but has always been too afraid. And truthfully, I've always wanted to know what's written inside his origami chatterbox. I've watched with envy as he hands out fortunes at school, always wondering what my fortune might be. My *fate*. But also a little afraid to know.

He positions the chatterbox over his small fingers, holding it out for me to see. Across the folded, diamond-shaped paper, four words are written in shaded blue pencil—the same color as Jude's eyes.

East, *West*, *North*, *South*, they read.

I know he wants me to choose one, and I blink down at the chatterbox, sensing that I don't want to get this wrong. This might be my only chance to have my fortune read by Jude—he likely won't offer it again, certainly not for free. I swallow, lifting my eyes. "West."

West is the direction I'll go when I leave this town. West is the direction that Swamp Wells Road heads away from our house, over a long hill that winds its way into Favorville, and then to a larger town called Park Grove, and then to the ocean. Wide and flat and endless. From there, you could set out across the Pacific to any continent in the distance.

Jude expands the paper origami, counting off the letters that spell "west," then opening the chatterbox wide to reveal more words inside. But instead of navigational directions, I see names—ones I recognize. Jude senses my hesitation, and he says, "They're names from classic novels."

I scan them quickly: *Gatsby, Pip, Sherlock, Inigo*.

I ask myself which feels the most *true*, the most right in this moment, but they all feel the same.

"Everyone hesitates here," he says, a tug at the corner of his pink lips. "One day I wrote 'Veruca,' for Veruca Salt, on every triangle. I wanted to make it easy. Give only one option. But still . . ." He lifts a shoulder. "Everyone hesitated. They stared at the name Veruca like they couldn't decide, even though there was only one choice." For a second Jude grins up at me, looking me clear in the eyes. But I drop my gaze—afraid he'll stare too long and start to sink closer and closer until he can't imagine a life without me. He clears his throat, like he felt the shifting in his chest, like he knows he needs to make this quick. "Fate will give you the fortune you need—it doesn't matter what name you pick."

Before I can doubt myself, I say, "Pip."

Jude nods. "Good choice." And he quickly flicks the chatterbox open and closed, then open again, until he lands on four different names: *Huckleberry, Moby Dick, Jane, Ichabod*.

The Beautiful Maddening

I don't let myself overthink it, I don't hesitate, I just say the name that my eyes land on first. "Ichabod."

But it's Jude who hesitates this time, who stares at me a moment before opening the chatterbox to peel back the paper. He unfolds the carefully creased angles, flattening open the origami to reveal what waits beneath.

But under the Ichabod name . . . lies a blank triangle.

It's the only triangle that doesn't have several words—*a fortune*—waiting beneath it.

"I always leave one blank," he explains, his tone shallow, like it's lost all its weight. *Its courage.* "But no one ever chooses this one. After all these years, I started to think no one ever would. But *you* did." He doesn't look at me, just stares down at the white triangle, no fate waiting for me.

No fortune to be read.

"Does that mean I don't have a fate?" My chest feels scraped clean, an empty cavity, like a cruel darkness has seeped under my vulnerable flesh.

"No," he answers, running his thumb over the blank paper. "It means you make your own fate. It hasn't been decided for you." He quickly folds the origami back into its original shape, then slides it into the oversized pocket of his cardigan. But before he turns away—as I expect him to—he reaches out suddenly, like a snake snapping at its victim, and grabs my left hand, pulling it toward him.

I let out a little squeak, caught off guard, but when I look up at Jude, his eyes are closed, fluttering like honeybee wings, and he places his other palm flat against mine—as if we are two sheets of paper laid one on top of the other.

"You shouldn't touch me . . . ," I say, starting to pull away, but he holds firmly to my hand—not painfully, but enough to keep me from slipping from his grasp.

I watch his eyelashes flap, his bottom lip sag, and I feel the strange heat of tears against my own eyes—a loosening in my chest I can't quite explain. Jude's mother is from Germany, his father from Tampa, Florida. But his mom was a fortune teller when she lived in a small town outside of Hanover—at least that's the rumor. People came to her home and sat in her living room over a pot of black tea. She was a seer of fates.

And now Jude can see them too.

"Your family has caused so much heartache in this town," he mutters, tilting his small-angled chin, the voices of Humphrey Bogart and Ingrid Bergman blaring from the speakers behind me, the flickering images of *Casablanca* cast out onto the lawn and through the line of trees. "You want to leave Cutwater . . . don't you?" I nod, but he doesn't see; his eyes are pinched closed. His palm becomes too warm against mine, sweat beading down his forehead. I want to pull away, but I also want to hear the rest—I want him to finish. "Tears and rain . . . it's all the same." His eyebrows pucker. "Forsaken Creek . . . is the only way to leave."

"What?" I narrow my eyes at him.

Jude's head sways a little, then his swimming-pool-blue eyes break open at the same moment he releases my hand, letting it fall to my side. A tingling numbness spider-crawls across my palm, as if I've just felt an electrical shock.

"How does the creek . . . help me leave?" I rub my hands together, trying to work out the nervy sensation.

The Beautiful Maddening

Jude blinks at me, then reaches forward, pushing his index finger into my chest, right over my heart—sharp and pointed. "This must break. This must weep, and then . . ." He breathes. "You will finally be free."

I shake my head at him. "I don't understand. . . . What does that mean?"

But Jude pushes his hands into his cardigan pockets, and his eyes water like dew on cut blades of grass. "It's your fate. . . . It's for you to interpret, not me."

"But what does the creek have to do with anything?" I lean closer to him, anxious suddenly, disoriented. Confused.

Someone starts laughing to our left, a deep, rolling belly laugh, and Jude's eyes snap toward the sound.

"Jude," I press, but he's backing away from me. "Please."

From his pocket he pulls out the origami chatterbox again, and without another word he heads away from the ticket booth, away from me, toward a group of juniors seated on a large beach towel.

He has more fortunes to give tonight, more fates to hand out, and he's already spent too much time beside Lark Goode. But as I pull in a warm breath of air, my mind crunching and churning over the words he spoke, the sky makes a low rumbling sound. A second later rain begins pinging against my forehead, the start of a storm darkening the skyline.

I turn and run home through the rain.

SIX

Maybe Jude is full of shit.

I lie in bed, listening to the gurgle of Forsaken Creek as it meanders beneath the floorboards before cutting its way out into the tulip rows. My fate was decided long ago, on the night I was born: doomed to bear the Goode last name.

"Forsaken Creek is the only way to leave," Jude said.

If only I could sail away on a paper boat—like Archer and I used to make. But the creek is a shallow, wild thing. Not deep enough to carry me far away from this life. So Jude . . . must be full of shit. Yet the other part of his fortune, about my heart needing to *break* and then I'll be free, felt a little too William Shakespeare. Like he was only trying to scare me, threaten me with the same heartbreak my family has caused this town. Because how could a broken heart set me free from this place?

The only freedom I need is a train ticket.

And after tomorrow, after our birthday—once I'm officially eighteen—I'm leaving.

The morning sun finally rises through the window, baking the wet, swampy soil behind the house, but I lie in bed, letting the hours

The Beautiful Maddening

pass, listening to the lonely quiet. Around noon I finally slip from bed. I pass the open doorway into Archer's empty room: my twin never came home last night, and it looks like I will spend *our* birthday alone.

In the kitchen I open the freezer and pull out the paper bag. I've been saving it, tucked at the back behind bags of frozen peas and expired Tater Tots. I'm not sure if Archer even knows it's here.

I remove the two tiny cakes inside, still shimmering with golden sprinkles, and place them on the kitchen table—beside the growing pile of Archer's unopened love letters—and they look just as perfectly sweet and delicate as they did the day Dad gave them to us. Months ago now.

He rarely visits Cutwater—he stays away, working on a fishing boat in a small coastal town that he said suffers its own curses and torments: boys who drown in the harbor, witches risen from the deep. But there is a small cake shop near the waterfront that sells a variety of peculiar flavors, promising to blot out unwanted memories, to help people forget the things they'd like to wipe clean from their mind. Dad chuckled when he said it; he thought it was an absurd notion. Still, he brought back two cakes for his two children. Archer and me.

"For your birthday," he said, handing me the paper bag.

"Our birthday isn't for another three months," I replied.

But he lifted a shoulder, like he'd lost track of time or it didn't matter either way. He knew he wouldn't be here for our birthday. It was too painful to stand in this house with his two children, borne by a woman who carried a curse around inside her bones. Our father fell victim to this curse. And when tulip season ended, our mom's belly beginning to grow, our parents knew it wasn't love. Not truly. It was only the tulips that had held them together for a few summer nights.

Love ruins everything.

I leave one of the tiny cakes on the kitchen table for Archer, and I carry the other one into my room, placing it on the windowsill to thaw in the sunlight.

I find the old suitcase that once belonged to our mother, stuffed under her bed, and I drag it down to my room. There are no tough decisions to make about what I should pack and what I should leave behind—I don't own enough things for this. Instead I pull every item of clothing from my closet, carefully folding it all into the suitcase. Two pairs of shoes and one pair of flip-flops. A few small trinkets from atop my dresser: A tiny silver rabbit, which likely once belonged on a charm bracelet that Archer found out in the woods, then gave to me for Christmas when I was eleven. A wooden bookmark that the middle school librarian gave to me in sixth grade with a quote on one side:

Books are a uniquely portable magic.
—Stephen King

I have a stack of two dozen sketchbooks on my bedside table, every page filled, and I lay these carefully atop my clothes. Jewelry, I own none. Cash, I have very little. Dad sends us money every month, for essentials, but whatever is left over after groceries and shampoo and light bulbs, Archer and I split. I've mostly saved mine over the years, while Archer spends his as fast as he can. I have nearly $500 counted and pressed into a wallet—that also used to be Mom's.

The Beautiful Maddening

Enough to get me out of this town and keep me fed until I find a job.

I sink down onto the window seat, legs curled beneath me, and watch the tulips tip and sway in the soft spring wind, and I wonder, *How long before someone tries to sneak through the dagger-sharp barbed-wire fence?*

I grab my notebook and press the flinty tip of my pencil to the page, right at Oak's collarbone. I shade in the sturdy lines of his shoulders, the curve of his lower lip, the way his mouth sat suspended just before he spoke, and the soft silhouette of the tree branches above him. I lose myself in the sketch, filling in the last of his hair—dark and short, slightly wavy at the ends—then I let the pencil fall to the notebook, staring down at him. *A boy I don't understand.* My fingertips stray across his eyebrows, his lips, the pale afternoon sunlight on his cheeks. I'm curious about him in a way I've never known before—but I also know I could never be this close to him in the real world. Not for long.

The light outside has dulled into late afternoon, and the tiny cake has now softened. Carefully I peel back the paper, and when the warm cake breaks apart on my tongue, I close my eyes, savoring the hint of lemon and mint and lavender. It tastes like a stormy night at sea, like a life I might have had if I'd been born somewhere else, instead of in this house—a birthday spent with family gathered around a homemade cake, blowing out candles and opening presents wrapped in silvery bows. Maybe I'd go into town with friends, see a movie, stay up late whispering in the dark, wrapped in sleeping bags on the floor of my normal room—no sounds of a creek rushing below us—giggling, refusing to sleep until the sun came up.

Shea Ernshaw

But in this life not even my twin is anywhere to be found.

Yet, for the briefest moment, it feels like the cake is stripping away the worst of my memories: the day Mom left, her silhouette vanishing into the dark. No goodbyes. No promises to return. Only a cold, empty house and nothing for breakfast.

Our world was cleaved in half that morning. And nothing would put it back together.

I swallow the last of the cake, my shoulders settling against the window frame, and listen to the constant gurgle of Forsaken Creek—even when snow carpets the ground in winter, the creek still flows, refusing to freeze. I push open the window—the sun gone to the west; the night revealing itself, warm and windless; insects thrumming from the field; frogs croaking along the muddy banks of the creek—and I sink into bed.

Tomorrow I leave this place.

I listen to the tulip petals brush together like silky paper. Some years the tulips stay in bloom for months; other seasons it's only a couple of weeks. The heat and cold have no effect on them—it's some other peculiar enchantment that causes them to wilt back into the soil. Sometimes they simply refuse to wither or decay, and they go on blooming, showing their vibrant petals well into autumn, into winter, even after the first snow falls. They follow no natural order, no farmer's almanac or rhythm of the seasons. They behave as they want.

I hear the click of the front door opening. Archer is home.

His footsteps travel down the hall, but he doesn't turn into his room. He keeps walking, until his shadowed outline is standing in my doorway. His hair is a little wild, cheeks flushed, like he's either

The Beautiful Maddening

just run home or been kissing someone on the front steps. "Everyone in town's talking about it," he says, as if he knows I'm still awake.

He walks across the room, the old, rotted wood floor creaking beneath him, threatening to collapse and send us both crashing into the creek below—but it won't, because this house refuses to die, refuses to sink into the swampy soil, when it should have decades ago. Archer stands at the window, looking out at the tulips. "They're bathing in the tulips, rubbing the pollen on their skin."

I exhale and push myself up, leaning back against the headboard. "They're drunk on them," I say. "It makes them feel like they're in love."

He looks back at me, jaw tensed, and the breezy calm that usually rests just beneath the surface of his disinterested eyes is briefly gone. "Lacy Bates said she'd pay me a hundred dollars for a single tulip. She likes some girl from her algebra class, and she thinks the tulip will help her odds."

"Love has always been a lie for us," I say. "Now it's a lie for them, too."

Archer turns fully, his tall frame casting a lean, moonlit shadow across the floor. It's unsettling seeing him like this, the nervous pulse at his temples. "They don't have much interest in me anymore either." He drags a hand through his dark hair, looking to the floor. "A whole tulip season wasted," he says. "Doesn't seem fair."

"Nothing about being a Goode is fair."

He nods, looks somber, tired even. Unlike him.

A long, frigid silence hangs in the air between us before I finally say, "I'm leaving tomorrow." The words are heavy on my tongue. Because even though I've been counting down the days until this moment, even though freedom feels so close that it makes me lightheaded, leaving my brother behind is the only thing that hurts. The only part of this that feels wrong.

He smirks a little, like he thinks I'm making a joke, but then his expression drops, his eyes swiveling to my packed suitcase. "You're serious? I guess I always thought you just liked talking about it, but that you'd never actually do it."

"You could come with me," I offer, daring to hope he might say yes.

Archer shakes his head, smiling, the light returning to his eyes. "You know I'd never survive outside of this town. This is where I belong. But you . . ." His smile pinches together. "You're better than this place, I've always known it. You know it too. I'm glad you're finally doing it—escaping."

I stand up from the bed, but Archer holds up his palm to me. "No goodbyes yet. Let's save them for the morning. You know I hate sentimental shit."

I laugh. "Okay, tomorrow."

He walks to the doorway, then stops and looks back at me over his shoulder. "Happy birthday, sis."

The air inside my bedroom feels heavy, humid, even with both windows open and a breeze sailing from the back garden, across my bed, then out through the front window facing the road. I crave the numbing quiet of sleep, but I blink up at the ceiling—knowing that this is my last night in this room, this house.

A faint tap-tapping enters my ears.

The Beautiful Maddening

I hold my breath, listening into the dark of the room, but there is only the sound of the creek rushing beneath the floor. Nothing else.

I force my eyes closed, willing sleep to take me under, when I hear another sound.

But this noise is different: softer, muted, like footsteps on wet soil.

I fling my eyes open and look to the front window—where I can see something resting on the sill. Something foreign.

The breeze tugs softly at the edges of the thing, and I feel a sharp twinge at the base of my neck—the part of my brain that tells me this isn't right. I force my feet to slide to the floor, then cross the room, while a chill scratches down my spine.

At the window I stare down at the thing.

A book has been placed on the windowsill.

Left here. Out of place. Where it doesn't belong.

In the moonlight I can just barely read the title: *Peter and Wendy*, by J. M. Barrie. I run my fingers across the black cover, the gold lettering—it looks old, a book that's been read many times over the decades. I lift my eyes to the open window, peering out into the dark, and catch a shadow slipping away through the tall grass toward the road.

"Hey!" I call.

The silhouette stops, seems to melt in with the dark, but when I blink again, he starts to turn, pushing back the gray hood of his sweatshirt, tilting his chin so his forehead and nose catch the soft moonlight, revealing his face.

He stands that way for a second, then another, as if deciding whether to run the rest of the distance out to the road or turn and walk back to my window.

Slowly he strides toward me.

Oak.

"You're trespassing," I say when he reaches the window, my voice hushed, eyebrow lifted, while my heart thuds strangely.

He is quiet and beautiful and almost otherworldly in this late, watery light, the spring air against his dark skin, the trees swaying behind him. "I'm sorry." His eyes are soft, and he seems different, bold, preternatural, as if he's emerged from the woods across the road like a storybook creature. "I wanted to leave you something . . . for your birthday."

I slide my finger down the spine of the book, feeling the subtly raised letters.

He watches me, and there are questions in his eyes, a paradox he's trying to unravel—a boy who has strayed too close to a cursed girl, standing in the moonlight, Forsaken Creek churning only a few feet away. He should leave, back away from the window. But I don't want him to . . . not yet. I like being close to him, a boy who still shows no sign of delirium.

A boy I don't understand.

"I wasn't sure if you already owned a copy," he adds, shoulders dropped, easy, his hands sunk into the pockets of his jeans.

I shake my head and smile. The books I've read are always borrowed, a library stamp on the inside flap stating the date it must be given back. "It looks old," I say, turning it over in my hands.

"My father has a library of rare books."

My eyes flick to his. "Does your father collect them?" I ask, hoping to extract any kernel of information about who Oak is.

"Yeah, and other things."

The Beautiful Maddening

"Then you probably shouldn't give it to me. It looks valuable." I hold it out through the open window, toward him.

But he doesn't blink; he looks straight into the beating heart of my chest. "He won't even know it's gone."

The warm spring wind plays against the tall grass behind him, and I watch his eyes, looking for any sign of love, for any hint that he's starting to tumble down a dark rabbit hole into madness. But his gaze is flat, unfettered, and I don't know how to feel. I've never experienced anything like it. Should I fear him . . . his lack of emotion when he looks at me?

How can the tulips have no effect on him? How can *I* have no effect on him?

"You came here just to give me a book?" I ask.

A wisp of hair strays across his eyes. "Is that okay?"

I love the way words slide carefully between his lips, how his skin reminds me of an autumn rainstorm, dark and cloying. Maybe it's him who's cast the spell on me?

"Did you come for a tulip?" I ask, the mistrust and doubt creeping into my thoughts. Maybe the book is simply a ploy to get close to me, to the house and the garden, so that he can ask for a tulip, like everyone else.

But his shoulders stiffen a little, an eyebrow lifts. "I don't care about your tulips."

"Everyone else in town does."

He runs a hand along his forearm, glancing up to the few stars visible in the heat-drenched sky. "They're just afraid they won't find love without them," he says, before lowering his green eyes back to me. "They're afraid of being alone." He slows his breathing, watching me like he's trying to make sense of what I am. "Isn't that what we're all afraid of?"

A pressure forms in my throat. He's talking about love, about loneliness, as if these are two ordinary things to be discussed by strangers in the middle of the night through an open window. But the way he says the word "love," it's as if it were nothing at all. A thin measure of air, a single grain of sand. Something that can be breathed in and let go just as easily. Dropped or forgotten. Meaningless.

"Not everyone," I reply, because I'm afraid of something else. . . . I'm afraid I'll only ever be loved *because* of the tulips.

Oak takes a step closer to the window, unfathomable green eyes piercing into mine, but his body is now tensed, like he's ready to turn and run if he needs to—if he starts to feel something for me that isn't natural, a deep obsession rising up from his gut. The curse spreading along his veins.

But it's me who feels something I don't like, a coiling need that I've never felt before.

"What are *you* afraid of?" he asks.

I bite down against the heat in my cheeks, because I can't tell him the truth: That I'm afraid the love others feel for me will always be entwined with the Goode family curse, that love will always be a lie for me. That it's something I can never trust.

And that now I'm also afraid of *him*. He scares me: The way my head thumps when he's only a few feet away. How I imagine him inching closer, how I daydream about what it might be like to feel his hand again—like when he pulled me away from the crowd at school. How I would like to know what he smells like when rain touches

The Beautiful Maddening

his skin, what his heartbeat sounds like in my ear, listening to the rhythm that keeps him alive.

But these treacherous thoughts can't be real, can't be allowed to cement in my mind, so I grip the book tighter in my hands. "I'm afraid I'll end up like every other Goode who's ever lived in this house," I answer. Plainly. Truthfully.

I feel him observing every flick of my eyelashes, every twitch of unease at the corners of my mouth. He looks at me as if I am a memory—like he can recall something in my eyes. Two moments in time. Two pools of darkness and light. As if I am something he has lost but found again. A girl from one of his books.

He takes another step toward the window, and my treasonous heart claws up into my throat. He nods to the book he's given me, my fingertips pressing deeply into the cover, holding on to it like a tether. Like it's the only thing keeping me from drifting away into the stars. "It's about a girl who leaves her ordinary life for an unexpected one," he says.

"What if I want to leave this world for one that *is* ordinary?" I pose.

"Most people are bored with ordinary."

"I crave it."

He smiles, a shiver in his eyes. "'Second to the right, and straight on till morning,'" he says, quoting the book I hold. "Maybe that's your way out of here, just like Wendy."

My heart pulses in my ears. "It's easier for fictional characters to run away from home than it is in the real world." I think of my packed suitcase, lying behind me on the floor, in the dark of my room. I'm almost gone. I'm almost free of this place.

"That's exactly what someone would say in a book just before they kill the villain and flee the castle and find true love."

I let out a tiny laugh, but it's mostly just air. "If only I knew who the villain was."

He smiles a little. *Only a little.* "I'm trying to figure that out too. And finding it harder and harder."

My mouth falls back into place, uncertain what he means. *Who is the villain of his story?* Who is the villain of mine?

But instead of moving even closer, instead of reciting more lines from the book he's given me, he blinks and straightens his shoulders back. "I need to get home." He looks restless suddenly, edgy, like he's stayed far too long, and he reaches for his own book in his back pocket—probably out of habit. The cover is creased, bent in half, and I envy it: the adoration he's shown the book, the time he's spent in its pages. The love he's given it. I exhale, pushing away the stupid thought.

He's already turning away, striding through the overgrown grass toward Swamp Wells Road, and I feel a pain in my throat, in the center of my heart—not wanting him to leave.

"Hey!" I call out.

He stops, soft green eyes glancing over his shoulder.

"Come back tomorrow," I say, I dare, I risk—when I know I shouldn't. "After sunset. I want to show you something."

For a second too long, he looks like he's going to say no—tell me that I won't see him ever again. Getting this close to me was a bad idea.

But his silent eyes flicker with something else, and he nods. "Tomorrow," he repeats. "Okay."

SEVEN

Oak might be the villain of my story.

He might be the thing that unravels me—makes me feel something I shouldn't. Something dangerous. A boy who is a paradox. Who defies all the warnings Mom recited to me before she left.

But every time I see him, the less I'm able to remember what it is I should really fear.

I sink back into bed, knees pulled up, and stare at my suitcase. *Nothing has changed*, I tell myself. I can leave the following day. I don't have a train ticket. I don't have anyone waiting for me. I make my own rules. I can spend one last day in Cutwater, with Oak, before I leave for good.

No harm in that.

I'm allowed one more day.

I stay awake and read *Peter and Wendy*, turning each page as if it will reveal some secret about Oak—tell me who he really is—but the story begins to feel like an omen.

A fable about the truth of who we really are, deep down. About the life we choose. And about loss. Wendy may love Peter, but she chooses the real world instead.

Shea Ernshaw

But my life is not a fable. It's much worse, because it's real.

I close my eyes and let the sound of the creek muddy my thoughts.

"Forsaken Creek is the only way to leave," Jude said. But his fortune might only be another fable. A made-up tale, a trick he learned from his mom.

I fall asleep just as the morning sun peeks through the damp woods, the book resting beside me in a streak of sallow light, and I dream of lands far, *far* away, where boys can fly and no one ever grows up.

But I wake not long after, a loud bang vibrating through my dreams.

I sit up, shaking off the haze of too little sleep, and I hear Archer's boots stomping down the hall. But he stops short before reaching my doorway, and I hear him enter Mom's abandoned room—a room we keep closed. A room we never step inside.

I throw back the bedsheet, still in last night's clothes, and hurry down the hall. Mom's doorway is still open, but Archer is no longer inside. I find him in the living room, moving toward the front door. "There's a whole damn crowd out there," he says, flashing me a look, then pointing toward the front window. "And they're asking for tulips."

It takes a moment for my mind to catch up, to realize what Archer is holding: our grandfather's old, antique shotgun. There's no ammunition for it—it's so ancient and rusted that it wouldn't matter even if there were—but Archer pulls open the front door and steps out onto the porch, holding the gun as if he's about to fire it into the sky.

A dozen of our classmates from Cutwater High have gathered at the end of the driveway, several cars parked along the ditch, one of them still idling.

The Beautiful Maddening

For years they couldn't understand why they felt drawn to the Goodes each spring. But now they do. *They know.* It was the tulips all along—because now they feel the ache, the pull toward the tulips.

And they want a bloom for themselves.

Yet none of them have mustered the courage to walk down our driveway. They stand, shuffling nervously, desperate for a tulip but unwilling to face the Goode twins, who might be witches, vampires, trolls who sleep beneath the floorboards of our house, who will rip out their eyes and swallow their hearts if they get too close.

Archer broadens his stance at the edge of the porch. "Get the hell off our driveway!"

The group falls quiet but doesn't move.

"Keep standing there . . . and you'll find out how serious I am," he adds, voice booming through the clear morning air.

Still no one moves.

A wretched need for tulips keeps them right where they are. And I wonder if there's a twisting pain inside them, a longing they can't ignore—a desire for love that overrides everything else.

A feeling I've spent my life trying to avoid.

Archer grumbles something, irritated, and he clomps down the front steps, over the creek, and starts striding up the driveway, shotgun at his side. He's fed up. He won't call the local police; he'll deal with this himself.

"Archer!" I call after him, afraid of what he'll do.

But he never reaches the end of the driveway. Maybe it's the look in his eyes, maybe it's just Archer himself, but in an instant the crowd scatters. They scramble back to their cars, climb atop bicycles, peeling away up Swamp Wells Road.

They don't stick around to find out how far Archer will take it.

He's a Goode, after all, and Goodes are both gods and monsters. Unpredictable and dangerous, with nothing to lose. Because everything has already been taken from us.

"They're vultures," he growls when he climbs back up the porch steps.

He's scared them off. But I know it won't last.

They'll come back with hope in their eyes. Tomorrow or the next day, they'll return. As the old tulips they possess wilt and fade, the effect wearing off, they'll need more.

They'll crave it.

Because the tulips bring them an even more potent intoxication:

l
o
v
e

And now that they've had a taste, one more will never be enough.

I dig through my suitcase, pulling out my jean shorts—the ones I cut off from a pair of thrift-store Levi's—and my favorite teal-green tank top with the three white buttons down the front. I pull them on, then face the mirror over my dresser. *What the hell am I doing?* I should have been on the first train leaving Cutwater, sketching the faces of the other passengers, daydreaming about the life waiting for me at the end of the tracks.

Instead I'm standing in my room, in this house, all for one last

The Beautiful Maddening

glimpse of a boy I can't explain. A boy who is a riddle I feel desperate to solve.

"Thought you were leaving today?" Archer asks. I turn, and he's standing in my bedroom doorway.

"I'm still leaving," I assure him, stepping into my sandals. "Just delayed it a little."

He squints down at my suitcase, partly unpacked. "Decided that you'd miss me too much, huh?"

"Hardly," I reply, striding past him.

"Seriously, though, why are you still here?"

I stop at the front door and look back at him. "Just something I have to do tonight."

"That's how it starts. *One more day*, and before you know it, twenty years have gone by and you're still in Cutwater."

I pull open the door. "That's not happening to me."

Archer follows me out onto the porch. "Sure, little sis. Ten bucks says you're not going anywhere. You'll still be in this house by the end of summer."

"I'm not taking your bet, *little* brother. Because I'm leaving . . . just not yet."

"Doubt it!" he calls.

"Watch me!" I move down the driveway, but I hear him laugh, and then the thump of the front door as he retreats back inside. These are the moments I *will* miss. The back-and-forth with my brother, my twin. When I'm gone, there will be a silence where he used to be.

The light drains from the sky, crickets sing from the tall grass along the back porch, and I stand in the shadow of a crooked birch tree beside the mailbox, waiting.

I don't want Oak walking up to the house like he did last night. I don't want to risk Archer seeing him, asking questions, making things unnecessarily awkward. So I wait.

There are no headlights on the road, and as the minutes pass, I begin to wonder if Oak will even show up.

Maybe he changed his mind. *He'd be smart if he did, if he stayed away*.

I tilt my eyes to the star-studded sky, breathing in the warm night air. Maybe I am stupid for staying in town, for delaying my escape. All for a boy who I'll never see again after tomorrow. Why am I wasting my time? Why am I standing out here in the dark?

I close my eyes, feeling foolish, thinking I should head back up to the house, when I hear the crunch of gravel underfoot.

Squinting through the dark, I see him. Oak is walking up Swamp Wells Road, hands in his pockets, wearing a gray T-shirt and looking like he was swept in on a summer breeze.

He came after all, like he promised.

"Hey," he says, casual and airy and full of secrets. And all my resolve to walk back to the house, to forget about Oak, melts away. Just like that.

"Sorry," he adds. "Were you waiting long?"

I shake my head, my thoughts tangled up. I'm not used to this: Meeting a boy after dark. Being this close to someone, getting to feel like an ordinary girl.

"Are you okay to walk a little farther?" I ask, not knowing exactly how far he's just traveled to get here.

The Beautiful Maddening

"Sure."

He doesn't ask where I'm taking him, doesn't question whether he should be this close to a Goode, but follows me around the side of the house, past the newly fenced garden, to the dirt path through the woods. The path leads us alongside Rabbit Cross River, where the water is cold and full and rushing, and the night air is like a warm breath against my throat. We haven't walked far when the path veers deeper into the trees, and we reach the train tracks that run east–west through Cutwater.

"We're almost there," I say, and he nods, seeming content just to walk. Unaffected by the scent of tulips always on my skin.

We make our way silently up the tracks, an owl hooting from somewhere in the trees to our left, until at last we reach the abandoned train car—left on an unused section of track. Rusted in place, a relic forgotten.

But not by everyone.

The door into the train car is slid wide open, the dark interior filled with empty beer cans, half-smoked cigarettes, and names painted on the walls. Kids from Cutwater have been coming here for years to mark their place in the world, to declare that they were here in this shitty, middle-of-nowhere town.

But I don't move toward the door; I walk to the metal ladder on the outer wall and hoist myself up to the first rung, then climb up to the flat roof of the train car. When I glance back down, Oak has already swung himself up the ladder without much effort and reaches the top quickly.

"You come here a lot?" he asks, turning in a circle to gaze out at the forest pressing in around us.

"Sometimes. In the summer."

I lower myself to the roof, stretching out onto my back—my heart a riotous thump in my chest—and Oak does the same. The metal roof is warm beneath us, heated by the sun during the day, but above us the stars feel close, drawn down by the spiky treetops. It always feels darker out here, swallowed up by the night.

I press my palms against the roof and close my eyes. "Sometimes I swear I can feel the train moving," I say. *Sometimes I swear I can feel it inching down the tracks, gaining momentum, a ghost train come to life.*

Oak presses his hands to the metal, his fingers only a millimeter from mine—the width of a snowflake, a tear, a strand of hair. "You want out of here that bad?" he asks, turning his head, his eyes almost black in the darkness. But his mouth is a calm, comforting line: a dangerous mouth, one that is far too close.

I breathe and pull my eyes away. He *should* feel drawn to me, but instead it's me who can't control my own thoughts—an unmistakable, fathomless feeling, like falling into an unknown darkness. And I keep waiting to snap awake, for the sensation to pull me back to the waking world. But it doesn't.

Through my lashes, I peer up at the starlight, counting the seconds and imagining the trees whipping by as the train carries us both far away from here. I don't know why I don't tell him the truth: That I was supposed to be on a real train this morning, leaving this place behind. That he is the reason I stayed.

"Don't you want to leave?" I ask instead.

He doesn't answer, an unnameable silence bending the darkness around us, shaped by the things he doesn't want to admit, doesn't

The Beautiful Maddening

say. But I know what it is to keep yourself secret, hidden, safe. And I smile, liking the quiet between our words.

"Everything feels different at night," he says after a long exhale. "Like it all has more meaning." He breathes, and I know there is more to this boy than what I can see beside me.

I tilt my head to look at him. A moment passes. Then another. Unfettered by noise, only our hearts thudding in our chests. A feeling that's hard to describe: like the ends of my eyelashes are lit with electricity, like the sky right before a summer thunderstorm—the mere seconds before the first snap of lightning. He's not looking for a response—it's the silence we both crave.

But then it comes . . . the low rumble I've been waiting for, and I push myself up to standing, squinting through the dark down the tracks. "There," I say, nodding.

Oak rises to his feet, his shoulder steady beside me, a boy who is a mountain, who is a *tree*, who is a heartbeat too close. Our eyes watch the tracks, where a beam of light is breaking through the forest.

A train is coming, only a few minutes behind schedule.

Never on time.

It travels on a track that runs parallel to this abandoned section— where we stand on the forgotten train car. The ground begins to tremble. This is my favorite part: the anticipation. The world shaking out of focus just a little.

The vibration grows stronger, the train moving quickly, only seconds now. I step to the very edge of the roof, closer to the other track, my heart climbing up from my chest—the adrenaline inching along my veins. This is why I come, the thing I want to feel.

Oak watches me, and I can sense the flicker of uncertainty in him. But he steps forward, filling the space beside me—this boy who stands so close, he could touch me if he wanted. He could pull Lark Goode into his arms and lay his lips against mine, but somehow *he resists*. Somehow he seems immune when others would have slid their hands along my floral-scented skin by now, begging me to love them back.

Somehow, *somehow* . . .

And yet.

A part of me wishes he would.

The light of the approaching train grows impossibly bright, filling the sky, flashing across the trees, sending the ghosts back into the dark. I suck in a breath just as the train slams past us. A rush of air and sound roars against my ears, the metal wheels rattling over every divot in the track, and I swear the air smells like all the places the train has been—sun-soaked beaches and snowy mountainsides and deserts where nothing grows.

This train doesn't stop here in Cutwater, doesn't even slow down; it passes through on its way to better places.

The wind screams against our faces, the stationary train car shuddering below us, vibrating up our legs, and I hold out my arms to feel the rush of the wind against my skin, my hair swept out in waves behind me.

Oak grabs my hand.

He touches me.

Clenches his palm to mine.

I flick my eyes to his, and I can see that the fear in his tensed jaw and sharp green eyes isn't for himself; it's for me—he's keeping me from tipping forward into the passing train as it shrieks past.

The Beautiful Maddening

My heart bangs against my eardrums, and I pinch my eyes closed: the heat from his palm, the wind against my face, it makes my body feel wrenched inside out, ripped free from the roof and sent down the tracks. A girl who once lived in Cutwater but was swept up into the sky by a boy and a train.

"Lark," I think I hear him say, my name against his lips, his voice like the first snowfall on autumn trees, cold and verdant and sanguine. I swallow, the pulse in my chest thudding louder, louder. . . .

Until all at once the train is gone.

Whoosh.

Slipped back into the night, the last of the roar echoing off the trees, carried away into the distance, and the wind goes with it. Silence falls over us, the lack of noise almost unbearable, ears ringing, blood spilling back down my veins. But I don't want to let go. I want to hold on to this moment, make it last, suspended like a raindrop against a cold windowpane.

But Oak slides his hand free from mine, and the moment is broken.

I feel lightheaded.

My heart is still beating against my ribs when I turn to look at him. "Do you want to go home?" I ask, breathless, senseless, reckless.

His eyes are blades. "No."

"Good. I have something else to show you."

A half mile down the train tracks, we reach a rarely traveled dirt road overgrown with blackberry bushes and cattail reeds—no cars have passed down this way in a decade—and we walk the length of the road until it dead-ends, a star-lit clearing opening up ahead of us.

At the edge of the meadow, an abandoned farmhouse stands against a line of evergreens, windows boarded, the interior dark, crowded with cobwebs and long-neglected ghosts. But at the other end of the meadow, where the ground slopes away, sits a clear, crescent-shaped pond with a view out to the rolling hills in the distance.

We make our way through the knee-high grass, the ground turning soft at the shore of the pond. Oak watches me, and I can feel the question in his eyes.

"I swim here . . . sometimes," I explain.

He hesitates, and the air feels tight in my throat. Maybe I shouldn't have brought him here. He looks uneasy, a flicker of doubt across his face. We've already spent too much time together—I've risked too much by bringing him here.

"The tulips . . . ," he says suddenly, not looking at me—like his thoughts have carried him far away from here. "I've seen them. In town. People are . . . They're acting . . ." He doesn't finish.

"I know." I rub my hands up my arms. "The flowers were never meant to be in the hands of anyone outside of my family."

He glances at me. "Why?"

I keep my eyes on the surface of the pond, unsure how to answer. In Cutwater, locals tell their own stories, their own legends about why the Goodes should be avoided. And now I feel strangled by my own thoughts, searching for the right answer. "The tulips are responsible for everything bad that's ever happened to my family. And now that someone has stolen the flowers, passed them around, I don't . . . I'm not sure what will happen."

The Beautiful Maddening

A cricket chirps from the far side of the pond, the night air brushes across my flesh, but it does nothing to cool me.

"It makes them feel like they're in love . . . ," he says. "The tulips." But I can't tell if this is a question or an observation. He's witnessed the tulips in town, and maybe he's trying to understand what they are—what I am. If any of the rumors are true.

"It's a lie," I explain, pulling in a breath. "It's not real love."

"How do you know?"

"Because my family has been tormented by love my whole life." Each word stings to say out loud.

But he falls quiet, the meadow a soft hush around us, until he finally says, "We're all tormented by something."

In his face I see the same hurt that I often find in my own reflection: anger and doubt and dread—a feeling that desperately wants to become a scream. "What are you tormented by?" I ask.

His eyes cut to me, and I wish so bad I could see his thoughts—understand all the things he won't say. Won't let me see. Understand why I feel a strange, biting ache inside me when I'm close to him. Why he can occupy the air only a few inches from me and not confess his love—not beg me to spend the rest of my days with him.

"The past," he answers, a bluntness to his words—as if this is all there is to say about it. I swallow, wanting to ask him what he means, what happened to him that he refuses to say aloud. But his eyes are sinking through me, steady and unblinking, in a way no one has ever looked at me before. He stares at me like I might already have the answers to my own questions. Like I am the riddle, not him.

Like he is the one searching for clues in my face.

Like the silence is its own kind of unraveling. Its own truth. Like the words we say won't reveal a thing. It's his eyes that tell me what I want to know. My heart battering in my ears that makes me want to be someone else.

A girl like any other.

Who doesn't fear the look of curiosity in a strange boy's eyes.

And this idea spreads like poison down my veins, making me feel lightheaded and wild. I pull my tank top over my head, peeling away my clothes. Because if I'm leaving tomorrow, I truly have nothing to lose. I'll never see Oak again. This is my last night in this town. A night to be reckless, a night to forget who I used to be, and start unraveling the layers of who I will become.

I stride down toward the water, and I can feel Oak's eyes watching me: silent, green and alive, as if he's watching me shed my skin.

The ground is soft and silty beneath my bare feet; the water laps against my legs, my waist, as I wade into the shallows. I skim my fingertips along the surface, glancing back at him. But he stands motionless on the shore: a boy made of the unknown. I'm certain this will all end badly, but right now I want to press this night into my chest and hold on to it for as long as I can. I want to let myself believe I can swim with a boy who has lightning in his eyes. Who seems indifferent to who I am. Who, maybe, won't fall in love with me. "You coming in?" I ask.

He doesn't move; he is a watercolor silhouette set against a darkly smeared sky. For a long second I think he's going to turn and walk away, too afraid, like he's realized how close he's strayed to a monster. And I swear I can see the conflict tugging at his features as he tries to decide if he should stay or run. If he's made a mistake in following me here.

The Beautiful Maddening

If it's already too late.

But he pulls his gray T-shirt over his head in one quick stroke, as if to prove a point—*he's not afraid of Lark Goode*. And the air gets tangled up in my throat as he moves through the grass, striding down into the water.

The pond ripples around us, two bodies beneath the cloudless, starry sky.

"The water's warm," he says, barely above a whisper.

"There's a hot spring deep underground." My chin dips below the surface. "It never freezes, even in winter."

His eyelashes are dotted with beads of water, like a million tiny worlds. "How did you know this was here?"

"I've lived here my whole life. You know things about a place when you've never left."

The wind slides across the water, gooseflesh pricks my arms, and I stretch my legs deeper into the warm pond.

"If I knew about this place . . . ," he murmurs, his voice endlessly cool, controlled, like he's careful of every word that leaves his lips. His eyes flash to the meadow, the shadowy hills spilling out into the distance like great sleeping giants. "I'd come here every night." His eyes scrape back to me, as if they could peel me open, and my heart starts battering against my ribs, drawn to him in ways that don't make sense.

With effort, I drag my gaze toward the abandoned farmhouse—anchoring myself to something other than him. "The bank owns that house," I say, my breath tight, my skin too warm. "You could buy it cheap after you graduate, then this pond and the meadow would all be yours. You could spend your days out here, until the end of time."

His mouth plays at the corners, almost a smile, almost a shape that makes me want to drift even closer. *Makes me want . . .*

But he shakes his head, the rising moon reflected back in his eyes, the pale light making dreams of the water's surface. "I'll be long gone after graduation."

"So you *do* want to escape this place?"

"Not an escape, a vanishing act. I want to get so far away, it will be as if I were never here at all."

I can tell there's more meaning beneath these words, but his chin lifts above the water, drops lingering against his lips, and the unfamiliar need inside me thumps in time with my heartbeat. I'm losing myself in the rhythm of his words, the shape of his mouth that I feel so drawn to that I almost forget how to breathe, how to be a girl cursed by love.

I turn and drift onto my back, my worthless body suspended on the calm surface of the pond, staring up at a cloak of summer stars. Trying to break the thread pulling me toward him. "Or we could just stay here," I muse, pulling the night air into my lungs, swallowing down the stars, reminding myself to breathe. "Let the years drift by, and soon they'll forget we ever existed."

"They'd forget me," Oak replies, his voice swept up in the moonlight. "But I doubt they'd ever forget you."

I look at him. *I'm losing this battle,* I think. *Reckless, reckless, reckless.* I can't let myself feel whatever this is: the torment of wanting something I know I can never have. Drifting in a pond beside someone who should be falling in love with me . . . but isn't. *Why?* And wanting, strangely, *impulsively,* to reach out toward him, to lay my fingertips against a boy named after a tree.

The Beautiful Maddening

No. Why are my thoughts so unruly, like they're forming in someone else's mind? I feel dizzy, drunk, dreamlike.

But he doesn't pull his eyes away. And neither do I.

"You're not what I was expecting. . . ." His mouth rests half-open, the muscles of his shoulders settling, finding relief in the weight of my eyes on him.

I try to sever the tightness in my throat. But everything inside me is humming. "What were you expecting?"

"You're just . . ." His voice trails away, and he runs a hand through his dark hair, water falling down his neck, across his shoulders. "I thought the Goodes would be more terrifying."

I almost laugh, but there is a seriousness in his eyes. "So you've heard that we're the undead who only come out at night?" I raise an eyebrow. "Or witches who turn our victims into a boiling stew or bury them below our house beside a cursed creek?"

His lips curl into a careful smile. "I actually heard that you're all vampires, drinking the blood of anyone who gets too close."

"Then you're taking a risk coming way out here with me. In the dark. With no one around. No one to save you."

The smile sinks from his mouth. "If you were going to kill me, I think you'd have done it by now."

"The night's still young," I tease, my voice not sounding like my own. I'm fooling even myself: pretending to be a girl who can swim this close to a boy I hardly know—a boy who watches me, unafraid, as if he doesn't know that his heart is in danger.

But so is mine.

The moon makes watery shapes across the pond, and he seems even closer now, like we are two madcap stars drawn together in the night sky by a gravity beyond our control. Unaware that each will obliterate the other when we collide. "How do you know I'm not descended from vampire hunters?" he says darkly. "And it's not *me* who's lured you here?"

His green eyes level with mine, only a breath between us. And there's something desperate in his stare, unguarded, a perilous glint that might destroy us both if we're not careful. Every nerve in my body feels like fire. "If that's true . . . ," I say, my chest now only inches from his, breathing, *breathing*, gasping for air as if my lungs have forgotten how to stay alive. "Then I'll have to turn you into a vampire first . . . before you kill me." The warm, traitorous wind seems to push us together, and in an instant my fingertips are against his chest, against his collarbones, his throat, *so close I can breathe him in*, and my face is inches from his, close enough I could sink my vampire canines into his soft flesh, warmth and blood and desire. My body feels electrified—a pulsing in my eardrums, in the deepest cavern of my belly—and I know I'm breaking every rule my mother taught me. Every rule our family lives by.

Don't get too close. Don't let yourself fall.

I fight my own thoughts, my own mutinous need, and I clench my eyes closed, trying to push the feeling away. But when I open them again, our eyes meet, and I catch a flicker of something in his: a tension forming along his jawline, every muscle in his chest overwrought and tight. Like he feels what I do. But I can't tell if it's lovesickness in his gaze—the tulips finally winding their way around his heart, tightening like a fist—or something else.

Fear.

I don't stay to find out.

The Beautiful Maddening

I release my burning fingertips from his chest and push myself back, wading through the shallows up to the shore. My feet reach the grass, almost to our pile of clothes, when his hand grazes mine, and I whip around to face him.

"Lark," he says, breathless, water spilling from the hard lines of his face. "I'm sorry." As if this were all *his* fault. As if he brought me here and led me into the pond. As if he were the one who was cursed.

But now he's *too* close, his breath heavy with each exhale, eyes pouring into mine.

And I want . . . *a thing I shouldn't.*

A *want* I can't seem to shake. To know the feeling of his mouth against mine, to know the relief it will bring and the heat of his skin and the feeling of the ground being ripped away.

"I never meant to . . ." His words break off, lost, and what's left is only the dark between us. The night swollen in our lungs.

"You didn't do anything wrong." I clench my jaw. I need to walk away.

I'm leaving tomorrow, I repeat to myself. This is stupid, pointless. Meaningless.

But his eyes fall to my lips, and I can almost breathe him in: salt and warm skin and pond water. I try to see what's in his eyes—the curse pumping through his bones? A dangerous need taking shape inside him that he can no longer ignore. Or is it simpler than that? The kind of summer longing stirred up between any small-town boy and girl. Fingertips and sun-kissed skin and trembling heartbeats— wild and nocturnal and left wanting more.

In the quiet his mouth is the only thing I see.

"Kissing Lark Goode is a bad idea . . . ," I whisper.

He breathes, and I swear he shifts closer—this boy who was only a sketch in my notebook days ago but now stands inches away, the night air buzzing around us, the sky tilting above. "I know you want me to be afraid of you . . . but I'm not. I don't believe any of the rumors about you." He swallows, doesn't look away. "I only believe what I see in front of me."

Every warning inside me spins out of control.

His eyelashes blink, and I'm so close that I could press my lips to his and forget all the ways this will ruin me. *Ruin us both.*

But I feel something cracking wide inside me, the throat-closing sensation of falling into something I'm not prepared for. A tangled-up-in-knots feeling.

And I feel myself tipping toward an edge. . . .

I glimpse what everyone else feels when they stray too close to Archer or me, when they grasp a tulip in their hands.

It's the beginning of something. . . .

A word I won't let myself say aloud.

I pull myself back from him, sudden and quick, severing the moment.

I can't let this happen. This lie. I won't feel the pain I watched my mother endure—knowing that our father never really loved her.

I will run from it. Always.

Because it's not real. What he feels in this moment, his heart racing in his chest, is only the tulips.

What I feel . . . will wreck me.

It will be the start of my unraveling. Of this boy breaking right in front of me.

I turn away, my lungs heaving, hating the feeling of separation

The Beautiful Maddening

from him, but I scoop up my pile of clothes. "I have to go," I say in a rush, sliding my eyes back to him, a twitch at my upper lip. *I love the way he looks in the moonlight,* I think painfully, achingly.

"Good night," I manage, instead of *I can never see you again.*

I catch the flicker of a smile against his lips—like he knows this isn't goodbye, *not really*, not in any permanent way, because this thing between us feels more unshakable than that—but still, I command my legs to carry me away, up through the meadow, before I can change my mind, leaving a trail of water behind me.

I leave Oak standing nearly naked beside the pond.

And I force myself not to look back.

EIGHT

I won't fool myself into thinking that love is anything other than madness. A delusion formed by old, spiteful tulips. A malediction. A sickness carried in the Goode family line—a thing for which there is no cure.

I felt the moon-mad lunacy taking shape beneath my skin when Oak stood too close—so close he could have touched me—carving its way along my pale bones. But I've spent my life at a distance, safely away from anyone who'd dare look my way. And I can't allow myself to forget who I am. I can't let anyone in. Even a boy with pond water on his eyelashes and a breath held dangerously against his lips.

The tulips may make others fall in love with us, but we are just as susceptible to love's intoxicating rhythm. We can become just as sick with love's affliction.

The truest kind of love.

Because we're human. Because love is treacherous in all its forms.

I bury my head in my pillow and try to sleep. But his voice is there waiting, words against my heated skin: *You want me to be afraid of you . . . but I'm not.*

The Beautiful Maddening

It wasn't what I really wanted. Not even close.

I wanted him to kiss me, desperately, gravely, the tall meadow grass licking at my knees, our skin wet from the pond, his hands so close that they could have strayed along my temple, tangled in my hair.

But I walked away.

It hurts to think of it now, a terrible grinding ache behind my eyes, in my throat—choking on everything I wanted to say to him but didn't—yet he keeps resurfacing, no matter how hard I try to push him away.

I crush my palms to my eyes.

But there are other voices too . . . in the night air, hissing, reaching out for me through the open bedroom window. Echoing, whispering . . . *giggling*.

I toss back the bedsheet.

The voices aren't in my head; they aren't a conjuring of the summer wind. *They're real.* My feet hit the cold wood floor, and I move to the window.

A tiny ember of hope itches at me: maybe Oak has been unable to sleep too, his mind cycling over thoughts of me, and he's come to climb through the open window and kiss me in my room while the moonlight peels away all the doubt still clinging to my skull.

But out in the garden is not a single shadow . . . but many.

There are four, *no*, five people skulking through the rows of tulips.

I yank open my bedroom door and find Archer already rushing down the hall. He grabs the shotgun from beside the woodstove, then bursts through the screen door onto the back porch.

But he stops short . . . staring out into the garden.

I see what he sees: the five thieves are not trying to steal the tulips, not exactly; they rip the petals from the white-and-bloodred blooms and rub them across their skin, their flushed cheeks and forearms, and along their scalps. They bring the petals to their noses and draw in deep breaths, trying to inhale whatever ancient magic lives inside each silk-soft flower.

As if they want to press them down into their blood and bones.

As if they want to become a Goode.

"I told those boys to stay away," I mutter, squinting into the dark.

Archer shakes his head. "It's not Tobias and Mac." He nods toward one of the figures as it steps into the moonlight.

Clementine Morris.

Soft-spoken, head down, brown hair always in her eyes—Clementine.

Who stood in the hall while Mac and Tobias swung their fists at each other. Who, at the drive-in, sat beside Tobias, his hands folded protectively around her. Clementine Morris, who had her fortune read by Jude during lunch while sitting with her friends from band class. I wonder what fortune he gave her, if he foresaw this—that she would steal tulips and find herself the envy, the desire, of her classmates, those who had ignored her only days earlier. Those who had teased her since grade school for her tangled, unruly hair, for her quiet nature.

But now she holds a tulip to her chest and sways in time with the breeze.

One of the other girls—Jada Reynolds, a sophomore who has a tattoo of a bluebird on the inside of her wrist—begins taking off her

The Beautiful Maddening

clothes, down to her bra, and lies on the ground among the scattered petals. A few rows away a girl I can't fully make out begins plucking off tulip petals and sticking them in her mouth, swallowing them whole. Another girl giggles manically, skipping through the rows, arms reaching for the tulips while her head tilts to the sky like she's calling down the moonlight, summoning some dark spell that will turn her into a Goode once and for all.

Archer glances at me, an eyebrow peaked into his forehead.

I would laugh—watching them roll around in our garden—if it weren't so unsettling. *They must be drunk,* I think. But I know it's another kind of inebriation: the delirious kind.

The kind our ancestors warned about.

"Fucking heathens," Archer says through an exhale, stepping to the edge of the porch. "Get off our property!" he shouts. "I won't tell you twice!" He grips the shotgun in his hands, even though he knows as well as I do that it's useless—the thing belonged to our grandfather, and our great-grandfather before that, an heirloom that's so old, it was probably used in the Civil War. And in truth, my brother doesn't need it: words uttered from Archer Goode's lips are nearly as unrefusable as law.

The girl who has been stuffing her face with petals abruptly stops, letting the remaining bits fall from her hands, while Jada pushes herself up from the dirt, eyes shivering open and closed, *open and closed.* They look mesmerized, stoned, like sleepwalkers who we've just awoken from some wondrously enraptured dream. I worry they're going to lunge toward us, try to rip us apart just as they have the tulips, but Archer stomps his foot against the wood porch, as if he's scaring away a pack of stray coyotes.

"Get!" he yells, louder this time.

And they scatter, like frightened animals, sprinting down the tulip rows, shoving themselves through a hole in the barbed-wire fencing they must have cut open, then into the dark of the woods beyond.

But Clementine doesn't move. She looks paralyzed.

Her mouth falls open, and she blinks.

"It was a dare . . . ," she says, voice broken by deep inhales. "The first time."

I frown at her, unsure what she's saying.

"We only wanted to see the flowers up close. To tiptoe through the Goode garden. We didn't know what they were, what they did. But . . ." She shakes her head, and I realize that she's confessing her crime, that even in her greed for the tulips, there still remains the guilt of stealing something that doesn't belong to her. "I can't go back to how it was. . . ." She looks like she's holding down a sob, her eyes watering, hands trembling. "Tobias never even looked at me before. Not until . . ." She looks down at the clump of tulips in her fist.

She stole the tulips. It was always her.

Sweet, mild-tempered Clementine Morris. And now she needs more.

"Jude said that a single tulip would bring me love. . . ." She blinks up at me, as if she knows I was watching her that day on the lawn, when Jude read her the fortune. "I didn't know what it meant. But Suzy remembered the tulips behind your house. We didn't really think anything would happen. We didn't even plan on stealing them at first. Until we saw them . . . breathed them in." She shakes her head, looks briefly lucid. "But yesterday I asked Jude for another fortune. He said that the love wouldn't last. I'd lose it just as quick as I'd found it. But I . . ." Her eyes brighten, her mouth twitches at the edges. "Maybe I can change fate." She makes a sound, almost like a laugh, then she quickly stuffs a handful of tulips into the pocket of her white shorts, before turning and darting down the tulip rows, then out through the severed opening in the fence.

She vanishes into the dark edge of the trees.

Jude told her that a single tulip would bring her love. He saw what the future held.

Archer walks out into the empty garden and picks up Jada's pink tank top from the dirt. He looks up at me, exhaustion, shock, and something else pulling at the features of his face. "Go back to sleep," he says. "I'll fix the fence." He glances at the place where Clementine and her friends fled into the woods. "But I don't know if it'll do much good now. If they want the tulips bad enough, they'll find a way in."

The morning sun finally scrapes above the tree line, and I find Archer on the back porch, seated on one of the old rocking chairs, staring out at the tulips.

"Did you sleep at all?" I ask.

He shakes his head.

My brother feels protective of the garden, of this house—maybe because we have so little, he doesn't want to lose what's left. Even the Goode name holds value to him, as if it stood for something once, as if somewhere in the lineage it might have meant honor or bravery, something worth defending. But I know better—there's nothing worth saving here.

I leave my suitcase on my bedroom floor, half-packed. I can't bring myself to leave my brother, not after last night, not with the nervy, bloodshot look in his eyes, waiting for someone else to sneak into the garden.

I'll wait a day or two, for things to settle, for my brother to ease back into the normal rhythm of his self-obsessed life . . . and then I'll leave.

Because he can't watch the garden day and night. The madness has already spread; they've had a taste of false love, and they'll come for more tulips.

And maybe we should let them.

Let them feed the desperation growing inside them, let them choke on the petals if that's what they want. I'm no longer certain if we're protecting them or ourselves.

Let them go a little mad.

Let them know what it feels like to be a Goode.

Maybe they'll see how terrible it really is.

Near sunset Archer is still on the back porch, his eyelids slipping closed, the shotgun resting on his lap. I touch his shoulder. "Go inside," I say. "Get some sleep. I'll keep watch," I assure him.

He mumbles something, shaking his head. But I grab his arm and help him stand, then lead him into the house. Inside I shove him into his room and close the door; I suspect he'll sleep for twelve hours.

But I don't go back out onto the porch. I have no interest in holding the gun and keeping watch over the tulips. Instead I carry

The Beautiful Maddening

my sketchbook out onto the front porch, ease into the wooden swing that my grandfather built long before we were born, and stare out at the black length of Swamp Wells Road. This is the view I prefer.

A road under the weight of stars.

A road that will lead me out of this town.

It's just a little delay, I tell myself. Another day won't make a difference.

With my headphones on—Sinéad O'Connor wailing about loneliness—I tilt my head back, the last of the setting sun now gone, and let my eyes stray across the star-pricked horizon. The quiet soothes my thoughts, and I watch as clouds pour across the skyline, dark and heavy, a summer storm gathering strength. They come almost every night this time of year. Rain and wind to cool the sweltering heat. And sometimes there is lightning, too, thunder that shakes the whole house.

I start to open my sketchbook, when my eyes catch a flash of movement—a shadow out on the road.

I sit up, squinting through the dark.

It could be Clementine, returned for more tulips—greedy, unable to keep away.

But the silhouette isn't trying to hide, to keep to the shadows; the person stands in the open, and now they're looking up at the house. I can't be sure if they can see me in the dark, or if they're just staring at the cursed Goode home.

I remove my headphones, keeping still and quiet, watching, and the shadow takes a step up our driveway, then another, moving toward the house.

I should wake Archer—if someone is coming to cut through our fence and steal more tulips, I won't be able to defend them on my own. *And I'm not sure I even want to.*

But the person stops, abruptly, looking back over their shoulder. I don't understand what they're doing.

They turn, and just as swiftly they start back toward the road—like they've changed their mind.

I stand up and peer down the drive—confused—and for the second time the figure pauses, hesitates, turning slightly to look back toward the house. And when they do, I see it: the outline of a book held in his left hand, just before he slides it into his back pocket.

"Oak?"

He spins around, and in the dark he looks not quite real—like the night will swallow him up at any moment. I walk to the front steps, and he must see me, because he moves closer, stopping only when he reaches the edge of the creek running below the front porch.

"What are you doing?" I ask.

He lifts his chin, hair brushed back from his forehead, and every feature of his face feels familiar. As if it's a face I've known my whole life.

"I'm sorry about the other night," he says, feet shifting in the dirt, voice windswept, roughened from the miles of pavement he's walked to get here. "I should have been more careful, I shouldn't have tried to . . ." His eyes skip past me to the house, then back. He was going to say that he shouldn't have tried to kiss me, and I wonder if he's afraid of the same things I am—that maybe he wanted to press his lips to mine only *because* I'm a Goode, because of the tulips—or if he's afraid of something else.

"You walked all the way here from Favorville just to tell me that?"

134

The Beautiful Maddening

He clears his throat. "I usually walk at night . . . and read."

I think about the book in his back pocket, about the dark stretch of road that leads from his county to mine. I think about the night air in his lungs, the thoughts stirring inside him. And all the things he might be thinking right now.

"I think books prefer the quiet, and the dark. It lets the pages breathe," he says, a soft twitch at the corner of his mouth, like he's saying things he didn't anticipate.

But I smile, liking this description. Liking the way words form on his lips. Liking the shyness that skips through his eyes, there and then gone. Like he's not used to the feeling, and he doesn't know how to push it away.

"I wasn't sure if I should come up to your house, once I got here." He looks me clear in the eyes now, the shyness gone. "I started to turn around and walk home." He glances past me to the porch swing. "I didn't think you'd be out here. That anyone would see me."

"I was keeping watch." My shoulders settle. "Someone broke into our garden again; they stole more tulips."

"I'm sorry."

"It wasn't who I thought it would be." I shake my head, thinking of Clementine and her friends. "But . . . my brother has been up watching the garden since it happened."

"And tonight is your shift?"

"Something like that."

He smiles, and the night feels more alive, the wind tracing my ears, the starlight sharper against his silhouette. "You want some company?" he asks.

I hold back my own smile; I tuck it down. "You sure you want to risk it?" I keep my mouth serious, giving nothing away. "It's nearly a full moon. This is usually when my family sacrifices helpless boys to the ancient gods."

His smile flattens, but only for an instant. "Then I'll have to warn any helpless boys if I see them."

I tilt my head, a smile reaching my eyes, still trying to understand why Oak isn't afraid, why he doesn't tip forward to breathe in my skin and confess all the ways in which he can't live without me. He is a boy I can't decipher. A paradox. Beautiful and strange.

We stare at each other, like two rivals sizing up the competition, trying to decide who's bluffing, who will flinch first. Who will make it out alive.

"Sure," I relent.

He steps over the creek and climbs the steps. We settle onto the porch swing, a soft wind stirring up from the nearby elms, sending a shiver through me. It'll rain soon, I can feel it.

"What do you listen to?" he asks.

I lift an eyebrow.

"On that old Walkman."

I realize the headphones are still around my neck. "They're old cassette tapes that belonged to my mom."

"Are they any good?"

"Some of them." I turn my eyes back to the dark sky, watching the moonlight as it's swallowed up by the clouds. "It's better than the silence." It makes me wonder why I'm so afraid of the quiet. What makes me crave the thrum of noise in my ears? Maybe because I hate the sound of the tulips, of Forsaken Creek, of the whispers in the halls at school whenever I walk by.

The Beautiful Maddening

Music drowns out the shrill, painful orchestra of my life.

I remove the headphones from around my neck, placing them in my lap.

"I know what you mean." His voice is a whisper, careful, but not weak. "It's hard to sleep most nights. . . . The silence is too suffocating."

I want to know about *his* silence—because I'm certain it's different from mine. But the hush of the wind, the quiet of the sky, stall the words on my tongue. I don't want to break this moment with questions that will surely open up parts of him he might not want to share. Not yet.

So I let the quiet pacify my thoughts. And I realize that I like *this* kind of quiet. With him.

Two humans watching a storm smear across the sky. Only a few inches between us. But as the minutes flit away, my mind starts to nag at me, old thoughts, old warnings seeping back in. "Aren't you worried . . . ?" I say, keeping my eyes on the darkening clouds. "I mean—don't you worry why you're here, why you walked all the way to my house? Why you're sitting next to me on my porch?"

"I'm here to help you catch your thief," he says, tilting his eyes at me, a soft, unaffected smile curling across his lips.

I almost smile back. "But what if it's not that? What if you're here against your will?"

"Like you're keeping me prisoner?" he asks with an even bigger grin.

"You know what I mean."

His smile fades. "You think the tulips lured me here?"

"Maybe." *Most likely.*

Shea Ernshaw

"Or . . . maybe I have more free will than you give me credit for," he suggests, lifting an eyebrow, his hand so close that he could lay it atop mine, his eyes so close that he could peer inside me and see all my secrets. And when he looks at me like this, it makes me feel like I've known him for lifetimes, like I've always known him, like we grew up next door to each other and we've spent countless summer nights together just like this. When his eyes blink slowly, lidded, when his mouth forms a barely there smile that I could almost mistake for sadness, I feel like I could stay here beside him for a hundred years. Like we are the oldest of friends, like we could tip into something deeper if we're not careful. Something dizzying and weightless and risky.

Something we are destined for.

But his mouth drives into an almost-serious line. "I'm here because I want to be here," he says. "I could leave at any time." He stands from the porch swing, shoulders broad, and takes a step toward the edge of the porch. "I could walk away right now, all the way home, if I wanted." He takes another step. "I'm serious. You better tell me to stay. Otherwise, I'm leaving. I'll really do it."

I watch him, trying not to smirk.

"Last chance, Lark," he warns, glancing over his shoulder as he descends the porch steps. "I'm going to walk home . . . in the dark . . . and the cold."

A short laugh falls from my lips. "You said you like walking in the dark," I point out. "And it's summer, it's not even cold."

He tilts his head at me. "The wolves, then, the wolves will surely get me. Imagine what a horrible death."

The Beautiful Maddening

"Okay," I say, unable to contain the grin taking up most of my face. "Stay."

But he raises an eyebrow. "I don't think you really mean it. It feels like you're just saying that to be nice." He steps over the creek, pushing his hands into his pockets, like he's preparing to make the long, dangerous trek back to Favorville. He looks at me one last time, forlorn and desperate, and when I don't say anything, he starts walking.

But I sit up straight. "Oak," I call, still grinning. "I want you to stay. . . . Please stay."

He swivels back to me. "You're sure? You're not just saying that?"

"Yes, I'm sure. I don't want you to leave. . . . I need you to stay."

He smiles, holding up his hands. "Fine, fine, I will if you want me to that badly."

I scowl at him, and when he climbs back up the steps, settling onto the porch swing, I shove him in the shoulder.

"I didn't know you were so desperate for me to stay," he says, shooting me a half smile, looking far too handsome in the filtered moonlight.

"You're lucky I'm not a real witch like everyone thinks I am," I tease. "Otherwise, I'd hex you and turn you into something awful."

"Even if you were a witch, I'd still stick around."

Our eyes meet, and it feels like gravity has untethered me from the earth. I let my eyes trace every detail of his face. I don't look away. *Of my own free will.* Because maybe I am a witch and he's a wolf and we have nothing to lose. Maybe this moment is all there is, and I want to feel the closeness of someone who isn't afraid of me.

I pull my knees up to my chest, and he leans back against the porch swing, causing it to tip slightly—enough to allow the sketchbook resting beside me on the swing to slide off the edge, landing with a thud on the porch.

Oak leans forward, retrieving it for me. But it's fallen open, and as he lifts it up, the pages flutter, revealing the sketches inside. "Did you draw these?"

I barely nod, a twitch of unease tugging at my chest.

"Wow . . . Lark. They're really good."

I try to force a smile.

"Are they real people?"

The pages have stalled on a sketch of Mr. Andrews, our postman. A portly man with reddish hair and a bent nose, like he was punched in the face at one time. "Yeah."

Oak turns to me. "Sorry, I should have asked. You probably don't want me looking at them." He starts to close the sketchbook.

But I smile. "It's okay. I don't mind."

Because strangely, the nerves in my stomach have settled. I trust him—a feeling I've rarely known, a feeling I hardly recognize. He flips forward through the book, past the faces of my classmates, my teachers, my school bus driver, and I tell him the names of the people in the images. Their stories. The pieces of their lives I've witnessed from afar.

The passage of time loses all meaning. His shoulder grazes mine, but he doesn't inch closer. Tonight is not like in the pond, when I felt desperate to touch him—to lay my fingers against his shoulders. Tonight I feel calm, the ease of our conversation, our laughter, soothing my usually guarded mind. As if we've done this a hundred times

The Beautiful Maddening

before, sat on the porch swing and talked like old friends. Like two people tipping toward something slowly, carefully, without much effort.

Tonight I let myself be here with him. I let myself feel safe. And unafraid.

I almost forget about the last sketch waiting at the back of the notebook. Until his fingers turn the page, and *he* is staring up from the paper.

Oak blinks. And my heart stops beating.

I tip back from him, swallowing, trying to think of what to say.

But he speaks first.

"Is this how you see me?"

I nod, but I don't think he notices. He is quiet, unmoving beside me.

"It's not finished yet," I say, worried he sees something in the image that he doesn't like. Worried he sees all my thoughts hidden in each pencil stroke. All the ways my heart has been unraveling onto this page. Worried it's not himself he sees, but *me*. The truth of what I feel when I look at him. "I know it's not . . ." I shake my head. "I mean, I don't usually show anyone my sketches. So you probably think it's . . . it's not really . . ." I don't know what I'm trying to say, but I feel suddenly anxious, fidgety, with his eyes staring down at the sketch. I feel *vulnerable*, certain he can see all the things I've been trying to hide. The ache in my chest when I think of him. The perfect slant of his eyes, his lips. I drew him how I see him in my dreams.

And now he can see it too.

I clear my throat, about to stand up, when he finally lifts his eyes and turns to look at me. But it's not disgust or disapproval I see in his face. It's something else—a thing that's hard to describe.

"Lark . . ." His voice falls away, becomes part of the wind and the storm.

I can't breathe.

I want to inch closer until there's no air between us. Until the beating of his heart drowns out my own.

I wish for things I would never say aloud.

But beyond the trees, the light is beginning to change. The sunrise approaching.

He breathes, and I watch every flicker of thought slipping past his eyes. I see the air held in his lungs; I see all the reasons why we shouldn't be this close. Why time feels unbending, immeasurable when we're together.

But above us, the stars begin to melt away.

The night ending.

And through the soft rush of the wind, I hear footsteps from inside the house.

Then the slamming of a door.

Archer is awake—probably crossing from his room to the bathroom. It's only a matter of time until my brother wanders into the kitchen, looking for caffeine. Only a matter of time until he discovers me on the porch, with a boy, looking like I've ensnared him. Like I've cast a Goode spell, making him mine.

But Oak doesn't pull his eyes away, and it feels like we're suspended in that gentle state between sleep and wake—like I could slip back into this dream with him, or rise and be reminded of who I really am.

The Beautiful Maddening

But when I hear another door close, and the sky turns pale and yellowing with the first hint of sunlight, I can't deny that the dream is over.

"I should get back inside," I say.

Oak nods, but neither of us stands.

Neither of us wants this to end.

"Thank you . . . ," I say as the stars fade from the sky. "Thanks for staying up with me."

I feel weightless as I force my legs to stand. He holds out the sketchbook, and I press it to my chest, never taking my eyes off him.

"Can I take you somewhere . . . ?" he asks. "Tonight, after sunset?"

I hesitate, looking to the front door. I feel the conflict inside me—the part of me that knows I should be on a train today. I shouldn't waste any more time with this boy. But my heart is a pendulum in my chest, knocking against my ribs whenever his eyes settle on me, and it's a feeling I can't ignore. No matter how hard I try.

And right now, *honestly*, I don't want to ignore it.

"Okay," I agree, forcing down all the parts of me screaming that I should end this now. I should tell him it's better if we don't see each other again. Instead I let myself live in the dream a little longer.

He smiles, then descends the porch stairs and steps over the creek. "Good night," he says, even though it's morning, taking several steps backward up the driveway, like he can't bring himself to turn away.

I don't care where he's taking me later tonight. The heat inside me is a roar. I only care that I'll be seeing him again. And this feeling is starting to feel like air, like something I'll die without.

I should be afraid that I'm losing control.

But I watch him walk away, and it's only warmth I feel. A dizzying euphoria that must be akin to what others feel when they're near a Goode.

NINE

Seated on my bedroom floor—listening to old Madonna tapes—I add a dozen stars to the skyline above the sketch of Oak. The portrait has become a record, an archive of all the moments we've shared.

A knock vibrates through the walls of the house, and I drop the notebook to the floor, hurrying out to the living room.

But I'm too late.

Archer reaches the front door before me, the shotgun already held at his side. "If you came for a tulip . . . ," he barks as he pulls open the door. "You can fuck off."

There is a heavy pause, feet shifting against the rotted wood boards of the front porch. "I'm looking for Lark," a voice answers.

I dart across the living room, peer over my brother's shoulder, and find Oak staring back. He's earlier than I expected—the sun not quite set—or I would have met him at the end of the driveway.

He stands with his hands slid into the pockets of his dark jeans, looking like he was blown in by a stray summer breeze and deposited on our front porch like Dorothy in *The Wizard of Oz*.

Archer's expression sours, pulls tight.

"It's okay. I know him," I tell my brother. But he shoots Oak a warning look before finally stepping back into the kitchen out of sight.

Oak blinks at me like he's briefly forgotten why he's here. "Sorry, should I not have come to the door?"

"No, it's fine. My brother's just a little jumpy."

I hear Archer let out a grunt from the kitchen.

But Oak seems to relax. "You ready?"

I flash my eyes back into the kitchen, where Archer is frowning at me, eavesdropping, wondering who the hell this boy is. But I look back at Oak and nod.

In the driveway sits a rusted gray truck, the hood sunburned and peeling, the side mirror on the passenger side sheared off—it's old, 1970s probably, the kind of thing that surely breaks down all the time. Hardly worth the scrap metal it's made of.

"Is this yours?" I ask as he opens the passenger door for me.

"I bought it when I turned sixteen. Been repairing it ever since." He smiles as if there's more to the story, but he moves around the front of the truck, then climbs into the driver's seat. Surprisingly, the engine fires right up.

The night is starry and clear, and he drives us to the far edge of town, past the lumber mill and the Rabbit Cross Bed and Breakfast, but when he turns down the red-gravel road, heading west, I flash a look at him. I know where we are, where he's taking me, and a coil of tension rises up in my gut.

Ahead of us, the road opens into a clearing, where I can see three other cars are already parked on Cutwater Ridge, overlooking the abandoned quarry. This is the place Cole Campbell invited me to,

146

The Beautiful Maddening

back when the tulips first bloomed. A place where kids from school park their cars and kiss beneath the moonlight. A place I'm sure Archer visits all too often.

I'm about to tell Oak that I don't want to be here, when he steers the truck away from the other cars and onto a narrower road that leads back into the trees—a road I didn't know existed.

"You didn't think I would take you to Cutwater Ridge, did you?" he says, shooting me a furtive look.

"Then where *are* you taking us?"

But he only winks at me.

The road is rocky and uneven and steep, but finally we emerge from the trees, and I realize where we are. The road has led us down the cliff, and now Oak parks the truck beside a large, glittering lake. The quarry has filled with water over the years, and there is a sandy beach leading down to the water's edge.

"How did you know this was here?"

"I told you, I don't sleep much at night."

Oak steps out of the truck and hurries around to open my door.

"It's beautiful," I say, walking toward the water, drawn by its still, mirrorlike surface. The moon sparks off the lake, making it feel like the sky has dipped into the water.

Oak bends down and begins taking off his shoes.

"What are you doing?"

"Going swimming," he answers, pulling his shirt over his head and then unbuttoning his jeans.

"No," I answer out of reflex.

"Why not? You took me swimming in the pond."

"That water was warm. . . . This water, I'm sure . . . is not."

He backsteps away from me, in only his boxers, smiling.

"I'm not going in," I add, defiant, shaking my head.

He sticks out his bottom lip, as if I've broken his heart, then wades in up to his knees. He cringes slightly, the cold unmistakable on his face, but he keeps going. "You're going to love it in here," he calls. "I promise."

"No way."

He turns, dives forward beneath the water, and when he emerges a few yards away, he lets out a whoop, brushing his hair back from his face, his skin dripping with cold lake water.

I can't help but laugh.

"It feels incredible!" he shouts.

"I didn't bring a swimsuit!"

"You didn't have a swimsuit at the pond," he counters. "And that didn't stop you."

I clamp my mouth shut, feeling chilled just watching him.

"Lark Goode . . . ," he says, his tone serious now. "Get in this water!"

I shake my head.

"You won't regret it."

I exhale, dropping my eyes. I take a few cautious steps forward, slipping free from my flip-flops and touching the water with my foot. It's frigidly cold, and I yank my foot back. "Nope!" I tell him. "Not happening."

He is the one who laughs now, and he starts wading closer to the shore.

"Don't you dare!" I say.

He lifts his hands in the air. "I'm not going to pull you in," he

The Beautiful Maddening

promises. Instead he holds a hand out to me, eyes bright and treacherous. His mouth curved into a persuasive grin.

I shake my head, but my resolve melts away, the fear dissolving on my tongue.

I strip out of my clothes, down to my underwear, shocked that I'm really doing this. Slowly I wade in up to my ankles, my knees, but the water gets colder the deeper I go, and I stop.

Oak reaches me and holds out his hand once again. I take it. "I trust you," I say, raising my eyebrows at him, hoping he won't try to throw me in.

"Only when you're ready," he promises.

I pull in a deep breath, hold it, and when I finally let it out, I nod at him. With his hand still in mine, I force my legs forward until I'm waist-deep, and I can see the ground drops away ahead of me. The water is dark, intimidating, but the moon is still bright, and I suddenly don't feel afraid.

I release Oak's hand, look at him one last time, and dive forward into the water. The shock of the cold rips the air from my lungs. But when I break the surface, I let out a gasp—he was right . . . somehow it feels incredible. Like shedding an old skin. One I no longer need.

Oak swims to me, and I tilt my head back to the stars, feeling—oddly, for some reason—like I might cry. Like I needed this more than I knew. Like the cold is swallowing up all the pain, all the hurt that's been tangled inside me. Like Oak is setting me free.

"Thank you," I tell him.

But when I drop my gaze, I see something in his eyes, something that makes me want to kiss him. Makes me want to drift forward and forget that I am a girl who cannot be loved. Let the moon

Shea Ernshaw

sink beneath my flesh and make me reckless and wild and unafraid.

I can see he's thinking it too.

He's thinking that maybe out here, in the cold, alone, our mistakes won't follow us home. That we have nothing to lose.

"You're really not afraid of me?" I ask, my lips touching the surface of the water.

He shakes his head. "I'm definitely afraid," he admits, watching me with heat in his eyes, something primal in every blink, every drop of water that falls from his lashes. "But I'm still trying to figure out who you really are."

"The villain, you mean?"

"No. A girl who seems to believe what other people say about her. Who pretends to be someone I should be scared of. But who is also so . . ." He shakes his head. "You're so unlike . . . I mean you're . . ." Again he loses his words, like he's certain he's saying all the wrong things. "I understand why you want to leave this town . . . because you're better than this place. Better than the stories that everyone tells about you." He swallows, looks me in the eyes. "This town doesn't deserve you. You're not the monster or the myth they've made you into. . . ."

My heart is hammering against my ribs. No one has ever spoken to me like this—like he sees some part of me that I've kept hidden, that I've forgotten.

I lift my hand—without thinking—and I touch his face, catching drops of water along his cheek. I run my fingers down his jaw as if they are brushstrokes, reciting him to memory, painting him onto paper. My fingers find his mouth, tracing his lips, suspended there— maybe the closest I'll ever allow myself to be. My fingers stall, and he

The Beautiful Maddening

watches me like he's going to shatter. Like neither of us will make it out alive. My eyes flutter closed as I absorb the cold of the water and the softness of his lips against my fingertips. And I feel more alive than I have words for.

I lift my eyes, and he's so close, I could press my mouth to his and finally know what it feels like. Know the warmth and surrender and taste of his skin.

But he speaks, and it crumbles the almost-moment. "You're shivering."

I blink at him, because I hardly feel a thing, hardly feel the cold. But he's right, my skin is pricked with gooseflesh, my bones vibrating.

"We should get out," he adds. There is still warmth in his eyes, but a flicker of doubt has edged along his mouth. Like some part of him knows we've taken this too far.

I nod, a storm of emotion breaking inside me, and we swim toward the shallows.

At the pond it was me who pulled away—me who felt the danger of getting too close to him. But tonight it's Oak who's severed the moment.

We wade from the icy water onto the beach and grab our piles of clothes, then head toward the truck. "I have towels inside," he tells me, the cold air piercing me down to the bone.

We're almost to the truck when I hear voices.

Up on the ridge.

In the trees.

Getting louder.

Someone is walking down from the cliff.

A moment later three shadowed figures appear from the tree

line, talking loudly, laughing. I narrow my focus through the dark and see Olive Montagu, Sebastian Marks—who I had ethics class with sophomore year—and Titha Roberts.

They draw closer, and I feel them eyeing us.

I just want to get into the truck before they recognize me.

"It's way too damn cold!" I hear Titha exclaim. They must have been up on the ridge, then decided to hike down to the water.

"I'm not getting my hair wet," Olive adds.

Oak reaches into the back of the truck and pulls out two yellow-striped beach towels. "You're trembling," he says, folding one around my shoulders. But I can no longer tell if it's the cold making my body convulse or the nerves building inside me. I reach for the passenger door, just wanting to get inside so we can leave.

Oak's eyes flick to the group as they pass the truck, and he seems unconcerned, as if there is nothing for us to fear. I watch as they head for the water, and I think we're in the clear—they'll just keep going. They haven't seen me. Or maybe they can't tell who I am—hair wet, lake water dripping from my skin.

But Olive's face turns in our direction, and I can see the recognition land in her eyes. "Oh shit!" she remarks, grabbing Titha by the arm. The others stop and swivel around, and I know it's too late—they recognize me.

Oak rubs the towel through his hair and starts around the hood of the truck to the driver's side, when Sebastian calls out, "You should be careful, man. You know that's Lark Goode?"

The air plummets into my stomach. My heart starts to race.

Oak frowns and takes a step back toward me, so he's partly blocking their view of me.

152

The Beautiful Maddening

"She might seem harmless, but she isn't. You'd be better off just leaving her out here. Save yourself, man."

Titha chuckles at this, but it's Olive's gaze that makes me the most uneasy. She takes a step closer to us, then another. Sebastian reaches for her but doesn't grab her in time; she's striding in our direction.

"Please!" she says, her eyes focused solely on me. "I only need one, that's it. Just enough to get him back." I remember Olive's desperation that morning in front of the school, the ache in her eyes as she grabbed at me. She wanted a tulip so Tobias would love her again. She felt the heartache a single tulip can cause. And she covets one still. "I'll pay you anything. Please!"

I feel paralyzed as I watch her move closer, hating that Oak is witnessing this, hating the look in her eyes. Wishing I could do something to make her see that a tulip won't get her what she wants. It'll only make things worse.

"Lark," Oak is saying, and I look up at him. "Get in the truck." He's opened the door and is urging me inside. I climb up to the seat, body shivering, the towel still wrapped around my shoulders. He closes the door behind me, then hurries around to the driver's side, swings himself in, and turns the key in the ignition.

Olive reaches the truck and presses her hands to the window. "Lark!" she begs. "I know you have them—that boy wouldn't be here with you if you didn't. Just one," she pleads. "You don't need them all."

Her pleas are all too familiar, the same appeals I heard that day on the school lawn. I stare at her, into her wide blue eyes, and feel a sadness for the pain the tulips have caused her. But before she can

153

reach for the door handle, Oak leans over me and slams his palm against the lock, ensuring she won't be able to get inside.

He puts the truck in reverse, and in an instant we're backing away from Olive, leaving her standing in the headlights, the lake shimmering behind her. Oak puts the truck in drive, hits the gas, and peels away, steering us back toward the tree line. He drives as if we're fleeing a real threat, a lake monster risen from the deep, a girl with heartache on her lips.

We are quiet the entire drive home, and when we pull up to my house and he kills the engine, I feel a hollowness inside me—certain how this will end. Oak may have brushed off all the rumors whispered about the Goodes, but it's another thing to see how my classmates react to me. To hear their warnings, to see Olive coming after me.

"I'm . . ." I shake my head, looking down at the pile of clothes in my lap. "I'm sorry for that. It's not . . ." My eyes turn to the window, looking out at my sad, sloped house, and I feel stupid for thinking this thing with Oak could ever be more than a delusion. A few days of pretending I could be like any other girl in this town. "Thank you for tonight." I don't let my eyes find him. I unlock the door and start to open it.

"Why are you sorry?" I look back at him. "Those kids are idiots. You don't need to apologize for the things that other people say or do."

His eyes are soft, gentle, but I still feel embarrassed. I still feel like I should say goodbye, leave his truck, walk to the house, and not look back.

And mean it.

But he keeps his eyes on me, refusing to let me go. "Can I take

The Beautiful Maddening

you somewhere else, since tonight didn't end like I'd hoped?" He releases his hands from the steering wheel. "I want to show you something. But it won't be for another few days, maybe more. The timing needs to be just right."

The air in my lungs feels caught, stalled between an inhale and exhale. "What is it?"

He smiles, and it destroys me. The way his mouth forms, tugging up on one side. "It's a place I've never taken anyone to before."

I thought he'd want to be rid of me after tonight, but he looks like a boy simply asking a girl if he can see her again . . . shyly, with a hint of hope in his eyes.

"Okay."

He nods. "You can keep the towel."

I open the truck door and step out into the night air. "Thanks."

"Good night, Lark Goode."

TEN

"Let them love us, never the other way around," Mom would tell Archer and me when we were young. She watched our father leave only days after she told him she was pregnant. Tulip season had ended—the summer was over—and the love he felt for her had faded with the season. He no longer remembered why he had followed Alice Goode around town as if she were the very air in his lungs. He returned for our birth—an obligation, a duty he felt—but he left again shortly after. He was simply a man who got tangled up in a curse he knew nothing about.

His heart was not his own.

This is why love cannot be trusted in our family.

Three days pass, and I begin to think Oak won't come back.

I wouldn't blame him.

Once he got home, once he had time to think about what had happened at the quarry, he probably decided I'm not worth the risk. I'm too messy, dangerous, bewildering . . . *bewitching*.

A girl you can never take home to meet the family.

A girl you don't want to be seen with, for fear of being followed, chased, or warned that you shouldn't be so close to her. A girl you

The Beautiful Maddening

always have to defend, a girl who over time you begin to wonder if you should trust. Or if all the rumors are true.

I'm not worth spending one more day with.

But on the fourth day, an hour before sunset, I hear the sound of a truck rumbling up the driveway. At first I'm certain it can't be him, but when I pull open the curtain on my bedroom window, I see his gray truck slow to a stop near the front porch.

I pull on a sweatshirt, step into sandals, and yank open the front door before Archer can ask where I'm going . . . or who is waiting for me in the truck.

I reach the passenger side before Oak even has time to open his door. I climb up onto the bench seat, and he looks at me. "Sorry I didn't call, but I, uh—I don't have your number. I didn't have a way to let you know that I was coming."

"I don't have a phone."

He smiles, as if he likes this answer.

"Any hints about where we're going?" I try, eyeing him, hoping for a clue.

"My house," he answers, starting the engine.

"We're going to *your* house?"

"I hope that's okay?"

I can't help but smile. "Yeah, I mean . . . of course." I've tried countless times to imagine where he might live, imagine his bedroom, his life in Favorville, but I've never been able to conjure it in my mind. Now I'll be seeing it for myself.

Windows rolled down, spring wind coiling through my hair, we drive west up Swamp Wells Road. I like this night already, feeling the air slice through my open fingers. Even Oak seems more relaxed than usual, an elbow resting in the open window, one hand on the steering wheel, his eyes clear and shimmering in the evening light.

The county line runs north to south through a forest of elm trees, and we cross into the outskirts of Favorville. The air smells different, like lilacs and ferns and spring mud, but we drive only a short distance before we turn onto a paved driveway that winds up a hill.

He lives just over the county line, not far at all—an easy enough walk under midnight stars.

But I'm not expecting the house that comes into view, perched atop the grass-lined hill at the end of the driveway. It stands two stories high, sunlit and towering, with a gray stone arch over the door, a modern slanted metal roof, concrete walls, and wood slats—it looks like it's straight out of an architectural magazine. I feel my eyes gaping through the truck window, tracing every angle, every surface—I can't believe a place like this even exists in Favorville.

Just to the right of the house sits a separate garage with four massive glass doors, a place to hold a fleet of cars, far nicer than the truck Oak is driving.

He parks on the far side of the circle driveway, and when I step out, I stare up at the row of windows on the second floor, wondering which one belongs to Oak—which one faces into a bedroom where he grew up, his clothes neatly organized in an oversized closet, a bed with fresh white sheets tucked perfectly at the corners. Maybe he has photographs pinned to his wall, memories with childhood friends, tokens from traveling carnivals, movie ticket stubs—the road map of a normal life.

A home like this creates a boy who has a plan, colleges lined up, a career path, a future that's been predestined. But he's never mentioned any of these things.

The Beautiful Maddening

My mouth hangs open, and I want to ask him a hundred things, want to know every detail, but he walks to the front of the truck and nods at me. "This way."

I follow him around the side of the house, across a neatly mowed lawn, to where a river is winding through the elm trees below—the low evening sun gleaming against the water. "Is this Rabbit Cross River?" I ask.

"Same as the one behind your house." His eyes flick softly to me.

The same water that pours past my house makes its way across two counties, eventually snaking behind his—although the ground behind my home is a low-lying swamp, while the land behind his is grassy and treed, with a view out over the valley.

I peer back up at his home, wanting to go inside—curious about the clues that wait within its walls about who Oak really is—but instead he leads me down to the river's edge, where a small rowboat lies belly-up on the sandy bank, green with a painted white stripe down the side.

He drags the boat out into the slow-moving river, his arms flexing from the effort, then reaches out a hand to me.

I know we shouldn't touch—the closeness is dangerous, and I fear I won't want to let go—but I allow my fingers to fold into his, and he helps me into the boat, one hand grazing my lower ribs, my spine, his touch making it hard to breathe as his eyes drag over me.

But once I'm seated on the wooden bench, he releases his hold on me, then shoves the boat the rest of the way into the river, swings himself easily over the side, and takes up the oars in his hands. I draw in a deep breath, reciting all the warnings I've told myself over the years, yet they don't seem to stick. I lose myself in the steady rhythm of Oak's arms as they pull the oars through the crystal-clear water, a motion he knows by heart, guiding the boat down the center of the river.

"Do you come out here a lot?" I ask, trying to distract my thoughts, my hands pressed to the wooden bench beneath me, my heart feeling light and windless as we move away from his house, following the lazy current of the river.

He draws in the warm forest air, the low light through the trees dappling his face. "Every morning, before sunrise."

I like the image of this: him waking when the light is still pale and soft, rowing up the river and back, sweat at his temples, his torso and shoulders strengthened a little more each time from the effort.

I lean against the side of the boat and trail my fingertips along the surface of the water, feeling lost in a dream that is pulling me farther and farther downstream—but I love this dream too much to force myself to wake. I love this impossible day, with him, the river widening around us, carving a path through the green forest, the evening sunlight peeking through the trees, the shore grassy and quiet, not a stirring of wind. I could drift for hours like this, watching him row with each practiced stroke, an easy smile finding his eyes whenever I look at him.

It feels like something I'm not allowed to have. This moment was stolen from a different life, a different girl. Yet I am greedy and selfish and will keep it for as long as I can.

A school of tiny silver fish whip past, slipping beneath the boat, then hurrying off downstream. "My mom used to say that if you eat a fish's eye, you'll be able to see underwater," I say.

Oak's eyebrows come together.

The Beautiful Maddening

"I never tried it, obviously." My gaze falls back to the river. "She was like that, always making up stories and riddles, her own kind of folklore. When I was younger, I loved it. But now . . ." I shake my head. "I realize that most of them were just lies."

"Maybe her lies were just a way to make sense of the world."

I look up at him, but his face is unreadable.

"Maybe." But I think about the lie she told the morning she left, the lie that was hidden in her silence. Her refusal to tell us the truth—that she was running away and never coming back. "She was a mystery, even to me."

Oak stares at me, like he understands what I mean.

I lift my hand from the river, waterdrops clinging to my fingertips, and I release an uncomfortable laugh.

"What?" he asks.

I shake my head, keeping my eyes on the shoreline as it drifts by.

"I just . . ." I swallow. "I can't believe that some part of you isn't afraid. Terrified, even."

He drives the oars into the water, steering the boat through a series of rocks jutting out from the shore. "Of what?"

"Of being this close to me. A Goode."

He smirks, and I like the way his green eyes crinkle at the corners. The way his mouth forms when he has a thought, a secret idea he's deciding whether or not to share. "I won't fall in love with you . . . ," he says decisively, like he's already made up his mind, but there is a shiver in his eyes, a tug at the edge of his mouth. "If that's what you're thinking."

"No?" I ask, raising an eyebrow.

"I'm not like everyone else in this town."

And this is precisely what ties my mind into knots. What I don't understand. *Why is he not like everyone else? Why does he seem unaffected by the tulips? By me?* I try to recenter my thoughts, but his eyes are too crushing, his mouth too perfect—*my sketch of him doesn't even come close.*

"The real question is," he continues, upper lip pulled into a merciless smile that makes my chest want to cave in, "can you keep yourself from falling in love with me?"

I want to laugh, a nervous twitch nearly breaking across my lips—I know he's making a joke, but I feel a pressure against my ribs, the truth of his words, and I don't know if I'm strong enough. I don't know if I can keep myself from crashing into something I won't be able to save myself from. Because when he looks at me like he does right now, I know it's possible. I know I could let my heart unravel and never look back.

And I know each moment I spend with him only makes it worse.

I know it might already be too late.

The river narrows, and we fall into a teetering silence, easy and untroubled. His arms flex, rowing harder, keeping the boat from plunging into the soft shoreline. The water heaves around us, splashing over the side, dampening my bare legs, but then it calms, flattens out again, and I tilt my eyes up to the halcyon blue sky, trees swinging by overhead. No moment in time, no river through the trees, has any right to be this perfect, this chest-swayingly beautiful.

No boy should look like him, no boy should say the things he does, and somehow sit only a few feet away and not lose his mind to the obsession that plagues others. He looks at me with something

The Beautiful Maddening

else . . . something simple, instinctual, a wandering faraway shiver. A thing I haven't deciphered yet. But God, I want to figure him out.

"Why does everyone call you Oak?" I ask.

His eyes flicker, a memory rising behind the green. "When I was young . . . my mom used to call me her 'little acorn.'" He smirks, looking the tiniest bit embarrassed. "But she said that I had the bones of an oak tree inside me and that someday, when I grew up, I'd be sturdy, even against the strongest storms. That I could never be ripped from the soil or upended."

"I like her," I say, trying to imagine a mom who would say such things and mean them.

"Me too." He glances out at the wide, slow stretch of water where the boat drifts for a moment, and he relaxes his arms, ripples feathering away from the bow. "She died when I was ten. She was sick for a long time." His jaw tenses, eyes steady. "She fought it . . . until she couldn't anymore."

Without thinking, I lean forward on the seat, closer to him: I want to touch him, lay my hand on his, press my fingers against his jaw until it relaxes. But I only shake my head. "I'm so sorry." I wish I had something more useful to say, and when he looks back at me, wetness rims his eyes before he blinks it away.

I sense that he's told me more than he's used to. These are memories he doesn't often let rise to the surface.

I sink back against the boat, the light of day fading around us, the sun inching below the tree line, and I wonder whether it's more painful to lose a parent to death or betrayal. Is *his* hurt worse than mine? My mother is still alive, but she chose a life that doesn't include us. Include me.

Dad left too, but it wasn't his fault. It was the tulips'.

Maybe it doesn't matter. Pain is pain. It digs deep no matter the method, the weapon. We both carry around wounds inside us, cut into the place where our heart used to be.

The river widens even more, becomes lazy and fattened, nearly as still as the pond where we swam, but Oak steers the boat to the shore and drags it halfway up onto the grass.

"Where are we?" I blink through the golden light of the setting sun, to a grassy hillside.

"Follow me."

I let my hand find his again, stepping free of the boat, but this time he doesn't release it. He squeezes his palm to mine, and he might as well have my heart in his fist—clenching tight, threatening to destroy me.

The sun is now gone from the sky, the air turned dark and warm, and we walk through the tall grass, up a gently sloping hill to where a row of trees grows toward the night sky.

At the line of birch trees, the land opens up, a meadow of wildflowers stretching out into the distance—soft and swaying in the moonlight. Yet it's not the wildflowers that stall the breath in my throat, it's the thousands—maybe *millions*—of winged insects fluttering through the night air.

Fireflies.

Tiny little orbs of light pulse golden and rhythmic among the dark, so many that it feels like candles set adrift in the air—an otherworldly sight.

I laugh, and the sound echoes through the trees, before I clasp

The Beautiful Maddening

a hand to my mouth. "What are they all doing here?" I ask, turning my eyes to Oak.

"I don't know. They shouldn't be here, in this part of the world. It doesn't make sense. But they come to this meadow every spring. My mom showed me this place when I was little."

I realize how special this meadow must be to him. I showed him my secret places—the abandoned train car, the farmhouse and the pond—and now he's showing me his.

"She used to tell me that there are all kinds of magic in this world. But not all of it has an origin. Or a reason. It just exists."

This place—fireflies humming all around us—feels like the most genuine kind of magic, a summoning of tiny winged creatures that should be witnessed only by kings and queens, a rarely performed ritual that bestows lasting luck on those who glimpse it before it's gone.

"It's beautiful," I hear myself say.

Oak squeezes my hand and pulls me out into the meadow, into the thumping, pulsing heart of the fireflies. Their wings sound like bits of paper rubbing together, and they look like confetti hovering in the airless sky, a kaleidoscope of dancing light. I laugh again, grinning, and I release Oak's hand to turn in a circle, feeling heady and buoyant, the fireflies amassing around us.

But when I tip my face back to Oak, I realize that he's watching me—his face soft and silent, like nighttime, like a thousand thoughts are trapped inside him but he's afraid to say any of them aloud. Half a dozen lightning bugs have landed on his shoulders, their incandescent lights pulsing slowly—like heartbeats. I reach out, and one of the insects lifts from his shirt, then lands on my index finger. I smile, holding it in the air between us, a beacon, a lighthouse, the rhythm of the light hypnotic.

"I feel like I'm in a dream," I mutter.

He is silent, and it feels like I'm drifting farther from the waking world.

"If you're the dreamer . . . ," he says, his mouth forming carefully over each vowel, "then please don't wake up."

Nothing feels real, his eyelashes, the lightning bugs pulsing around us like falling stars, the air in my lungs.

"I . . ." Oak's voice is a whisper, a rainstorm. A weight of words gathers in his eyes. "You don't know . . ." He breathes, and breathes, and breathes. "How hard it is to look away from you." He swallows and looks briefly startled by his own words, like he knows how treacherous they are. But he doesn't take them back.

"It's just the tulips . . . ," I begin, dissolving the meaning from his statement.

But he shakes his head. "No . . . it's not." His mouth settles into a line, eyes clear and sharp, and when he looks at me like this, I don't trust myself.

The firefly lifts from my hand, wings thrumming, and disappears into the crush of all the others. Oak takes a step closer, and I forget how to breathe. His hand strays across mine, his fingers tracing my palm. Circling my wrist. His face is a poem that hasn't yet been written, his lips are a question that only I can answer. He's inches away, and I want nothing more in this whole awful world than to sink into him, let his eyes drift down into my bones, and rip me apart.

"I told you before, kissing Lark Goode is a bad idea," I whisper,

The Beautiful Maddening

remembering back to the pond when I uttered these same words.

He drifts even closer, *too close*, his mouth hovering just over mine. Only a few centimeters separate us now—only air and wings and a heartbeat that's slamming against my ribs. He does something to me that feels beyond all logic. *All magic.* "Do you want me to kiss you?" he asks, out of breath, out of thoughts, out of any reasons why he shouldn't.

"I . . ." Only air comes out, because I *know* what I want—what I feel coiling tight in the lowest part of my stomach. But I also know I shouldn't want it, shouldn't want *him*.

I can't trust this feeling, this moment.

None of it.

His mouth hovers over mine, and I feel the soft, barely there graze of his lips. He smells like wildflowers and a hundred years of quiet, unspoken words. Ancient and alive. Like oak trees and sweat on summer-heated skin. He looks like fate. Like the very thing that might save me. Destroy me. Put me back together.

My lips part, the word "yes" suspended so delicately on my tongue that it feels like the thinnest shaving of glass. Cold and perfect and dangerous. But before the word can slip free, a fraction of a second before I can crush my mouth to his and tell him all the ways I shouldn't want this but I do . . . a voice echoes through the air.

Loud and booming.

A voice that isn't Oak's.

I snap my head toward the sound, and across the meadow I can just make out a figure at the far tree line. A silhouette. And it's shouting at us. "Who . . . ?" I start to ask, but Oak's hand is already clenching mine, yanking me away from the meadow.

167

We run through the flickering haze of lightning bugs, and they part around us, a sea of sunshine-gleaming orbs. At the border of trees, I glance back and see the figure moving toward us, still shouting, but I can't make out the words over the thrum of flapping wings. "What's he saying?" I ask.

"I can't tell," Oak says, darting a look over his shoulder. "But I understand his meaning."

"Are we trespassing?"

His mouth tugs at the corner, a wild, windless smile, and he pulls me down the hillside toward the river.

"Shit, Oak," I say as we run, the warm night air rushing around me. But when he flashes me a look, still smiling, I can't help but laugh. I wonder if this is what others feel when they clench a tulip for the first time. A delirious thrill, drunk on something that almost feels like love. Wasted on it. Soon enough the hangover will come, but right now, running hand in hand with Oak at my side, I feel more alive than I ever have.

At the river's edge, he shoves the boat back into the water in one push, and I splash into the shallows, clambering over the side. The man has reached the top of the hill, and he yells down at us, something about "keeping off his property," but Oak is already rowing us back upstream.

A grin spreads across his face, while my eyes water from reckless, giddy laughter.

Rowing upstream is much harder than rowing downstream, and Oak's arms tense with each stroke, his shoulders contracting. My

The Beautiful Maddening

head is whirling from the rush of sprinting down from the meadow, vibrating from the starry haze of thousands of fireflies, teetering from the feel of Oak's lips nearly touching mine. I feel untethered and windswept, a little madcap.

"You do that a lot?" I ask, still breathless. "Sneak onto other people's property?"

"Only every spring." A smile touches his eyes, and I tilt my head back, the night air streaming against my face, wishing I could feel this way every second of every day: heedless and wide open. Not a single thing in my way. He makes me feel like I could be someone else. *Like I already am.*

I tip my eyes, watching Oak dig the oars into the water, and a question rises inside me, one I've been curious about since I first saw him in the school parking lot. The last detail of my sketch that I never finished.

"What book are you always reading?" Even now, I know the book is there: I noticed it tucked into the back pocket of his jeans when we walked down to the river, and when we fled the meadow.

Without a word, he stops rowing, releasing one of the oars to reach into his back pocket, pulls out the paperback, and hands it over to me. I'm caught off guard—I didn't expect he would so easily let me see it—but I run my hand over the bent cover while he grips the oars again and resumes rowing us upstream. The book is clearly not from his dad's rare collection. It looks like it probably came from a cheap used bookstore—I know there's one or two in Favorville, shops where dusty, fifty-cent titles sit in stacks from floor to ceiling. Most of the books sit forgotten, left to molder for decades; not even the shop owners know what titles lie hidden among the crowded rows.

This one is no different—a piece of the corner has been torn away, the pages bent, like the book was rolled up at one point to swat a fly. But I can still read the title: *Lonesome Traveler*, Jack Kerouac. The illustration on the cover is an unusual watercolor, depicting a man holding a walking stick, I think. It's hard to tell exactly. The cover is so worn, nearly breaking apart in my hands.

I glance up at Oak, but his focus is out on the water, keeping a steady rhythm as he rows, not wanting to lose any ground with the current always pushing against us. The book might seem cliché in the hands of anyone else: mysterious boy who reads Kerouac while walking *lonesome* roads across a county line. But it doesn't feel that way. There is a genuineness to it, a boy who's searching for something and hoping he'll find it in the yellowing pages of this book.

"Is it good?" I ask.

He looks briefly serious. "Yeah, it's good. No one writes like him anymore."

I hold the book out, and he takes it gently, his fingers sliding over mine, before stuffing it back into his pocket.

"You only read used paperbacks?"

"More portable," he answers with a grin. "And they're cheap."

I feel my eyebrows tug together—he lives in a beautiful house atop a sun-kissed hill; I doubt he needs to save a few dollars on books, especially if his dad collects them. But there's obviously more to the story. More about him that I don't understand.

His hands clench the oars, eyes averted, before he asks, "Where will you go when you leave Cutwater?" It feels like he's trying to change the subject.

The river swirls past us, little ribbons of moonlight catching on

The Beautiful Maddening

the surface. "The ocean." I've only ever said this aloud to Archer. "There's a small town—my dad told me about it—just a fishing community, not much more. But there's a little cake shop near a marina, and it sounds so quiet and perfect, a place where no one has heard of my family. Maybe I can rent a room somewhere, a place overlooking the sea." I imagine it so clearly, it's like I'm already there. A place that waits for me.

I only need to board a train and not look back.

"The truth is, I don't really care where I go . . . ," I add. "As long as it's far away from Cutwater."

"And the ocean is far enough?"

I lift a shoulder, a stirring warmth expanding in my chest at the thought of leaving—just talking about it fills me with a hope so large, I feel lightheaded. "If I could afford it, I'd cross the Pacific. I'd buy a small boat, learn to sail, then I'd never be stuck anywhere for long."

"I could teach you to sail," Oak says.

"You know how to sail?"

"A little. My dad taught me."

A tiny shiver slides along my skin. It feels silly, impossible: talking like this, like it's something we could really do. The two of us on a sailboat, his practiced hands showing me how to steady the mainsail and navigate at night, while the wind grows stronger against our backs. Pushing us out into the deep, the endless ocean ahead of us, and nothing in our way.

I sink back against the boat, dipping my hand into the water, letting my fingers trail against the current. Because I know it's a future that won't really happen. Wherever I go, I will always be alone—

because I can never trust a life spent with anyone else. Love is a cruel, deceiving trick.

"Where will you go after graduation?" I ask—now I am the one who wants to change the subject.

"My dad wants me to go to college. . . ." His tone changes—almost imperceptibly—but I can hear the strain, the edge, as his arms pull heavily against the oars, the motion almost like a meditation, a thing he does to calm his racing thoughts. "But he doesn't get to choose my life . . . not anymore."

"Does your dad live here?" I think of the large, beautiful home looking out over Rabbit Cross River, wondering whether he has a father waiting somewhere inside—seated at a desk perhaps, inside a home office, a reading light switched on nearby. Or maybe he's in the kitchen, preparing dinner. Pasta and garlic bread. Windows open to let in the evening breeze.

But Oak breaks apart this image in my mind.

"No," he answers, digging the oars into the water, the moonlight darkening in his eyes—as if a storm has settled over him. "He's been gone for a while. Doubt I'll see him again."

Gone. A word I know too well.

Gone. A word that can mean so many different things.

A parent you learn to hate because they left, a parent you imagine returning one day and all the things you would say—all the vile, hate-drenched words that would rush from your lips.

He lost his mom.

And his dad too.

A life shattered, much like mine. And while I know there is more that he's not saying, a story beneath the rigid slant of his eyes, I don't

The Beautiful Maddening

press it. Because I know the pain that comes from talking about what's been lost, and when his jaw forms a stiff, unbroken line, I know I've strayed too far into something that hurts.

He rows even harder, driving the boat against the current, his breathing heavy, his face losing all its softness. We reach the shore below his house, and he steers the rowboat up onto the dirt, then swings himself out quickly to drag it the rest of the way onto land.

My heart is beating low in my chest as I step onto the shore, knowing that something is wrong. That everything about him has changed.

He stands for a moment, looking back at the river, but I stare up at his solitary, empty house. "Are we going inside?" I ask softly.

"Not today." He looks at me like he's trying to force a smile, but he's all hard edges and cold glances.

We leave his home on the hill and drive back across the county line, his truck chugging up the last rise on Swamp Wells Road, the silence growing wider between us.

I want to ask him what's wrong, what's changed, why talking about his dad made him turn to stone. But I sense the *asking* won't fix anything, and he'll cinch the armor even tighter around his chest.

We come to a stop at the end of my driveway, the truck engine still running, and I sit for a moment, waiting for him to speak, but his hands only twist against the steering wheel, his eyes unblinking, staring through the windshield.

"Thank you for today," I say, but my mouth tastes like metal. My heart is shrinking closed.

He nods but won't look at me.

I watch him for a half beat more, my bottom lip hanging open, like the right words might fall out, but nothing does. I open the door and step onto the driveway.

He backs away before I've even reached the porch, and I hear the roar of the old truck accelerating up Swamp Wells Road, back to his side of the county line.

And I start to doubt, to fear . . . that I'll never see him again.

ELEVEN

"So that's why you haven't left town," Archer says as I walk past him on the front porch. "My little sis found a boy to torment for the summer."

"I'm not tormenting him."

"Well, it sure as shit isn't the other way around. You're a Goode—we're the thing they break their hearts against. We leave the shattered remains of their weepy lovesickness in our wake."

I roll my eyes at him, opening the front door. "*You* do that," I say. "Not me." I step into the house and shut the door before he can answer.

In my room, I blink down at the suitcase, clothes now spilling out onto the floor.

I should go.

I should walk to the train station, wait for it to open in the morning, buy a ticket, and leave this place once and for all.

But my whole body feels numb, vibrating with a tiredness unlike any I've ever known. I kick off my sandals and sink between the sheets of my bed. I let sleep pull me under, and I dream of the river, of fireflies buzzing in the air between Oak and me.

I dream of his lips touching mine, faintly, carefully. I dream he doesn't let me go.

Not for anything.

Archer must see the strain in my face when I emerge from my room, the morning sun spearing through the trees, slanting into the old house, and he hands me a cup of lavender-and-lemon tea, nodding silently. He doesn't ask again about the boy. He doesn't ask if I'm leaving Cutwater.

He gives me the quiet I need to reassemble my thoughts.

Three days pass.

I should leave Cutwater. I don't know why I stay. Why I move numbly through the house, while my brother paces at the windows, the useless shotgun resting beside the front door. When a car slows down along the road, or someone strolling by pauses to stare up at the house like they're considering making the long walk up the drive to ask for a tulip, Archer grabs the gun and rushes out onto the porch, shouting at them to "get the hell away from our house."

He's doing the thing he does when he feels like our lives are out of control: he assumes the role of parent, guardian, protector. He takes the helm of our lives as if he could steer us back on course. But I know it's already too late for that. This family has been sinking for generations— all we can do now is abandon ship, scramble aboard a lifeboat, and run for our lives before we're swallowed up by the wet dirt.

But maybe this is why I stay.

My brother is anxious, fidgety, not himself, and it feels wrong to leave him right now.

The Beautiful Maddening

I tell myself I'll wait another day.

I tell myself it has nothing to do with Oak. That I'm not waiting for him to walk up the driveway, to knock on the door and tell me he's sorry. Tell me why he turned cold and quiet that night on the river.

I'm not waiting for a boy.

I could leave at any time.

I sit at the end of my bed and stare down at the image of Oak. The portrait is done, the book cover in his hands now sketched in, but still I find myself shading in the trees around his face, adding tiny fireflies in the background. I keep my pencil always pressed to the paper, wearing it down, trying to understand what happened. What changed in his eyes.

But there are no answers in the gray pencil marks.

Archer has fallen asleep in the old armchair beside the unlit fireplace, his chin tipped back, mouth open, snoring gently—he sleeps only in short bursts now, jerking awake at the tiniest sound. Quietly I open the front door and step out onto the porch, needing the fresh air, but also *hoping* . . . hoping I'll see Oak striding up the road, a book in his hand.

Regret in his eyes.

I sink into the old porch swing, my mind churning over every second we spent together, trying to unearth some clue, discover a piece I might have missed. A reason to explain why my heart stings every time I think of him. And why his heart doesn't seem to feel a thing.

Shea Ernshaw

After an hour, the air turning windy and cool, a shadow comes into view out on the road. . . .

I flinch upright.

But when I narrow my gaze through the dim light, I can tell—it's not Oak.

Mrs. Thierry ambles to a stop at the end of our driveway, her dog, Peebles—a massive Great Dane—tugging at the end of a leash. She lives a half mile up the road in a two-story, Victorian-style home half-shrouded in vines and blackberry bushes that she refuses to cut back. She glares up the driveway, the evening light—shades of orange and raspberry ice cream—melting into the trees behind her, and she looks as if she's casting some malediction, damning those who live in this house with an evil scourge.

But we're already the damned.

She mumbles something, spits onto our driveway, then inclines her head so her shaky voice will carry. "You'll curse us all with those flowers." Her words are sandpaper and gravel. "Just like old, nasty Fern Goode did the day he moved here." Mrs. Thierry knows the history of my family as well as anyone, because she's older than most, and meaner. I also suspect many of the rumors about my family began with her: she loves a good gossip, a tall tale, and I can imagine the stories forming behind her gray eyes. "You're stirring up things you shouldn't, letting locals carry around those tulips."

"They stole them," I shout back, pointlessly, because maybe it doesn't matter how they got them, only that the tulips will indeed stir up old, bad magic.

She and I stare at each other for a long moment—knowing that she wants the same thing as me: for the Goodes to leave this town

The Beautiful Maddening

and never come back. But at last she clicks her tongue and turns away, wobbling on up the road. She has a tendency to sway dangerously far toward the center line, cars speeding past, honking. But she is a woman who not even death can touch; she is unshakable, a woman who will surely live far longer than any of us.

"What did Mrs. Thierry want?" Archer asks when I step back into the house. He's awake, standing in the kitchen, his hand in a mason jar of homemade granola—given to him by a girl with strawberry-red hair and sad blue eyes who left it on our front porch a week ago.

"To remind us how doomed we are."

He snorts, like he finds this funny, but then his expression drops, as if he knows how true it is, and he falls quiet.

Dark settles over the house, and I lie awake in bed, my heart feeling like shredded paper. I want to see *him*, ask him what happened. But I also know it's better left alone.

Better if I don't see him again.

I should never have let myself get so close to him in the first place—his lips hovering against mine, soft and careful . . . but also *careless*. Needful and aching, the desire spinning upward in my chest like the lightning bugs flitting around us. I *wanted* him to kiss me, wanted all of it, wanted every second to shatter and burn apart like a storybook unraveling.

But all this *wanting* makes it impossible to push him away, to ease the twisting ache in the center of my ribs whenever I think of him.

I need to scrub him from my memory. I need to forget.

I need to leave.

A week flits by, and I keep telling myself that *tomorrow* is the day.

Tomorrow I'll repack my suitcase, tell my brother goodbye, and walk until I reach the train station in town.

I promise myself that I'm staying only because my brother still seems on edge, because he's worried someone else will sneak into the garden. And I don't want to leave him alone.

I vow that by the next sunrise I'll be long gone.

Still . . .

I watch the road. I feel a sense of waiting growing heavy against my rib cage.

But Oak doesn't come to the house—he doesn't leave books on my windowsill; he doesn't stroll down Swamp Wells Road under the cover of night. My heart feels knotted and aching and unnatural—and I hate it.

I don't understand it.

It makes no sense.

I hide the book he gave me—*Peter and Wendy*—with the sketch of him tucked inside the pages, stuffing it into the very back of my closet, pressed up against the wall, behind damp, forgotten clothes and an old handmade doll from my childhood.

I try to push him away. Cut him free from my mind like a rotted, gangrenous limb.

But . . .

It doesn't work.

I walk down the tracks to the forgotten train car, and I lie on my back, staring up at the stars, imagining Oak lying beside me—every

The Beautiful Maddening

one of his exhales stirring loose the constellations above, rearranging the night sky. And when the other train roars down the tracks, I stand and feel the wind against my face. But Oak isn't there to keep me from tipping over the edge. So I escape to the pond, strip free from my clothes, and sink beneath the surface, wishing the water were the same weight as his hands.

Wishing we had another chance.

I wish for stupid things.

"He's not just going to materialize," my brother says, finding me on the front porch staring down the empty driveway at the darkened road. Sunset an hour behind us.

"I wasn't looking for—"

My brother raises an eyebrow. "You're full of shit, little sis."

I pull my knees up on the porch swing.

"You should have left a long time ago, after graduation, but you're still here. You're waiting for him."

I frown. My hatred for this town, this house, has always been at my core, the center point that every decision pivots from. My reason for leaving. And yet, beyond all reason, there is now a second center of gravity. Sturdier, more dangerous than the first.

A boy. Who I need to forget.

"Even if he came walking up that driveway, could you trust anything he said? Anything he felt?"

"I'm not waiting for him."

He cuts his eyes over me and smirks. "You might be able to lie to yourself, but you can't lie to me. I know why you sit out here on the porch every night, watching the road. You're hoping that boy will appear."

I exhale and look away from my brother. I know the point he's trying to make, but I don't want to hear it.

"It's fine, I get it. But eventually you'll need to decide what you want more: freedom from this town, or that boy." He sinks onto the swing beside me and begins shelling peanuts from his pocket, tossing the brown husks over the railing into the creek, where they're carried away beneath the house, then out through the tulip garden to the woods beyond.

I stand up.

I can't take it anymore: this conversation, the waiting, the hole burning its way slowly through the soft muscle of my heart.

"Where you going?" Archer asks.

"Out."

"It's supposed to rain!" he calls.

But I stomp down the steps, over the creek, and down the driveway—without a word.

It's not just the desperation I feel to be rid of this house, of my brother and my room and my notebook filled with the sketches of people I can never get close to; it's the ticking in my skull for every day that's passed, every hour, when I should have left this all behind. I should be counting the miles that separate me from this town.

But I can't, not until I see him, not until I understand what went wrong.

This is the truth.

It's not my brother that has kept me here.

It's Oak.

The Beautiful Maddening

I walk through the warm evening air, headed west, toward Favorville.

This is a bad idea.

But I don't care.

Time unravels around me—I cross the county line, where the ground slopes up and the air feels crisp and mild and less humid—until I find myself walking up the long driveway to Oak's house.

I don't know what I'll say to him; I haven't rehearsed it in my head. I have no plan. Maybe I'll tell him he's an asshole for showing me the meadow, for taking me down the river, for getting so close to kissing me, then dropping me off at my house without a word.

Or maybe I'll stand mute in front of him, forgetting all the reasons why I'm angry.

Because my heart is a savage thing.

And it can't be trusted.

The air drains from my lungs the closer I get, and when I reach his house—built perfectly atop a grassy, moonless hill—I look back the way I came. I could leave now and he'd never know I was here. The specter of a girl slipping back into the quiet, loathsome, starry night. But I'd return home and my mind would continue to churn over the same questions.

It wouldn't fix a thing.

So I choke down the doubt and move up the stone walkway to the front door. I knock twice and wait, but there are no footsteps from the other side. I press the doorbell and hear the soft chime echoing across the expansive house. A scattering of lights is visible through a narrow window, a lamp in a corner, another down a hallway. But the rest of the house is dark. It's late; he could be asleep. Or he could be out wandering back roads, trying to lose himself in a story.

I cross my arms against the night air, against the cold, empty feeling sinking through me—I came all this way for nothing. Above me, the sky is beginning to fill with clouds, dark and baleful, a summer storm pushing west. But I don't turn and head back down the driveway. . . . I'm a Goode, after all—stubborn, persistent—and I walk around the side of the house.

I want to be sure.

Down the slope I can see where the rowboat is pulled ashore.

But it's not the only form in the dark.

A silhouette is seated beside it, angled toward a book in his hands, a few feet from the river's edge.

My heart ratchets up into my throat, and before I can convince myself that there's still time to leave, my legs carry me down the hill to the river.

I'm afraid to blink, afraid he'll vanish into the night—only an echo, a shadow spun together in my mind. But the closer I get, the more real he becomes. Calm, restful, knees bent—reading in the dark. I feel a pang of hurt in my chest that doesn't have a name, or even a word to describe it.

He doesn't hear me approach, doesn't lift his head until I'm only a few feet away, and his eyes suddenly snap up from the page.

Dark lashes.

Mouth tucked into a line.

He is beautiful at night, under the stars. Nameless, tenuous. But the calm I saw in his face is now gone.

He closes the paperback and stands up quickly. "What are you doing here, Lark?" His voice is like melted wax, burning my skin.

The Beautiful Maddening

"I . . ." My own voice fails me, crumbles, and I look away, back the way I came to the road in the distance. *My way out of here.*

"You shouldn't have come," he adds, but I can hear the doubt in his voice, a molecule-sized flicker of hesitation. He doesn't believe his own words.

I meet his eyes—finding the part of myself that won't turn around and go home until I have answers. Until I understand. "I don't know what happened before, the other day, on the river," I say firmly. "But I know something changed. I just need you to tell me why. . . . I need you to talk to me."

He looks to the ground, a wretched silence breaking across his face, like he's recalling that day in the boat: remembering the words we spoke that made his heart close up, made him regret taking me down the river and up to the meadow. "I need to tell you something. . . ." He swings his gaze back to me, the green rims of his eyes looking like they could pierce me clean through, a blade and a balm all at once. "I should have told you earlier." He scrapes a hand along the back of his neck, his eyes filling with fear, with a hurt I don't understand. And I'm afraid of what he's going to say.

That it was all a mistake.

Him and me. And the what-if that lingers between us.

I root my feet to the earth, trying to hold myself together.

But the sky cracks open instead—a mantle of storm clouds scraping across the horizon, turning everything black—and a second later a downpour of summer rain crashes over us. I wince, the sound deafening, drops exploding against the earth, pinging off the boat, and I'm surprised when Oak reaches out for me, takes my hand in his, and pulls me toward the house.

My breath shakes in my lungs as we run, and we're soaked by the time he pushes through a back door and we step into a quiet, dark room: a mudroom lined with boots and sneakers against one wall, coats hanging from hooks on the other. Organized and tidy. Clean.

Rain spills from my hair, drips from my clothes onto the floor.

"Wait here," he says softly, releasing my hand and vanishing into another room. A light is switched on somewhere, and I can see a kitchen illuminated ahead of me. I step into the massive space, with a gray concrete floor and white countertops, cream-colored walls and a lemon scent. I blink, trying to take it all in. It's the kind of home I've read about in books but never imagined I'd see in real life.

Oak appears behind me, holding out a large white towel. "Here," he says, his voice changed, all its sharp edges gone. He folds the towel over my shoulders, but it isn't enough; my whole body trembles, the cold saturating my skin. "You need dry clothes," he adds, clutching my shivering hands in his, before turning and slipping away into another part of the massive house. I sense that he doesn't want me here: His home is a place he wants to keep private. Secret. A part of his life he doesn't share.

The cold sinks even deeper, my bones feeling like they're rattling against my skin. I clutch the towel around my shoulders and step carefully into the living room—searching for a source of heat. But it feels like a museum, hardly lived in, all modern, clean lines and cold walls. Not the kind of place where a family wakes up on birthday mornings, the smell of waffles rising through the air while the sound of laughter echoes down the halls. This is a home of ghosts. Of a past left to die.

A fireplace stands against the far wall, and I find a switch on the

The Beautiful Maddening

right side that ignites the fire. A quick burst of light illuminates the vast room, and I hold my hands toward the gas-fed flames, the heat starting to dry my shivering skin.

Above the fireplace, the mantel is lined with framed photographs—the first sign that a family resides inside this catacomb. I scan each one, photos of Oak as a young boy, with warm green eyes and dark hair cut short. His mom is in several of the images, a woman with amber skin and long, dark hair and bright, beautiful eyes. I see Oak in her, in the kind, gentle slant of her face. I peer at photographs of their family at the beach, at an amusement park, Oak waving from a Ferris wheel. A few depict Halloween costumes, and several show the family beside Rabbit Cross River, Oak and his mom sitting in the same green boat he took me in days ago. His father is visible in only a handful of images—he was likely the one always snapping the photos. He is a tall man, like Oak, with broad shoulders and gray eyes. He is handsome, and there's something enigmatic, perplexing, about him—the same unnameable quality I see in Oak.

At the end of the row of photos, a stack of books rests on the mantel. They are old books, small, and most of the spines are so worn, they're unreadable. They look like poetry volumes. But it's not the books that my eyes settle on, it's the corner of something beneath the stack.

A single, loose photograph. I don't know why my eyes linger on it, why I feel compelled to pull it free from under the books—there is a throb at my temple, a prick of curiosity from some unknown place inside me.

I slide the photo free, holding it carefully between my fingers.

The light from the fireplace dances across the image, and my mind tumbles over itself, confused, off-balance, unsure what I'm looking at.

Oak's father is standing on a dock, nestled in a harbor, the mast of a sailboat rising up behind him, the afternoon sun slanted over his features.

But the woman standing beside him . . . is not Oak's mom.

It's someone else.

A woman with sable hair and dark, bewitching eyes. A woman with betrayal in her smile, a woman who left everything she knew and broke apart her family without a word.

The woman is not Oak's mom.

She's mine.

My eyes shiver over the photo, trying to take in every detail: Oak's father with his arm around her waist, her shoulder leaning into him.

My head thuds.

My heart begins to scream in my ears.

When Mom left, she fled Cutwater without a word. There was a secret inside her, a lie, a deceit. But I've always wondered if she left with someone she'd met. A man she kept secret from us. A man who couldn't resist a woman with the Goode last name. A man who finally helped her escape this town.

And now, fingers trembling, I wonder if this is the secret.

Tears well quick and icy behind my eyes, but the anger is scalding in my chest. And when I look up, Oak is standing at the edge of the hallway. Watching me.

He's shirtless, wearing a dry pair of jeans. But his eyes fall, and he sees what I hold in my hand. His face loses all meaning.

The Beautiful Maddening

"Did you know?" I ask.

He doesn't answer, his chest rising quickly with each inhale.

"My mother? And your father?"

His jawline contracts, all the lies reflected back in his face. "I wanted to tell you," he tries. "I was going to . . ." He doesn't finish, but he doesn't look away from me either.

My head spins, confused. Mom never mentioned Oak's dad— but she rarely talked about the men in her life. She swung easily from one romance to another. Like Archer, she never took love seriously, never considered the crumpled hearts she left in her wake. It was always about survival. And she didn't care who got hurt.

"My mom left with your dad . . . ," I mutter, trying to piece it together. "And you knew it. All along?" The photo in my hand starts to feel heavy, like it's gaining weight, like it's going to slip from my fingers and fall into the fire, burning to nothing. "Is this why you were following me, why you came to my school that first day?" I try to remember how to breathe, but the air tastes like dust. Like everything he never said. "Because you knew who my mom was?"

His throat tightens, and he sways a little on his feet. "It's been three years since my dad left. . . . I kept waiting for him to come back," he whispers. "But he never did." For a long moment he is silent, breathing, like he's searching for the right way to explain. "I finally got up the courage. . . . I wanted to see for myself." He shakes his head. "I needed to see the family that ruined mine." There is hurt in his eyes, a raw kind of pain I've never seen in him before, and it tangles up all my emotions. "I wanted to hate you. . . ." His green eyes drive straight through me. "But when I saw you outside the school, I felt something . . . like . . ." He winces. "Like something was burning me from the inside out."

My hands shake, not wanting to hear this.

He felt what the tulips wanted him to feel. *Love.* A pull toward me, unexplainable, perilous. He felt an ache, a need, a desire that wasn't real.

It never was.

I swallow, the feeling inside me like a sudden storm, a sea crashing against rocks, violent and terrible.

Everything between us has been a lie from the start.

He takes a risky step toward me. "I wanted to know if I could be around you . . . and not feel something. I wanted to prove to myself that I was stronger than my father, that I could resist a Goode."

I feel like I'm going to be sick. I thought he was immune; I thought the tulips had no effect on him. But maybe I only *wanted* to believe it. *Needed to.* I was stupid. Wrong. He felt what everyone else does, but he fought it, resisted, for as long as he could.

This is why he's tried to keep his distance, why he pulls away when we get too close—because he feels himself falling, *tumbling*, an urge to be even closer to me. The enchantment digging its way under his skin. That day in the boat, I asked about his father, and it must have reminded him of why he came to find me in the first place—it reminded him of the promise he made to himself, not to fall in love, not to repeat what his father did.

"He bought it for her," he says, nodding to the photo still in my hands. "Only a few months after they met, he bought her that sailboat. He was so in love with her."

I bite down on all the pain cracking through my ribs, making

The Beautiful Maddening

my heart feel shriveled and black and worthless. "Was she ever here, in this house?" My eyes dart around the living room, trying to imagine her seated on the low gray couch, trying to imagine her at ease within these cold walls.

But Oak shakes his head. "No. He never brought her here—he knew how I felt. I had heard about the Goodes at school, heard rumors. I told him that she couldn't be trusted, but he didn't care." He dips his chin, eyes to the floor, breathing. Oak thought the Goodes couldn't be trusted . . . but he is the one who lied. "One morning," he continues, "he said he was taking a trip with her. They were going to take the sailboat out, leaving from the coast. That was three years ago. He just never came back."

Three years. I know the weight of those same years.

"Have you heard from him?" I need to know . . . need to know if his father cares enough to write, when our mother hasn't bothered to send even a postcard.

Oak nods. "He calls sometimes, doesn't say much. They were in Europe a couple of months ago—Spain, I think. I know he feels guilty for leaving, and I think hearing my voice just makes him feel worse." He blows out a breath, looks exhausted and angry and broken. "But he also sounds . . . I don't know . . . happy, I guess. Like he really loves her."

I cringe, knowing that my mother is more to blame for all of this than his father. Maybe she loves Oak's father, or maybe she is only using him. Either way, she used the tulips—our family's charm—to convince him to take her far away from the town she always hated.

She convinced him to leave his son behind. And never go back.

She is the villain.

But if his father still thinks he loves her, then the enchantment hasn't worn off, hasn't left her flesh. It trailed her even after she left Cutwater. But eventually she will lose him, her charm will run out, the allure will wear off—it won't last forever—but not before she hurts everyone in her orbit.

Oak's eyes flick back to mine, and I don't want to admit it, but we both have known the same pain. The same years of waiting. The same loss.

We both have been abandoned because of love—the wrong kind of love.

The lying kind.

We both have made vows to ourselves—not to end up like our parents.

And now . . . here we are.

Tears leak down my cheeks; I'm unable to press them back down. He takes a step toward me, like he's going to wipe them away, but I shoot him a look not to touch me. "You lied," I tell him. "You knew all along, and you didn't say anything."

"I'm sorry. I never should have kept it from you." His eyes are dewy points of light, pinpricks of hurt. "I screwed up. But I wanted to believe that I could see you and not feel anything." I can see the anguish in him, the tears pressing against his eyelids. "I had to prove it to myself. But it became harder and harder not to think about you, not to . . ."

I shake my head, *not* wanting to hear any of it, and I clench the towel tighter against my chest.

"I've tried to stay away . . . ," he says, voice rough, like the words are a burden he's carried too long, and I think I see his lips

The Beautiful Maddening

trembling. Pain tucked into every crevice. "I thought I could fight it, but . . ." His chest swells. And my heart starts to crash against my ribs: fearful of what he's going to say next but needing to hear it, needing to know what thoughts have tormented him. Needing to know why I shouldn't just leave and hate him forever. "I went to the abandoned train car, the place you took me that night. I stood on the roof and tried to think of all the reasons why I needed to forget you. But they were all the wrong reasons . . . because it's not . . . because I . . ." He shakes his head, exhaling like it's the last breath he'll ever take. "I told myself I would never see you again and that eventually it wouldn't hurt so bad. But I don't think that's true either, because seeing you now . . ." I try to look away from him but can't. My eyes are buried in his. "I don't think a girl like you can be forgotten. Not really. Not ever."

His words peel back old scabs, breaking my bones all over again. "You only think about me because I'm a Goode, because you can't help it. What you feel isn't real." It hurts to say this, I wish it weren't true, but I know he can't trust his own heart. Every unshakable thought he's had about me . . . *is a lie*. What he feels when he sees me is a lie.

I am the monster. The daughter of the woman who took his father away.

"No," he says, jaw tensing, eyes flashing to the fireplace. "I don't believe that. It's . . . it's not your last name. It's not this town or anything that could grow from the ground behind your house." He scrapes a hand through his dark hair, like he's not getting the words out quite right. His eyes click back to mine, the dark centers of his pupils cut through with pain. "Lark, tell me you don't feel anything . . . and I'll believe you. If it's only me, then it must be the tulips, then I've been stupid this whole time. I've imagined this whole thing. But if you feel something . . . then it's not your family, or those flowers. . . ."

My lungs have stopped inhaling, and it feels like a broken knife is cutting apart every inch of my swollen heart, leaving it in shreds on the floor of his beautiful home. And he won't take his dangerous, savage, painful eyes off me. "I can't . . ." *I can't let myself. . . . I can't admit how he makes me feel.*

Because he's lied. And I feel betrayed—not just by him, but by my own mother. By everything that's happened. My family has broken *his* in ways that I can't make right.

There are too many hurts between us for there to be room left for anything good.

Still, he moves closer. I tell my legs to walk away, I tell my body to run, but my muscles are useless—as if there's a gravity in him I can't pull away from.

"Tell me something, Lark, anything," he presses. "Tell me you hate me. Tell me you never felt a thing for me. Tell me you never want to see me again."

I want to be angry. I want to tell him I'll never forgive him for what he's done, the secret he kept, but it's not what I feel at all. I feel my whole body spinning into dust, into nothing; I feel every *need* inside me growing out of control. My heart is a drum in my ears. "I—I," I stammer, my lungs caving in. "I don't feel anything for you," I lie. *Because I feel everything.* Because I have to keep my distance, because he doesn't understand what will happen if I allow myself to tip too far into something we can't return from. We can't trust.

The Beautiful Maddening

He exhales, but his eyes stay on me, unflinching.

"I've seen the lives those flowers have ruined, just like they ruined yours," I tell him instead, trying to make him understand. The truth I can't escape. "You once said that the people in this town want the tulips because they're afraid they won't be loved without them. But I never told you what *I'm* afraid of." My head pulses, words pressing against my teeth. "I'm afraid the tulips are the *only* reason anyone will ever love me."

I'm afraid I am a girl who will only ever know false love. Conjured by a flower that blooms each spring outside my bedroom window. I'm afraid I'm a girl who is unlovable otherwise. But mostly . . . I'm afraid of what will happen if I let myself fall for him.

I'll end up losing him.

Like my mother lost my father once tulip season was over.

Heartache is always waiting on the other side of summer. Once the tulips wilt and die, so does the delirium of love they cause.

Oak's eyebrows pull together. "So you'd live your life afraid to let anyone love you?"

"If it keeps me safe, keeps my heart from breaking a hundred times, then yes."

He takes a brave step toward me, and I can see all the pain crashing against the shore of his eyelids. "You're not afraid of being loved . . . ," he says, defiant, cavernous. "You're afraid that you'll fall in love, and everything you've ever believed was wrong. You're afraid that love is the only thing that will save you. That love is the only thing you really want."

I breathe, anger and pain bleeding into something that feels like truth. "You were afraid too," I point out. "You were afraid of *me.*

And you lied," I remind him. "You only came to my window that night, on my birthday, to see how close you could get to Lark Goode without falling in love. But you failed. You're just as weak as the rest of them." The words sting; they slice against my tongue.

I am the monster, I remind myself.

"I'm not like the rest of them, and neither are you," he says, moving even closer, unfazed by my words, and I want to yell at him, tell him to keep his distance or we will destroy each other. It's the way of Goodes. It's how it's always been. "I don't believe in the curse, Lark. I spent so much time blaming your family, your mother, for what happened. But it was *my* father who chose to leave, who decided that *she* was more important than staying here with me." He exhales, his chest deflating. "Maybe your family *wanted* to blame the tulips for everything that's ever happened to them, and maybe the town wanted a reason to explain what they felt for the Goodes, because they couldn't accept that they might be drawn to a family like yours. The tulips are just an excuse. A story we tell ourselves to make sense of what we feel." My breathing slows, and a strange quiet settles over me—his voice makes every knot inside me slip apart, my heart easing into a rhythm it knows only with him. "This thing I feel when I'm with you has nothing to do with the garden behind your house. And I don't want to wake up one day and regret not telling you this. I don't want to wake up and wonder where you are, wonder what might have happened if I had."

The warm air from the fire suddenly feels too warm.

"I never should have lied to you," he says, temples tightening all the way down to his jawline. "I know I hurt you, I know I pushed you away, and I'm sorry." I can see the tears breaking against his eye-

The Beautiful Maddening

lids. Watery edges of regret. "I should have told you all of this sooner. I should have stood at your window and told you that it's my fault. And I know . . . it might already be too late."

Confusion rips at me. *I want to believe him.* Maybe it was never the tulips. Maybe we wanted to believe in a curse so badly to make sense of *this*—this fever that weaves tight around our throats and makes it hard to breathe. Maybe there is nothing to fear in the garden behind our house. It was only ever a story we told to make sense of the heartbreak and misfortune that has always followed us. We wanted to believe it, and so we did. And the town did too. The only real sickness is our belief. A fable, a folklore we can't shake.

Maybe the only thing I can actually trust is what I feel right now. Here.

With him.

"Lark . . . ," he says softly, so close that I can smell the rainwater on his skin. "If you never want to see me again, just tell me."

He's giving me another chance, and my mouth falls open. *I hate you,* I should say. *I hate you for this secret you kept from me.* But the lie no longer has weight. Meaning.

Neither of us has trusted love.

Neither of us knows how.

So I do what I shouldn't: I reach out for him.

My cold fingertips find the warmth of his collarbones, feeling the pulse at his neck. He is the river and the midnight air that soaks into his skin when he reads beneath the stars.

I want to believe he's right.

I need to.

He lifts his arm, the muscles of his chest tensing, and he touches a strand of my wet hair—as if it's as close as he dares to get. But it's not enough—*he's never close enough*—and I don't care that a part of me is still shouting that I need to leave, I don't care that I've made promises to myself, because my heart is now a piston, firing out of control, about to break my rib cage into a thousand jagged pieces of bone.

I stare up into his impossible eyes, pleading for something I'm certain only he can give me: *relief, hope.* Meaning in the torment of his hands on my skin.

I want so bad to hate him . . . but instead I am breathless and desperate, and I want only one thing.

This feeling will break me. I'm certain of it.

"It's not just you," I admit.

His thumb slides down my cheek, across my chin, my bottom lip, and he looks at me like he's forgotten everything that came before this moment, all the words spoken between us, all the near misses when we pulled away from each other.

Maybe we don't have to make amends for the mistakes our parents made. Maybe we don't have to punish ourselves; maybe we don't have to resist what we feel because we're afraid of ending up like them. We have to make our own mistakes.

We have to risk everything so that we feel *something*.

So that we live.

I lift onto my tiptoes, and I graze my lips gently across his—air and rain and a thousand hours that I've spent tracing the outline of his mouth, that I've imagined the softness of his breath against mine. And now . . .

Now . . .

The Beautiful Maddening

He sucks in a breath, and I dig my fingers into the back of his neck, feeling the heat of his skin. Feeling myself tremble at the same moment his lips sink in, tracing the delicate, never-before-touched curve of my mouth. Rainwater falls from our flesh, dries up, evaporates just like my heart. My fingertips graze his wet hair, while his hands slide beneath the towel, finding my waist, my hips, and it feels like we're tumbling backward, heat and breath and all the lies between us. But none of it matters. He lifts his mouth and kisses my throat, the soft place beneath my earlobe.

I feel weightless again, lost in the warmth of his fingertips as they trace the landscape of my flesh that no one has ever touched. I kiss him back, tasting the rainwater on his skin; I kiss him so desperately, I worry we'll both break. His hand slides along my ribs, beneath my soaked tank top, and I swear it feels as if my heart is pounding so loud that it'll rattle the walls of his house.

His mouth is on my throat again, tracing every freckle, his hand now against my belly. He takes a deep breath, stalls, and I close my eyes, falling, *falling*, tipping recklessly into something I never want to wake from. His mouth is on mine again, desperate, both of us losing ourselves in whatever this is: lust or love or a madness.

"Lark," he whispers against my flesh, and I feel a deep, dangerous unspooling inside me. A rupturing behind my eyelids, a feeling like I want to cry and laugh all at once. A feeling in the very center of my being, a thing I've always feared, a thing I've been warned about.

Love.

It tiptoes up the base of my spine, careful and quiet, as if I might miss it, as if it's only a whisper. Hardly there at all. A thief. A pickpocket.

But once it lands in my chest, it thunders through every muscle and bone, splitting apart every cell . . . and there's no denying it.

This is what I've spent most of my life trying to avoid.

But when it settles behind my eyes, I feel tipsy and inside out, like I'm drifting away. I feel inhuman, a speck of stardust. A riddle and a blade of grass. Nowhere and everywhere.

I feel like a girl who is having her first kiss.

Who fell for a boy one perilous summer and never looked back.

I *let* myself feel it all. I draw in a ragged breath, my skin alight, and I stare into his eyes, trembling. Maybe Oak is right: It was never real, *the curse*. It was only ever a story, a thing told to Archer and me, a fable my mother believed in, a tall, *tall* tale.

I lay my lips on his and he kisses me back. The chill that tunneled across my skin when we ran through the rain is now gone; only warmth is left. His hands slide back down my ribs, and I kiss him, knowing I'll never lose him again. I kiss him for all the times I wanted to but never could. I kiss him without fear, and I pull him to me, scraping my fingers across his collarbones. I want to know every feeling I've denied myself. I want to make up for lost time. I want to know what it feels like to wake up in his arms, the morning sun shivering across our bare skin. I want to lose every part of who I used to be.

His hands are in my hair, and my heart feels like it's going to explode. Break clean through my flesh, kill me instantly.

But it's something else . . . that destroys me.

Something else.

His voice against the soft flesh of my ear, vibrating against my eardrums, delicate and small. But with the weight of a hammer.

The Beautiful Maddening

"You smell like flowers," he murmurs. The words sound far away, as if uttered beneath water, whispered against a cold wind whipping down from a mountaintop.

I pull my head away, and he blinks, looking briefly confused, like he never intended to say the words. As if they'd been spoken by someone else.

"What did you say?"

He shakes his head, eyebrows crinkling together. "I—I didn't mean . . ."

"You said I smell like flowers."

"I just meant that . . . I shouldn't have said it. . . ."

I shake my head and slip free from his hands. *Fuck.* I smell like flowers because I am a Goode. Because the scent of tulips is laced like poison along my skin: it lives in my hair, pollen dotting my eyelashes, the perfume of love and desire inescapable. And with only a few words from his lips, I know the truth. His hands trace my flesh only because of the flowers that grow wild and dangerous beside a cursed creek.

Even if he doesn't believe it, even if he convinced me for a brief, dreamlike moment that the tulips are only a story told to make sense of the past. His voice has shattered the illusion.

I can never escape the lie the tulips tell on my behalf.

He desires me because I am a Goode. Nothing more.

"Lark . . . ," he begins.

But I stagger back from him. And it feels like being dropped from a cliff.

"It's not real . . . ," I hear myself say, but my thoughts are already breaking apart, coming undone.

201

"It *is* real . . . ," he insists. "I'm sorry I said that, about the flowers, it was stupid. I didn't mean anything by it. I don't even know why I said it—it just came out."

I allow my eyes to scrape up to his. "You said it because your thoughts aren't your own. Your mind isn't your own. This is all . . ." I shake my head. "I shouldn't have come here."

"Lark, no." He tries to step toward me, but I take another step back, then another.

I can't believe I let myself trust this feeling, trust him, trust this moment.

Love is a lie. And it always will be.

But it's not his fault. . . . It's mine.

I am a Goode. I am the monster.

"I'm sorry," I say to him. "I understand why you lied, about your dad and my mom. But I should have known better. I should have stayed away."

My legs carry me back, and Oak stands frozen, the firelight making ribbons of light and dark across his chest. The hurt in his eyes is so heavy, I can't bear to look directly at them.

"Please, Lark, don't go. Don't walk away."

I risk a glance at him, feeling my own tears welling against my eyes. "It's not your fault, how you feel," I say. Words that burn. That cut me apart. "But you should try to forget about me. About this summer. And by winter you won't even remember why you spent a single day with me; it'll all seem like wasted time."

"No," he mutters.

But I force my eyes away from him, yanking open the door, and I duck out into the storm.

The Beautiful Maddening

Raindrops explode against the asphalt. The air fills with its warm, atmospheric scent. And my heart is ash.

Mom's words repeat in my head: *Never trust your heart, never trust love.*

I run, the wind howling against my face, the air burning in my lungs, my bare feet smacking against the pavement. I can still feel the places where Oak's hands touched my skin. The scent of him pressed into my flesh: of the river behind his house, wet earth, and a long, winding road.

I left my sandals beside the back door of Oak's house. But I'm not going back. I won't risk it; I can't trust that my heart won't tip back into his arms. That I might forget why I left in the first place.

All the fear that lives inside me, the warnings I've repeated to myself my entire life—*never get too close, never make eye contact, don't let them love you*—force my legs to pump even harder. My heartbeat cracking against my eardrums.

I reach our driveway and sprint toward the house, over the creek, and gasp for air on the front porch before pushing inside. Archer is leaning against the kitchen counter, sipping a cup of coffee, the shotgun at his side—like he intends to stay awake all night.

"What happened?" He sets his mug on the counter.

But I march past him and out into the garden. The tulips sway innocently, a section of the crop now headless, ripped from the soil, but most of the garden is untouched.

Over the years several of my ancestors have tried to destroy the tulips: Uncle Sergie mowed down the whole garden with a riding lawn mower one night while drunk; my great-grandmother Pip tried to dig up the bulbs with a shovel, uprooting most of them in hopes that a local man who bred horses on the other end of town would stop loving her. But it didn't work. The tulips always returned the following spring, and the locals kept falling in love. *Obsession and desperation and misery.*

I head for the toolshed and find a pair of large, rusted shears. They're heavy, haven't been used in a decade, but I make for the garden, determined. At the first row, the tulips churn around me as if they sense something, feel the malice of my intention, and I swing the shears up, snip off three beautiful tulip heads, and watch the blooms hit the ground like they've been decapitated.

"What the hell are you doing?" Archer shouts from the back porch.

"They ruin everything," I say, shearing off another five tulips.

I hear Archer's footsteps on the porch stairs, but I keep hacking at the tulips, watching the blooms roll across the soil, the air fragrant and alive with their terrible scent. But just before I can snip off another towering clump, Archer rips the shears from my hands in one swift move. "You think destroying the tulips will be this easy?"

I turn on my brother, my ears pulsing. "I have to try."

Archer holds the shears at his side, and I eye them, ready to snatch them back, but he gives me a look, his eyebrows raised. We both know that I won't be able to wrestle them from him: he's stronger, and he'd win this battle one way or another—just like when we were little kids and he'd swipe my favorite stuffed rabbit from my bed and run into the woods, knowing I couldn't catch him.

His eyes flatten, trying to unearth the truth from his sister.

The Beautiful Maddening

"What happened tonight? You went to see that boy?" He squints, his upper lip curling a little, like he's found it. Discovered the thought I've been trying to hide. "You started to fall in love with him, didn't you?"

I don't answer.

"Shit, sis. You know better than that."

I exhale, craning my head back to stare up at the moonless sky, every star vivid and sharp like needlepoints. "I really liked him," I whisper, I confess, heat rising behind my eyes. "I thought . . . I don't know, that maybe it was real."

"First rule of being a Goode: never believe anything that feels like love."

I lower my head, looking down at the pile of tulips at my feet, and I feel suddenly afraid that I'll never leave this house—just like Archer. That all my plans are impossible. *Improbable.* And I'll never be any better than everyone else who couldn't find a way out of Cutwater.

That I'll stay here forever.

Archer grips the shears, using them to point to the garden. "Without the tulips, what do we have, Lark? We're just two orphans living in a shit house, in a shit town, with no future. But these flowers give us power. Control."

"But we'll never have love. *Real love.*"

He turns away from me briefly, like he's hiding something, a thought, a memory he doesn't want me to see. Then his eyes swing back. "I'll take power over love any day."

He starts toward the back porch, then pauses, turns to face me again. "If cutting down the garden would end the curse, someone in this family would have done it long ago. This garden . . . this is our life. It's all there is. The sooner you accept it, make it work in your favor, the less miserable you'll be." His eyes soften, pity forming at the corners. He feels bad for me. "I know it's hard. But we have to be tougher, more resilient than anyone else in this town, or this life will destroy us."

My eyes drop to my feet. Tulip season *will* end, winter *will* come, yet we will still be the Goodes. And the curse will not end for us. We will never be rid of it. It will start all over again next spring.

My brother leaves me in the garden.

The screen door banging shut behind him.

I've known a lifetime of lovesickness; I grew up watching Mom push away unwanted affections, our doorbell ringing at all hours of the night, men standing on our porch pleading with her to love them in return—their voices waking me from sleep.

I grew up with this maelstrom of forsaken love all around me. And when I scan the garden, I see what others do: the beauty of each rare bloom, white petals cut through with an ancient red incantation. But I also know the tulips are made of darkness. They are a plague. And they will ruin us, one way or another.

I push in through the back door and march down the hall. My heart is a twisted knot, my body is still razed with memories of *him*, and I peel away my clothes.

In the Goode family, love means destruction. It means pain.

I step into the shower and turn on the water as hot as it will go. I need to rid him from my body. *I need him gone.* I allowed myself to believe, foolishly, that maybe Oak wasn't affected by the tulips. That he was drawn to me like any normal boy enchanted by any normal girl.

But now I know the truth.

The Beautiful Maddening

I scrape at my skin. I tilt my head back and let the water stream down my face, mixing with the tears, washing me clean of the girl I used to be. But it's no use.

I can still feel every place his hands pressed against me, his fingertips at my hip bone, his mouth beside my ear. I touch my lips, remembering the way it felt when he kissed me. *And I want to feel it again.*

No.

I am a girl who is cursed.

I can't strip away my name—I can't undo who I am. That part of me will never be washed down the drain.

I leave the shower and crawl into bed, knees pulled to my chest, naked, hoping that by morning I'll forget who he is. I'll forget a boy named Oak who once touched me like I was his gravity—the only thing keeping him from drifting away. From disappearing. A boy I still want just as badly as I did before I stepped into the shower.

The feeling has burrowed in deep.

An ache in my belly, a pulse behind my eyes.

A thing that's hooked its claws into me and won't let go.

TWELVE

Heartbreak should kill you.

But it doesn't. It keeps its victims alive, tortures them until there's nothing left but a hollow cavity beneath the ribs.

Is this how everyone else feels when they fall for a Goode? Is this the torment Archer and I—but mostly Archer—have been inflicting on others?

I wake to the scent of toast burning and the sound of Archer cursing in the kitchen.

I drag myself from under the comforting weight of the blankets, pull on a sweater and shorts, and pad down the hall—still feeling tangled up in Oak's arms, in his betrayal. In the stilled way he looked at me as I backed away to the front door. And fled.

"Morning," Archer says gently—his tone changed from last night.

The kitchen table is set with two glasses of orange juice, a plate of french toast—burned at the edges—and a mason jar of fresh maple syrup. "You made breakfast?" I can't remember my brother ever making a meal for us.

He lifts a shoulder, setting two forks on the table. "We didn't do anything for our birthday."

The Beautiful Maddening

I slide into one of the chairs, waiting for my brother to reveal his true intention—certain this is all some prank—but I fork a piece of french toast. "Where'd you get all this?"

"It was a gift," he says with a wink. *Of course it was.* Some love-sick girl probably gathered a dozen eggs from her family's chickens, then baked a loaf of bread, leaving it all on our front porch for Archer Goode.

But I don't argue—maybe a meal will fill the hole left inside me where my crumpled heart once lived.

Archer sinks into the opposite chair, his mouth sloped. "I understand why you did it," he says, voice earnest. "Why you tried to cut down the tulips." He looks to the front window, a softness in his expression that wasn't there last night. "We've always known that love is a slippery thing in our family. You have to be careful, Lark."

A *slippery thing*, as if it were as minor as a stubbed toe, a sliver in the finger. As if it weren't a whole broken heart—a vital organ.

I press my tongue against my teeth, trying to keep the hurt from breaking against my eyelids. "It's over now," I say. "I won't see him again."

I don't tell him about Oak's father, about the photo of our mother beside a sailboat. Because maybe it doesn't matter who she left with, only that she's gone, abandoned us, and she's likely never coming back.

My brother reaches out and touches my hand on the table, squeezing, and I feel several stray tears leak down my cheeks.

"We're strong," he says. "We have to be."

Right now I don't feel strong. Right now I'm certain I'll never be free of the scent of Oak on my skin.

"I know what it's like. . . ." Archer releases my hand, eyes dipping to the plate in front of him. "Last summer, I . . ." He pauses, tapping his foot against the floor, looking uncomfortable. "It was Stella Lu, she bumped into me outside of Lone Pine Coffee—actually no, that's not right. I bumped into her." He stops tapping his foot, a smile catching at the edge of his mouth. "I saw her walking by outside, and something struck me—she just seemed . . . I don't know." He shakes his head. "We've gone to school with her since we were kids, but I saw her that day and I just wanted to talk to her, *really* talk to her. I walked her home, and when she smiled at me, it was like switching on an overhead light. Like I had been in the dark for years, fumbling around, and then suddenly she was there, a flashlight in a basement." His eyes find the window, and he smiles out at the morning sunlight. "We spent every day together for nearly a month."

I think back to last summer, and I remember seeing Archer with Stella a handful of times but didn't think much of it—it seemed like every other temporary fling my brother finds himself in, brief and over all too soon. But the way he's describing it now, it was something else entirely.

"We went camping one weekend, took her dad's truck, drove all the way up to Jackjaw Lake. It was warm, and we slept under the stars. I was careful, kept my distance as much as I could, because I knew . . . I felt myself . . ." His voice breaks, and he looks away.

"You were falling in love with her."

He nods, still staring through the window. "It was different with her, *I* felt different. She made me want to be someone who . . . I don't know. Who was just better, I guess. I know that sounds dumb."

I shake my head. "It's not dumb."

The Beautiful Maddening

He nods to himself, then settles back into the chair. "That night . . . I kissed her and I felt it happen. I felt my chest almost widen, like I was becoming something else. More awake somehow. I felt . . ." My brother's eyes start to water. "I fell in love with her. And I thought it would be okay; I thought she would still love me when tulip season ended." He scrapes a hand across his eyes. "But that night, I didn't know it, but the tulips wilted in the garden, and when the sun rose, she was already packing her things outside the tent. She woke up, looked at me, and felt nothing. She probably couldn't even remember why she liked me in the first place."

I feel a tightness in my chest, knowing all too well how this story ends.

His shoulders drop. "After that night it hurt too much to see her. That empty look in her eyes—like we'd never spent all that time together. Like it meant nothing to her. I was a mistake she made, nothing more."

I realize suddenly that *this* is why he skips school, why he hates going to class. It's because of her. The one he dared to fall in love with. "You never told me any of this," I say. "You never even mentioned her. I just assumed she was . . ." I catch myself. "I'm sorry, Archer. I'm sorry I didn't see how heartbroken you were."

My brother is silent for a long time, and I feel my own heart twist inside my chest, knowing that he held this in and never said a thing. The creek rushes beneath the floorboards, carving away the soil, generations of pain and loss buried in the walls of this house. Fate inescapable.

"No," he says, drawing in a deep breath. "It's okay. I sure as shit won't let myself feel that way again. I keep my heart stuffed down deep. I let them love me, but never the other way around." I watch my brother's face change, the hardness settle behind his eyes. "Safer this way."

I want to tell him he's wrong . . . but I'm beginning to wonder if this is the only way. Better never to love at all than to feel the pain of losing it an instant later. This is the way of Goodes—nothing lasts, love is deep and dizzying for everyone around us, yet we don't get to feel a thing.

And I allowed myself to feel something I never should have.

I push myself up from the table, my appetite gone.

Archer gives me a quiet look, like he understands what I'm feeling more than I know. "It won't always hurt this bad," he offers. "But I'm not gonna lie, for a while it's going to hurt like hell."

I look to the back window, at the garden, where the remaining tulips bend in the wind, tall and swaying. Unnatural. *We'll never be free of this place,* I think. Even if I leave Cutwater, will the curse follow me? Will love always be a lie?

Even if I travel far away from this town, where no one has heard the Goode name, where the rumors and lore cannot find me, it may not be enough to rid the scent of pollen from my flesh.

How far will be far enough?

I shiver, the cold finding its way back in.

I start toward my room, needing the silence and the dark beneath my blankets . . . when there's a knock at the front door.

My eyes flash to Archer, but his cut to the shotgun leaning against the wall.

I'm certain Oak is not standing on our front porch, but it could be someone desperate for a tulip, someone drunk on the feeling of love. I

The Beautiful Maddening

watch my brother stand, then move to the front door and open it slowly.

The morning wind slides through the open doorway, but Archer is motionless.

I ease toward him, trying to peer past his shoulder—trying to see who it is.

But Archer's eyes fall to the ground, blinking, before he bends down to pick something up.

He turns, and in his hands he holds a newspaper.

The *Cutwater Gazette*.

"Why is there a newspaper on our front porch?" My voice is mostly air.

Archer doesn't answer, and I move closer to read the headline, the room starting to spin out of focus.

CUTWATER HIGH STUDENTS AFFLICTED WITH

UNEXPLAINED HYSTERIA

I skim the article quickly, my eyes catching on several words— sentences that feel like sharpened thorns scraping across my bones.

Locals blame longtime residents known as the Goode family . . .
Tulip farm may be the cause of the unusual phenomenon.
Symptoms are abnormal . . . including delusions of love.

I step away from Archer—I don't want to read any more.

"They're calling it a modern-day tulip mania," he says, glancing up from the article.

"They're not wrong." I sink back into the chair, facing my uneaten plate of toast. "Who do you think left it?"

Archer folds the paper in half, then drops it onto the kitchen table. "Mrs. Thierry was at the end of our driveway when I opened the door."

We are silent, staring down at the newspaper—we've spent our whole lives shrouded by whispers and rumors about our family, but this is the first time our name has been printed in the local newspaper.

"It's a shit newspaper anyway," Archer says.

It might be a tiny newspaper for a tiny town, but it's still the Goode family name stamped in black ink on the front page, for all to see.

The air leaves my lungs, and I lift my eyes to my brother. "We'll get them back."

He frowns. "What?"

"We'll get them back," I repeat. "All of them. We'll find the stolen tulips and we'll stop whatever's happening."

He sinks into his chair, tilting his head. "How?"

"Bait and switch."

My brother and I walk to town, taking the alleyways, keeping out of sight.

Mrs. Thierry said that we were "stirring up things" we shouldn't by letting others possess a tulip. Stolen or not.

I intend to fix that.

We reach Aubrie's Flower Shop, on Second Street, and we gather

The Beautiful Maddening

all the ordinary tulips arranged in glass vases, then ask the shopgirl for any others she has in the back. She eyes us, wary, watchful, but I tell her that they're a gift for a sick relative, and she nods, like she has no intention of questioning our motive. She just wants us out of her shop as quickly as possible.

Archer pays for the blooms with money I never knew he had, and by the time we've left the shop, we have a good five dozen tulips balanced in our arms.

Leaving town, we keep to the shadows, making sure we aren't seen, then hurry up Swamp Wells Road.

Archer drags out the rusted red wheelbarrow from the side of the house and parks it at the end of our driveway. The tire is flat, it hardly rolls, but we fill the wheelbarrow with the purchased tulips. Then I use a piece of cardboard from the shed and hastily write out a sign:

TRADE IN YOUR OLD TULIP FOR A FRESH ONE.

NO COST.

"Do you think they'll really do it?" I ask, unsure if anyone will believe our lie.

Archer sinks into one of the two lawn chairs that he carried down from the porch. "I guess we'll find out," he says with a wink. He's confident. And I hope he's right.

Because this feels like redemption.

If we can find all the stolen tulips, if we can recover the flowers that should never have left the garden, maybe it will set something right. Like turning back the clock, to before Clementine and her

Shea Ernshaw

friends snuck into the garden, stuffing their pockets full of tulips. Back before Oak left a book on my windowsill.

Maybe if we can undo what's happened, it will right all the wrongs.

It'll repair this wound beneath my ribs.

We sit like this for an hour, Archer flipping the guitar pick through his fingers while he tells me stories about the time he got locked inside the library up in Favorville with a girl named Shelly Shellington. He tells me about the time he fell into the rosebush outside Layla Black's bedroom window, and how he was picking thorns from his backside for two days after. We laugh, and I almost forget why every part of me hurts.

"Thank you," I tell him. "For helping me with this." I nod to the flowers. "Even if it doesn't work." My brother—who has always felt like a passing shadow I happen to share a cursed home with—now won't leave my side. And I think: maybe this is the only way to survive—with those who understand what it feels like to be crushed by love.

A few cars pass on the road, slowing down to read our sign, but always they keep going. "They don't trust us," I say. "Maybe because anyone who tried to get close to the house in the last couple of weeks was met with a shotgun." I give my brother a teasing look. "They probably think this is a trick."

Archer shrugs. "Maybe. But they're also desperate."

Only a minute later he's proved right.

A blue SUV pulls off onto the side of the road, and Cole Campbell jumps out, something held in his closed fist. He doesn't say a word, but when he reaches us, he opens his palm, revealing a flat-

The Beautiful Maddening

tened, dead tulip. "Can I get a new one?" His mouth is tensed, a look of fever in his eyes.

"Help yourself," Archer replies, and Cole quickly drops the lifeless tulip to the dirt, then yanks a new one from the wheelbarrow. He scurries away to his car as if he's afraid we'll change our minds and ask for the tulip back.

Cole has just pulled back onto the road when another car veers off into the driveway, slamming on its brakes. Olive Montagu gets out of the white Honda, nearly tripping over her leather sandals to reach us. She drops three flattened tulips into my lap, her eyes wide and wild and red at the edges like she's been crying. "You swear it won't cost me anything?"

"Not a penny," Archer answers, but I stare up at her, thinking of the night at the quarry when she came after me, begging for a tulip. I think about Oak witnessing the madness in her eyes as we sped away in the truck.

But now she only eyes me briefly before swiping three tulips from the wheelbarrow, then making her way back to her Honda.

Within minutes the end of our driveway is crowded with cars left running while our classmates dispose of their old, wrecked tulips, then greedily grab new ones.

Word has gotten out, and now they've all come to replenish their supply of tulip-induced love.

What they don't seem to notice, what none of them point out, is that the new tulips look nothing like the Goode tulips. The wheelbarrow is filled with an assortment of bright sunshine-yellow, pale pink, brazen red, and even a few stark-white blooms.

They are clearly not Goode tulips. But maybe it's the desperation they feel, the greed—they want to believe these are the real thing. And what do they really know of Goode tulips? They've never seen the crop behind our house until this summer. Maybe the blooms in the wheelbarrow are a different variety, a slightly different color, sure, but a Goode tulip nonetheless. Because if the Goode twins are handing them over, they must be real.

It's only Lulu Yen—when she stands in front of us, holding out a few worthless, torn tulip petals, asking if she can still get a new tulip—who frowns down at us and asks, "Why are you doing this? Giving them away?"

"Figured we should get rid of them," Archer says with a shrug. "No use keeping them to ourselves."

She hands over the petals, then takes a bright pink tulip from the wheelbarrow. "You could sell these, you know, make a lot of money."

For a moment Archer blinks at the tulip in her hand, like he's considering it, then clears his throat. "We're just spreading the love," he answers stupidly, as if we're giving away friendship bracelets at a summer fair.

Lulu nods, clasping the fresh tulip in her fingers, before striding away.

After another hour the crowd starts to thin, the last of the stolen tulips having made their way back to us, until we're left with a few dozen dead and dried Goode tulips.

Our classmates don't realize they've just swapped genuine, curse-laced tulips for useless ones.

The delirium they felt, the lovesickness, will not return.

They will feel nothing.

The Beautiful Maddening

Archer steers the wheelbarrow back to the house, while I gather the old, dead Goode tulips from the dirt.

I thought I would feel different, knowing we've retrieved the stolen flowers—we've taken back what should never have been stolen.

But I feel hollowed out.

Maybe we've stopped the madness from spreading. We've prevented things from getting any worse. But I haven't remedied the source of my own pain.

Maybe this was never a story about a curse, about stolen tulips and mismatched love.

It was always something else.

Something simpler.

A tiny love story.

A *lost* love story.

And a summer I can't get back.

Four days evaporate behind me.

Locals no longer come to the house, begging for tulips. They got a free tulip. And although they must have figured out it is the wrong kind, a flower that contains no magic—a flower that can't bring them desire or affection—no one has marched up to our house complaining of such things.

Maybe now they can begin fitting their broken hearts back together—the lovesick and feverish dusting themselves off, a little rattled, a little hungover after a summer of delirium. But it wasn't their fault. It was a sickness, a poison, that plagued a handful of

Cutwater High students—a wickedness that most would rather not speak of.

A summer when they loved the wrong person. When they felt a wild, unnatural euphoria whenever they held a rare, blood-streaked tulip between their fingertips.

But they all know what it really was. . . .

The Goode family.

And with renewed fear, they will keep their distance, they will whisper our names in Lone Pine Coffee and on back porches, they will cross the street when Archer or I draw near.

We are to blame for what happened this summer.

I watch the garden, wishing the tulips would finally decay back into the soil. Maybe then I would feel like I could leave. Like the summer was truly over. Like there was nothing worth staying for.

No flicker of hope. No last chances.

But the tulips remain—even as the sun blazes over Cutwater, the afternoon heat turning the swampy soil to dry, cracked mud. Even when the creek below the house fades to only a trickle.

The tulips are defiant, refusing to die.

Footsteps on the front porch.

It's well after dark, and I'm seated on the living room floor, working on a sketch of Mrs. Thierry—shading in the deep creases around her eyes, her dog, Peebles, standing at her side, nose to the air—losing myself in the drawing, as if I'm shading over the memory of *him*.

Oak was a lesson. A lie. I learned the hard way, the worst way,

The Beautiful Maddening

just like Mom warned. What we had was only the start of something. Those first fragile moments together—the almost, the could have been but never was. The promise of something. And maybe that's what makes it so hard—not knowing what it might have become.

Eventually I'll forget.

But the sudden scrape and shuffle of footsteps sends a dreadful spike of hope straight through me.

Archer shoots me a look, and he reaches for the shotgun in one swift motion as he moves for the door. He pulls back the curtain on the front window, peering outside.

"Who is it?" I ask, imagining a boy, tall and shadowed on the front porch, eyes shaped by sadness, a thousand promises on his lips. A boy who could crack me open again.

But my brother doesn't answer. Instead he lets the curtain fall back into place, and he yanks open the door, letting in a cool evening wind.

Peering past my brother, I see the half outline of a boy.

But it's not Oak. It's Randy Ashspring—a junior—his light brown hair shaved close, his brown eyes all soft and pleading. He's tall, taller than Archer, and he stands with arms crossed, legs set wide on the front porch, like he's ready for a fight. I think he's going to ask for a tulip, beg for one, but instead he says, "She thinks she loves you. . . ." He stares down at Archer, and I understand at once why he's here. He's not the first angry boyfriend or girlfriend to get the courage to confront Archer directly. "She broke up with me, and she thinks she's going to run away with you."

I see Archer's shoulders relax; he's heard this so many times before, it's lost all its meaning. "Who?" he asks, sounding disinterested.

"Gabby Pines," Randy replies, his voice pitched, offended that Archer wouldn't already know this.

My brother blows out a long, tired breath—like he's finally growing weary of his own games, of the love he encourages, then must try to fend off. "Give it a month, man," he says, reaching forward and patting Randy on the shoulder. "Soon enough she'll lose interest in me and go back to you."

I see Randy's mouth gape open, about to say something else, but Archer closes the door in his face. My brother turns, shaking his head, and I can't help but smirk. Randy looked so dumbfounded—maybe he thought he'd have to fight Archer for Gabby's love, or maybe he was ready to drop to his knees and plead with Archer to leave Gabby alone. He didn't realize that Archer couldn't care less about most of the people who fall for him. And when the tulips finally sink back into the soil, the attraction that others feel for Archer will fade. He'll still be a Goode—he'll still be a touch more irresistible than anyone else in this town—but the charm will be diluted enough that someone like Gabby will likely go back to her boyfriend. The one she's meant to love.

I sink onto the couch as Archer starts for the kitchen, when there's another sound outside—a car this time, coming up the driveway. Archer frowns, flashes me a look, before turning back. "Who the hell . . . ?" he says, pulling open the front door.

I push up from the couch to get a better look.

And I see what he does: an old white Chevy truck kicking up dust as it roars toward the house, then lurches to a stop near the creek.

My throat dries up.

The Beautiful Maddening

My heart stops beating.

Dad . . . is home.

I watch, unblinking, as our father ambles stiffly out of the truck, his face sunburned, looking tired—like he's been driving all night—and when he peers up at the house, I feel my lungs cease to draw in air.

Archer and I watch as our father steps over the swollen creek and climbs the stairs. His brown hair is windblown and uncombed, and the sleeves of his green flannel shirt are rolled up to his elbows, revealing skin that's dark and weathered from working long hours on a fishing boat off the Pacific coast. He reaches the front door, shoulders dropping as he exhales.

"I saw the article," he says, raising an eyebrow at us. "One of the guys I work with found it online, showed it to me, remembered that I used to live in Cutwater."

He tips his eyes at us, waiting for a response, but both Archer and I are mute, standing side by side as if we were ten years old again and had been caught sneaking Mom's peanut butter cookies from the cupboard in the middle of the night.

"Start talking," he says.

Archer tells him everything. Every last detail about the stolen flowers and how we traded the real Goode tulips for fake ones.

Dad is quiet, eyes heavy—he seems exhausted. But finally he rubs his hands across his sun-scorched neck, then walks into the kitchen for a glass of water. He looks like he's been at sea for some time, his back always bent to haul in the nets, seawater in his hair, the salty air in his lungs.

Shea Ernshaw

"It's late," he says finally, staring down at the floor. "And I'm tired."

Archer gladly retreats to his room, but I stay, watching Dad walk out onto the back porch, where he stands at the railing, breathing in the muggy summer air. I follow him out and lean against one of the rotted wood posts that hold up the roof. It's a strange thing, seeing my dad here, in this house that he tries so hard to avoid. He used to visit once a year, near our birthday. But since Mom left, he's been coming more often. He worries about us, I suppose, but not enough to stay. Not enough to save us from this house. This life.

He wants out just as bad as I do. And he makes sure to stay away more than he's here.

"Looks like they got quite a few of them," he comments, nodding to the headless stalks.

"I may have cut down a couple as well," I admit.

He nods, like he understands—like he's considered destroying the garden a time or two himself.

I clear my throat, looking up at the man who feels more like a stranger each time I see him. "We could sell it," I say, an idea I've considered over the years. A way out. "This whole place. Then we'd be rid of it."

The garden did this to us, broke us all apart, sent us scattering. He was a victim of this house—of the woman he loved one summer with a Goode last name.

A woman he was *tricked* into loving, because of the tulips.

But if we sold the house, the land, we could walk away—all of us.

His eyes sag, and he draws in a long inhale. "It can be hard to

The Beautiful Maddening

separate the difference between right and wrong. Between fate and free will." He stares out at the rows of perfect blooms, the flowers that have ruined all of us. "I don't know what this garden is, why those tulips have a way of wrecking everything, but I know that this home belongs to you and Archer. And it needs to stay that way."

I want to tell him that he's wrong; I want to remind him of how Mom let him fall in love with her even though she knew it all would end when tulip season was over. But mentioning Mom hurts me as much as it hurts him, so I keep my mouth shut.

"I'm sorry . . . ," he starts to say. "I'm sorry I'm not here more. I'm sorry for leaving—it's just too hard for me to . . ." His eyes begin to water.

"It's not your fault," I tell him.

He winces at hearing these words, like the fault can no longer be pinpointed, not exactly. When I think of Oak, I feel the same way. It's his fault he lied, kept the truth about his father from me. But it's my family—*my mom*—that broke his. It's the Goode tulips that caused everything that happened between us.

In the end it all leads back to me . . . and this garden.

Love is a malediction in this family: a plague that tightens around the heart.

He was merely swept up in it, just like Dad.

Neither of them can be to blame for how it all started.

And this is why our father stays away—this is why it hurts so bad when he walks through that front door, when he sees Archer and me. *We* are the ghosts of his past. Of a time when he had no control over who he fell in love with.

And this is the point: *free will*. The right to choose who we love, to trust our hearts to know the difference between what's real and what's not.

This garden takes that away.

"I hate these flowers," I say under my breath.

Dad is quiet, thinking, while the wind briefly sways through the garden, a frog croaks from the muddy creek, and the stars reveal themselves behind a thin sheet of clouds. "You can't blame the tulips for everything." He looks at me, and I feel wrung out, a husk left to wither in the sun. "You might not like who you are . . . ," he says gently. "Or the life you were born into, but there are always things to be learned from your past . . . from your mistakes." I swallow down the tears, and it feels like he can see the crumpled remains of my heart, even if he doesn't know how it got that way. "And I hope you make a lot of them in your life. I know I have."

Tears break over my eyelids, and Dad pulls me into a hug, folding his broad arms around me. I can't remember the last time my father hugged me, and I worry my legs will collapse—I worry all the torments inside me will crack apart at once. "It's the only way you'll become who you're meant to be," he says, his own chest rattling with emotion. "Don't be afraid of who you are, Lark." He releases me but keeps his hands against my shoulders, holding me up. "Not all Goodes are bad."

I wipe at the tears dripping from my chin. "Can I come with you?" I plead, my voice tiny, a little girl again, all my strength gone.

He breathes, his eyebrows angled down like he's considering it. But when his gaze lifts, I know what he's going to say. "Sorry, buttercup. I got a job up north, in Alaska, for a few months, not a good place for you." He releases my shoulders, and I teeter. He reaches

The Beautiful Maddening

into his back pocket, pulls out his wallet, and extracts all the cash inside. A few hundred dollars, I'd guess. "I always thought you'd leave as soon as you graduated."

"Me too," I answer.

He holds out the wad of cash to me. "You deserve to see what life is like beyond this place, then decide for yourself where you belong."

I hesitate, staring down at the money.

"But I should warn you, the world isn't any easier beyond the borders of Cutwater. Life is hard no matter where you put down roots."

I nod, and he pushes the wadded bills into my hand. But when I look up, the softness in his eyes has changed. Gone rigid. He looks on the verge of tipping over a cliff, like a shadow has crept over him again, the memories of his own past getting too heavy to hold up. This house is a reminder of what he's been trying so hard to forget. A feeling he'll never get back. And I think he's been running from this town, and us, taking jobs farther and farther away, in hopes that eventually the past will rework itself, and it will be like we never existed at all.

"I leave in the morning," he adds, offering up a tight smile. "I just wanted to check on you, make sure you hadn't burned the place down, before I headed up north." His gaze sways out over the tulips, eyebrow lifted.

The light is gone from his eyes, but he touches my cheek, and I sense that this is goodbye. He'll likely be gone before sunup tomorrow.

The longer he's here, the more pained he looks.

I doubt he'll sleep; he'll toss and turn in the bed he once shared with a woman he thought he loved. Until he didn't. And in the early dawn hours I'll hear the sound of his truck rumbling down the drive.

He'll escape this place, leave it in his rearview mirror.

And I don't blame him.

I stay on the back porch, watching the tulips bend and twist in the breeze, stirred up by a wall of evening clouds. I think about all the tragedy that's burdened this family.

And I know I will never allow myself to get close to someone again. Like I did with Oak.

I sink into one of the rocking chairs, knees pulled up, head resting back. I listen to Forsaken Creek rushing beneath the floorboards, spilling out into the garden. I watch the dark rain clouds push away to the east and the sky become still and starry.

I search for something.

A way to heal this emptiness that was cracked wide inside me. I look for reparation. But it's not out there in the garden, under this somber summer sky.

It lives somewhere else.

THIRTEEN

I can't wait any longer.

I won't be the girl who lets just one more day pass, one more month, one more year. Just another girl who forgets to leave Cutwater. And ends up like everyone else in this town. Bitter and regretful, still dreaming of the life they might have had if only they'd mustered the courage to leave.

The next morning, after Dad is long gone, I stuff the contents of my life back into my suitcase.

I scan my closet, to be sure I haven't missed anything . . . when I find it.

I tried to forget, push it away from my mind, but the copy of *Peter and Wendy* rests beneath an old, moth-eaten sweater. I sink onto the edge of the bed and open the cover, finding the sketch of Oak tucked inside.

My eyes pinch closed, and I consider just crushing the portrait in my fist and throwing it away—destroying everything that's left of him. But instead I run my thumb down the curves of his face, suffocating on each detail: the way he stares up from the paper, his eyes dangerous and full of sorrow. Unforgettable. *Unforgivable.* In them I see all the words never said between us.

All the days I'll never get back.

I fold the sketch of Oak, creasing the paper across the pencil lines of his face, folding it into halves again and again until I hold a tiny square of paper in my palm. Tears soak the paper. My heartache held within its folded edges. I slide it into the pages of the book, hiding it away. Promising myself I'll never look at it again.

Archer walks by my doorway, peers inside, sees the suitcase. "You're really doing it?"

I nod.

"Okay," he says, like he knows it's real this time. "When?"

"There's a train at ten p.m. Last one of the night." In the dark I will leave Cutwater behind, and when the sun begins to rise, the Pacific will stretch out to greet me.

"I'm proud of you." He exhales, pulling the guitar pick from his pocket, tapping it with his thumb. "Make sure you say goodbye before you go."

"I will," I promise.

Standing alone in my room, I know what I need to do.

I retrieve my notebook, the stub of a pencil, and leave the house.

At the end of the driveway, I stop and stare up at the house that I have hated for so long. I open my notebook and press the pencil to a blank page. I sketch the sunken walls, the roof with its sagging eaves, the windows that look like eyes weeping from the moisture always clinging to the glass.

I draw its likeness in my notebook, among all the faces I've sketched over the years. The faces of people I've been too afraid to ever really know. My notebook is filled with memories, of ghosts, of my past. Filled with a town called Cutwater.

The Beautiful Maddening

This is what I will take with me.

So I never have to return.

"You running away?" a voice croaks from behind me. I turn, and Mrs. Thierry is standing a few paces away—she must be out for her morning walk, her dog, Peebles, sniffing at the tall wildflowers growing up beside our mailbox.

I snap my notebook closed so she won't see the sketch.

"The only reason to draw that house"—she nods up at the Goode family home—"is if you plan on leaving it behind."

I don't answer her.

She laughs from the back of her throat, like she already knows the answer. "Locals claim they're leaving Cutwater all the time." She raises a coarse eyebrow at me. "But they don't mean it. They always come back."

Peebles makes his way toward me, huffing at my shoes before he looks away, disinterested.

"I'm not coming back."

Her eyebrows pull up into her forehead, and her hand trembles against the leash as Peebles tries to tug her forward. "What about that boy of yours, the one named after a tree?"

My knees nearly give out—maybe I shouldn't be surprised that she knows about Oak. Mrs. Thierry knows nearly everything that happens in this town. Stolen kisses and secret lovers. Girls who run away and promise never to return.

"He's not *my* boy," I reply.

Mrs. Thierry cackles, drawing her thin lips against her coffee-stained teeth. "'Course he is. He walks by your house nearly every evening, slows at the end of your driveway, then keeps going.

Even a fool can see the broken heart inside that boy's chest."

What about my broken heart? I want to scream. What about the sharp edges left behind, the scraps rattling around beneath my ribs? Can she see that? See the blood spilling from my wounds?

"That boy is walking around looking for something he's lost," she adds, raising an eyebrow at me.

I glance up the road, toward the county line—in the direction of a home belonging to a boy with sad green eyes and too many lies on his tongue.

Mrs. Thierry watches me like she's calculating something, trying to see all my damaged insides. "It's good you're leaving—it's time," she says. And I wonder if she's ever tried to leave Cutwater, if she's longed for a different life. "I fell in love with a Goode once," she says, nodding slowly. "Your great-uncle, Albert Goode. And still . . . when I look at that house"—she nods behind me—"my heart feels bruised in places that refuse to heal. Your family has never been any good at love. You manage to ruin it for yourselves and everyone around you. Nothing to be done for it."

I sway a little on my feet. I never knew about Mrs. Thierry and my great-uncle Albert, who I have no memory of. But maybe this is why she wobbles past our house each day, looking like a woman who has been wronged by our family. She made the ill-fated mistake of falling in love with a Goode.

"I'm sorry," I say, because it's all I can offer. "I'm sorry my family has taken so much from so many people." *It's taken everything from me,* I think.

Lips pulled in, she squints at me. "Your family is cursed deeper than the soil that grows those wretched flowers—they're cursed

The Beautiful Maddening

down to the bone." She tips her eyes closer to me. "Get yourself as far away from this house, this town, as you can." She turns toward the horizon, the morning sun edging higher through the trees. "You know . . ." Mrs. Thierry looks back toward the Goode family home. "Locals used to toss coins and tokens into that creek that runs below your house. They feared it, but they also believed it held magic from long ago. That it granted wishes." She makes a low grumble in the back of her throat. "It was an unlucky happenstance when your ancestor Fern Goode bought this swampy plot of land and built his house over that creek." She grunts again, nodding toward the line of water meandering toward the house. "Yes, unlucky indeed. But some people are drawn toward bad luck—it calls to them, a hand reaching out for their throat. And your family has paid the price ever since."

The weight of my whole life sinks into my stomach, and I peer up at the house where I was born. We have been jinxed by love: we chase it, run from it, wish we'd never known it at all. We are tangled up in it—and it always leaves us wounded and alone.

Makes us bitter. Makes us monsters.

But it has tormented this town, too. Those who've had the bad luck to call Cutwater home. It has taken pieces of their hearts, ripped from their chests and never given back. Mrs. Thierry has suffered; she is a woman with memories of a man who took her heart but never loved her in return.

And I see her now—I see the sadness held at the edge of her frown. I see what we have done to her.

The tulips. The Goodes. This creek and the swamp.

All of it is to blame.

"You say people always come back to Cutwater after they leave,"

I say through my teeth, turning back toward the house. "But not me. When I leave, I'm leaving for good."

"Curses and folktales are for the Old World, not for this one," Grandma Georgie used to say when she was still alive, her eyes shimmering like a campfire in the dark. I remember very few things about her: the jingle of her cheap chandelier earrings, the burst of her laugh like a bubble popping in the air, and how she didn't believe the tulips granted us any enchantment—no unusual attraction, no charm that made us irresistible.

"If there was any magic in those tulips when Fern Goode brought them over the Atlantic, it's long gone by now."

She was a skeptic. She thought our family was foolish to tell such stories now, to talk about the tulips as if they had any power over us. And yet Grandma Georgie found herself entangled in more passionate romps and romances than Archer.

She was known to seduce even the hardiest of men in this town, the ones who seemed so sure-footed that no woman could ever pull them astray. But Grandma Georgie was a rarity, a woman who cared not for the consequences of infidelity—she lived with her heart held out in front of her for all to see. A woman who ran toward love with her arms wide open, bellowing with laughter the whole way.

I envy her—even if she was a little mad, a little too far off center to know what was good for her.

But as I stand at my bedroom window, watching the last of the sunset streak pink and golden over the garden, thinking of only one thing—*one person*—I no longer know what's true or right or good.

The Beautiful Maddening

Goode.

I should feel relief, knowing that my freedom is so close. But instead I feel only regret . . . for everything I've left unsaid.

If I could go back. All the way to the beginning. I'd tell myself *not* to fall for him, so recklessly, wildly. I'd tell myself he is no one at all. Not worth staying for, not worth sketching, not worth remembering.

I'd tell myself these lies.

To save myself from this pain.

I close my suitcase and drag it out into the living room, placing it beside the front door.

Thunder tumbles across the sky in the distance, a storm that may reach us or pass us by. I scan the house, taking in the details one last time—old, sagging couch, wood coffee table with candle wax burned into the surface, a rug that should have been tossed out long ago—when Archer appears from the hall. We stare at each other, both of us unsure what to say, but then he crosses the room and wraps his arms around me. I can't remember the last time my brother and I hugged, and the tears leak from my eyes to his shoulder. He smells like the tulips—a scent that is born into our blood.

"I'll call you when I get there," I say, pulling back from him. "Let you know where I'm staying."

He wipes at his eyes, and I can see he's trying to hold back the emotion rising to the surface. "It's hard to imagine what tomorrow will feel like, when you're not here." He shakes his head, draws an inhale. "But I'm proud of you. Get as far away from this place as you can."

I nod.

Shea Ernshaw

"I'll come visit you," he promises.

"No you won't," I answer, knowing he'll never leave this town.

He laughs, eyes watering. "I hope you find whatever you're looking for out there."

"I hope you find something good here."

"You know me, I'll be fine." He lifts a shoulder. "I was actually thinking of renting a place in town, getting out of this house."

"Seriously?"

"Mr. Sanchez has an apartment above the guitar shop. He said I could rent it cheap if I worked at the shop."

I smile at my brother. He may never leave this town, but maybe he'll escape this awful house. "You deserve something that's all yours."

He will always be the boy who chases love headfirst: without caution, without fear. He crashes into it, scraped knees and bruised elbows, he leaves fire and smoke in his wake, but he keeps on moving forward. He doesn't look back. He doesn't scan elm trees for old lost loves.

He's braver than me. But maybe he's also growing up a little, making decisions for himself that aren't bound by our family's destiny.

"Hold on . . . ," he says. He turns and jogs back into his bedroom, then emerges moments later. He grabs my hands and shoves something into my palm.

I peer down at a wad of carefully folded bills. "Where did you get this?"

He folds my fingers over it. "Been saving it," he says.

I lift an eyebrow. "Archer, seriously, where did you get it?" Doubting that he came by it honestly.

The corner of his mouth curls into a smirk. "Been giving guitar

The Beautiful Maddening

lessons for the last couple of years. When you're at school, I've been working."

I shake my head at him.

"I don't tell my twin everything," he says with a wink.

I hold the cash out to him, trying to give it back. "Archer, I can't take this. And Dad already gave me everything in his wallet."

But he pushes my hand away. "I want you to have it. You're going to need more than you think to start a new life out there. It's your getting-the-hell-out-of-Cutwater gift."

I feel the tears coming. "Thank you." I can barely meet his eyes, and he pushes me gently in the shoulder. I glance around the tiny house one last time, taking in every last detail.

The home that raised me. The home that cursed me.

I wonder if I'll miss it. If I'll think of it fondly, years from now, the dark memories fading with time.

Or if it will always feel like a place woven with the worst kind of shadows.

I swivel around, and Archer has grabbed my suitcase and is carrying it through the front door. I hear him descend the porch steps, hefting my suitcase over the creek. "I should have tried to borrow a car," he calls from outside. "Then I could drive you to the train station."

"I'm fine to walk," I answer.

I start for the open door, when my eyes flash one last time over the kitchen table, stacked with unopened mail. Love letters addressed to Archer. Most still unopened. Evidence of the madness that plagues us each summer. But there's something else among the heart-adorned letters.

A postcard.

I almost blink it away; I almost don't squint down at it. *Because it can't be.* But the handwriting is familiar. Sloped back on itself, loopy, carefree, written by a woman with deceit in her fingertips.

I move closer, staring down at the postcard.

I hear Archer walking up the steps, back through the door.

But my eyes find the return address, landing hard on her name. *Her.*

"Shit," I whisper.

A postcard from Mom.

I start to reach for it—my hands beginning to shake—but Archer is faster, and he snatches it from the table.

"What are you doing?" I try to grab it from him, but he back-steps away, into the living room. "Archer! Let me see it."

He shakes his head. "No."

My eyes flatten, confused, but a sharp, thorny memory tugs at me: moments when Archer hid something from me just like this, when he held a letter behind his back where I couldn't see.

A secret he's kept.

I lunge forward, and Archer tries to turn away, but I grab his arm and rip the postcard free.

"Lark," my brother shrieks. "It's not . . ." But he never finishes his thought; he must see the color drain from my face.

In my hand I hold a postcard addressed to both Archer and me.

"Why?" I sputter, my eyes clicking to his. "Why were you hiding it?"

His face crushes into a line. "She doesn't deserve to send us let-

The Beautiful Maddening

ters. She doesn't deserve to tell us where she is or pretend she's part of our lives."

The postcard trembles between my fingers.

"She sends them as if she thinks we care."

I feel my eyes widen, the realization sinking heavy through me. "There are more of them?"

My brother shifts from one foot to another, the creek roaring beneath us, filling my ears.

"How many has she sent?"

He turns, staring out the front window. "She's been sending them since the beginning," he admits coolly, but there is no regret in his voice. Only bitterness.

"She's been sending us postcards for three years?"

He nods.

"Archer, what the fuck?" I want to tear him apart. "You've been hiding them from me?"

He crosses his arms, closing in on himself like a little kid. "I was protecting you. She left us, Lark." He finally looks at me, and I can see the tears forming. "She abandoned us. And then she sends us postcards as if she's just on vacation, like we should be happy for her, living a life out there without us." He laughs, short and blunt, but it's an awful sound.

"Where are they?" I grip the postcard in my hand so tight that it starts to bend. "Where are the rest of the letters?"

Archer's face sinks—he looks like a brother who knows he's done a very bad thing but it's something he can't take back. "I threw them away," he says to the floor. "I didn't even read them."

Shea Ernshaw

My blood is fire, my heart a battering ram. I want to step forward and shove him in the chest; I want to shout. Too many hurts are fisting together inside me.

But I look down at the postcard still in my hand, the only one not destroyed.

This is why Archer often insisted on retrieving the mail himself—I always thought it was because most of the love letters were for him. But it was because he was keeping a secret from me. All this time.

"I should have told you," he says now, but I'm already backing away. He never let me decide for myself what to feel. All these years I thought she didn't care enough to even send a letter. It stacked more pain on top of the mountain of hurt. But she's been writing to us all along.

She never forgot about us . . . not entirely.

"Lark," Archer says again, but I won't meet his eyes.

"I don't want to talk to you right now. There's nothing you can say to make this right." He's blocking my path to the front door, so I turn and escape out the back door into the garden, gulping in the warm evening air. I stare down at the postcard, my whole body shaking.

Moonlight breaks through the low clouds, lightning snaps in the distance, but it doesn't rain. The sky is dry and sharp and awful.

I run my fingers across the smooth paper of the postcard, reading Mom's words through a blur of salty pain, each letter a piece of her—the *o*'s like yawning mouths, the *t*'s like tall steeples, towering over the other words.

We found a port in Sardinia, off the Italian coast. The weather has been warm but windy, and Lark, you would love the old

The Beautiful Maddening

stone buildings and the faces of so many beautiful people to
sketch. Archer, are you still playing the guitar?
I'll be at this hotel for the next two weeks if you want to write
back. Would love to hear from you both.

Love always,
Mom

Her return address is a place called Casa Gallasso. She's been writing to us, hoping for a response, for a letter back that never comes.

I feel ripped apart.

Archer denied me the chance to write to her: to tell her I hate her, love her, want her to come home, and never want to see her again.

He kept this from me. He didn't think I was strong enough. Didn't think I could handle seeing her words written with an airy ease, blithe and carefree, while she sipped espresso at some small café, the afternoon Mediterranean sun tanning her ageless skin. Living a life out there, without us.

My eyes rise to the field of tulips, the sound of thunder rolling across the skyline from somewhere far away.

I hear the front door shut, and I know Archer has left. The guilt or maybe the anger too much for him to bear. I won't see him again before I leave—and I don't want to.

Everything feels ripped apart.

I blink out at the garden—the thing that is to blame for all of it. For Mom leaving, unable to get away from this house fast enough.

For Archer loving all the wrong people and keeping Mom's letters from me. For Oak lying to me, loving me, when he never should have. For my own heart being turned inside out.

This garden has plagued me. It's ruined me.

I walk out into the tulips, the hurt of it all like a fist around my dried-up heart.

My knees sink to the soil, and I let out a sob.

What if freedom from this house won't really set me free? What if I'm no better than Mom—running away from the things I can't face?

I read the postcard again, swiping at the tears, but they won't stop falling. They leak into the already-wet soil. This damp, swampy land, this sinking house. I hate it all. I cry, and the sky answers back, thunder rumbling along the belly of the clouds. I dig my fingers into the dirt, ripping up the ground, and the rain begins to fall. It doesn't begin gently—it falls in sudden sheets. And with each gasping breath in my lungs, the thunder shakes the air, rattling the earth beneath me. I think about fate, about Fern Goode choosing this awful patch of ground on which to build a home, dooming every generation that came after him, to suffer the same heartache, the same loss of love, the reminder of the tulips growing right outside our windows. I think about the magic in this soil, the curse, the bad luck that lives in my veins.

I think how unfair it is that one man's decision to plant a few bulbs in this swampy dirt would plague me since birth.

Why can't I choose something different?

Why isn't there a way out, a way free from this dreadful life?

Why can't I destroy what's been sown into the soil? Destroy what Fern made, so I can begin again?

The Beautiful Maddening

Tears well against my eyes, stream down my cheeks. How much pain can one girl bear in a single day? In a single life?

Love is more than desire: It's power. Deceit. You can command armies with love; you can alter the world. As long as I'm a Goode, no matter how far away I travel, these tulips will still bloom, and they will still curse my blood. I will never know if the love others feel for me is real.

Real freedom is not a town on the Pacific coast where no one knows my name.

Freedom is a swamp of destroyed tulips that will never bloom again.

I tilt my chin up to the sky and I scream. I tell the storm that I hate this place, every last inch of it. I beg the rain to take it away, to rip this land up from the bedrock and carry it out into the woods, as if it were never here at all.

With my broken heart beating hollow and empty inside me, I weep, and I plead, and I wish this house had never been built over the creek; I wish Fern Goode had never sailed across the Atlantic. I wish these tulips had never pushed their way to the surface, greedy and full of false love. Full of lies. Full of spite.

And strangely, with force, the storm replies.

My feet, my knees, feel suddenly cold and wet. The ground beneath me turns soft, muddy, as if a tide were rising up from the dirt, a lake bubbling to the surface. I wipe at my eyes and turn back to see Forsaken Creek has swelled beyond its banks and is now spilling outward like a dam that's burst.

I push myself up, water swirling around me, rushing with the force of a river.

The sky snaps again, lightning flaring across the horizon, and the rain throws itself over me like tiny pebbles stinging my skin. I push through the rising swell of the creek, now flooding through the garden, and wade up to the porch, grabbing the sagging railing to pull myself up the steps.

I stand for moment, staring out at the downpour—stunned. I've never seen anything like it. Nearly a foot of water now surges among the tulip stalks, making them sway and bend against one another. Threatening to snap.

But it's not only the garden that heaves against the force of the water. The porch beneath me begins to shift unsteadily, the posts in the ground starting to lose their footing.

My heart thuds. This is not a normal rainstorm; this is something else. Violent and unnatural. A torrent that is only getting worse.

Shit.

I turn for the door and scramble back inside. But the sound of the storm beats against the roof, and I can hear that the creek—usually a gentle stream spilling over rocks—is now a roar, tearing away the soil beneath the floorboards.

I sprint down the hall and duck into Archer's room to be sure he hasn't returned, but I find his room empty. The lights overhead flicker, then go out. There is a loud *pop* sound from the kitchen, and I know one of the circuits has blown. We've lost all power. The usual hum of the refrigerator has gone quiet, and back in the living room, all I can hear is the screaming wind, the echoing thunder, and the creek below the house becoming turbulent and angry.

For a moment I stand frozen, unsure what to do.

But the house doesn't give me time to decide. . . .

The Beautiful Maddening

It begins to shake and teeter beneath me.

I hear a loud crack, followed by another.

The house is separating from its foundation.

This is bad. My eyes cut to the front door, but the wall tilts strangely, like it's going to buckle. The window above the kitchen table shatters, glass exploding to the floor. I swivel around, and the garden is churning in the wind, everything blustery and tempestuous beyond the windows. But it's not the world outside that's swaying; it's the house where I stand. It feels like standing in Oak's rowboat, pitching from side to side as the floodwater lifts it up from the soil. I can't stay here any longer. My legs take a staggering step, and I find myself slipping back, the house now tilted, the couch beginning to ease away from the wall and slide toward me. I nearly drop to my knees but somehow stay upright, feet scrambling across the wood floor.

I reach the front door, grabbing the knob with both hands. But it doesn't swing open. It's wedged shut. The walls of the house have shifted, buckled, and I yank at the knob, panic rising in my chest.

But it won't move.

Shit. Shit. Shit.

Water begins to bubble up beneath the floorboards, cold and churning.

Fear wells up inside me, and I scream, eyes darting around the room. In the kitchen, rain pours in through the broken window. I stagger toward it, wet shoes crunching on the glass. A jagged layer of glass remains at the bottom of the window; if I try to climb through, I'll tear my flesh apart.

But I don't have a choice—the house begins to tilt onto its side, water spilling up from below. I slide a chair in front of the window and step up, when I hear a thud against the outer wall of the house. I pause, listening, and I hear it again, another loud smack.

My heart races, fear pulsing against my eardrums, unsure what's causing the sound.

Thud, thud . . . crack.

I back away from the window, from the wall, afraid the whole house is about to collapse in on itself. The creek sounds like a torrent, a river expanding and swelling outward, swallowing up everything.

My eyes flash to the front door just as it cracks inward, wood splintering along the wall. I blink, trying to focus through the dark, and I think I see someone standing in the open doorway.

The figure moves toward me, shadows melting into shadows, and I almost slink away, my nerves vibrating, but a hand reaches for me.

"We have to go!" the voice says.

I can't speak. Can't think.

"Lark," he says. "Take my hand."

I feel his palm grip mine, and he's pulling me through the doorway, free of the house. But half of the front porch is gone, broken apart. I shake my head, stunned by the amount of water swirling around us. The house has drifted back, farther into the woods, and Swamp Wells Road feels impossibly far away.

"We need to hurry," he says, and my eyes look into his for the first time.

The boy I never thought I'd see again.

I open my mouth to speak, to ask him what he's doing here, but he's already stepping off the broken porch into the water, standing waist-deep. "I won't let you go," he says, his hands now reaching

The Beautiful Maddening

up for me. My ears ring, the storm thundering overhead, the house cracking and snapping behind me, but I reach out and he folds his hands around me, lifting me off the porch and into the water. Into his arms. My eyes flash back to the house, where the creek is carrying it away, into the trees, into the dark. Swallowed up by the storm.

Oak's hands are braced around me, keeping the creek from sweeping my legs out from under me, and slowly we wade through the deep water, until it turns shallow, and we manage to reach the grassy bank. I want to sink to the ground, but Oak won't let me. "It's not safe," he says, urging me up the edge of the creek that has now become a river, until we reach Swamp Wells Road. His truck is parked on the wet pavement, the ditch along the road surging with water.

He opens the passenger door and lifts me inside.

The sound of the storm is instantly dulled. Only the thump of my heartbeat fills my ears. I close my eyes, telling myself to breathe. Telling myself that this is all a nightmare, and if I focus hard enough, I'll finally wake.

But when Oak opens the driver's side door and pulls himself inside, all the noise comes roaring back into focus. The rain against the metal roof, the wind howling against the windshield.

He turns the key in the ignition, and heat begins pouring from the vents. I realize for the first time that I'm shaking. Oak wraps something around my shoulders, a sweatshirt, and I open my eyes, holding my hands toward the vents.

Finally I look to the window, and I see what's been lost.

The sky is gray and wet. At the end of our driveway . . . the house is gone.

Not even a memory of it remains. The creek carried it away, pulled it out to Rabbit Cross River, where it will surely break apart, board by board, year by year, dismantled along the banks. Our past taken with it. But it's not just the house that's vanished.

The garden has been ripped from the soil.

Every bulb, every petal, torn away.

The creek took it all.

Gone.

I'm finding it hard to breathe, to slow my thoughts. Witnessing the loss of everything.

"I'm sorry," I hear Oak say. As if I should feel sad, as if I should begin to cry. But I feel tangled up, spun inside out. I feel something intangible, unnameable. Unfathomable.

Loss, but also . . .

I lower my hands from the vents, my body no longer trembling. "What are you doing here?" I ask.

He breathes, is quiet, then absently reaches into his back pocket, retrieves the paperback he always keeps there, and tosses it onto the dashboard, settling back into the seat. The book is wet, soaked through, pages warped. But the heat from the dash will dry the paper. I stare at it as he clears his throat. "It looked like it might rain, so I thought I'd drive somewhere, instead of walking." He blinks through the windshield at the storm. "I drove over the county line without even thinking about it. . . . I—I didn't plan to come here." His voice is crisp, careful, like he doesn't want to reveal too much, like he's trying to keep himself hidden beneath the soft edges of his lips, which I can still remember against mine. But I already know— because Mrs. Thierry told me—he walks by my house each night. A

The Beautiful Maddening

ritual. A habit. A torment he can't shake. He comes here each night, whether he will admit it or not. "I was driving by your house when I saw the water."

"Nothing happens by chance," Mom would say. "Life is a series of predestined moments, timed perfectly, orchestrated by hidden threads that bind us to our destiny."

But I don't know if I believe anything she said anymore.

I close my eyes, listening to the rain, trying to make sense of everything.

"My suitcase . . . ," I say, suddenly remembering, sitting up to peer through the window, but also knowing . . . it's long gone. Carried away with the flood. I've truly lost everything. All that's left is the postcard in my shorts pocket and the cash in my wallet.

"You're leaving?" he asks, knowing what a suitcase means.

"Tonight."

He tilts his head back against the seat, his face a galaxy of memories—as if he can see every thought, every moment we've spent apart, every night I waited for him at my window but he never came.

The silence between us is like a needle pressed into an open wound. Sharp and precise. He is everything I've tried to forget, seated beside me.

"You deserve more than this town," he says through an exhale, like he's doing everything he can to keep himself steady. "I'm glad you're finally getting out." He blinks, and there is almost a smile in his eyes, like he once loved this about me—my dream of escaping this place.

"I always thought I'd be leaving something behind. . . ." I stare at the place where the house once stood. "But now there's nothing."

Not even a suitcase. No dry change of clothes. A hairbrush. Another pair of shoes. Even Mom's Walkman is gone. It was all taken by the creek.

This is the destruction of my whole life.

I think of Archer, somewhere in town—oblivious to everything we've both just lost.

The rain begins to slow against the hood of the truck, the thunder echoing farther to the east.

"I need to get to the train station."

Oak's eyes narrow as he turns to face me. "We should wait here. The fire department, or someone, will probably come. Your house is . . . it's gone. This storm might get worse."

"No," I say, feeling like I can breathe for the first time. "No one's coming. No one cares about that house. They'll hardly notice it's gone. They'll hardly notice when I'm gone."

Oak stares out the window, and there is hurt hanging in his forest-green eyes—pain that has no name. "I'll notice."

FOURTEEN

Oak drives me up Swamp Wells Road.

The worst of the storm dissolves overhead, lightning shivering in the distance, only a soft rain continuing to scatter across the windshield.

Seated in Oak's truck, smelling the familiar scent of tires and sunlight, I'm reminded of early-summer days when we drove with the windows rolled down, my hand floating through the warm air. It feels like a hundred lifetimes in the past. And for a single moment I pretend I am still that girl—naive and hopeful. I pretend we are two teenagers in love who will give this thing a shot out in the real world. I imagine his hand is reaching across the truck to grab mine. That we are leaving this town together.

Fleeing. Starting over.

I am a stupid girl.

He slows the truck, steering down Aspen Avenue, and the seconds are moving too fast. The truck rolls to a stop in front of the train station, and Oak puts it in park. His hands grip the steering wheel, like he's afraid to let go. Like he can't trust his own hands.

I draw in my bottom lip, not knowing how to sit beside him and not touch him—sink into his arms and breathe in his scent. River and wind and wilds. Not knowing how to say goodbye.

My eyes settle on the paperback on the dash. *Atonement*, by Ian McEwan.

A love story, tragic, if I remember right.

He follows my eyes. "It's about a man who loses the one he loves, all because of a lie. A rumor."

"Some rumors are true," I answer in reflex.

He shakes his head and says, voice so low it's nearly lost to the rain, "I don't give a shit about the truth."

Another long silence. Watching the rain against the windshield.

"I wish it were different . . . I wish I . . ." I want to say, *I wish I weren't a Goode.* But I can't apologize for what I am. We did this to each other. We broke each other's hearts. And wishing for a different past is useless.

He nods, breathing shallow, and his shoulders settle like he knows this is really the end. "I hope you get everything you want."

This hurts worse than anything. Worse than the time we spent apart.

His hands twist around the steering wheel, and I know . . . this is the last time I'll see him, and none of it feels fair.

"I don't know what else to say," he mutters. His jaw tightens. He is a brick wall seated beside me—no part of him begging me forward, urging me into his arms.

"I don't think there's anything left to say." The words are almost enough to shatter me—my own words . . . are lies. Because I want to say a thousand things; I want his hand to touch mine; I want him to say that there will never be enough words, never enough moments

The Beautiful Maddening

between us, never enough time. Because he's missed me so much that it's felt like death.

But he doesn't.

He closes his mouth, a subtle nod tipping his chin down, like he understands that it's too late for that. There's no going back.

He breathes, then finally speaks—saying the worst thing of all—so softly, I almost don't hear it. "It was just a summer thing . . . anyway." My eyes flash to his, but there is nothing there. No comfort. No regret. Only his words, and they feel like a rusted blade driving straight down to bone. Twisting. Shattering what's left of my insides. Ripping me apart. But I manage to nod, *agreeing*, even though I don't mean it.

This is the end of our story.

The tulips are gone, torn away with the flood, and maybe now . . . what he felt for me is gone too. The enchantment, the allure, has worn off. A thing he can't pinpoint, a feeling that was once alive inside him, has evaporated with the storm.

His heart no longer aches to reach out for me.

When I leave, when I'm gone, he won't miss me.

He'll hardly think of me ever again.

I wish I felt the same.

I wish I felt nothing.

But when my eyes skim over him, I know my thoughts are just as wrecked as they've always been. He rubs a hand down his forearm, and I think how impossibly beautiful he is, how he was the boy who made me forget, for a few brief weeks, how dangerous love is.

I want to say so many things, but I know it doesn't matter now. "Goodbye, Oak" is all that comes out. I touch the door handle, about to step out into the night, but he reaches for me, and I feel his hand against my arm. Gentle but pleading.

I don't even realize I'm crying until I turn and Oak is touching my face, wiping at the tears, pulling me into his arms. Maybe it's pity he feels, the last lingering remnants of compassion for the girl he once thought he couldn't live without.

I press my face to his shoulder and I breathe in his scent—the river at night, the sun against his tanned skin. Too long I've craved this, to feel him against me, to hear his heartbeat in my ear, beating wildly.

"I'm sorry," he whispers. "For everything."

I'm sorry too, but I don't say it. I don't know how.

I lift my head from his shoulder, and his horrible, beautiful, painful green eyes lift a millimeter to meet mine . . . and every part of me cracks into a billion unsalvageable pieces, dissolving onto the floor. *Don't look at me like that,* I want to scream. *Don't hold me so close that I can smell the wind in your dark hair. Don't let each word hang against your lips so slowly that I can imagine myself suspended against your mouth, tumbling, falling, smashing into you.*

Fuck. I still love him. And I hate myself for it.

I try to swallow, to dampen my throat enough to speak, but all the right words are now the wrong ones.

I miss you.

Don't drive away.

I love you.

I always have.

. . . I still do.

His mouth is only inches from mine; it hovers so close, I could—

The Beautiful Maddening

Tears stream down my cheeks, and I want to scream—I want to be a million miles away from here and I want to be nowhere else. I want . . .

I want . . .

"Lark . . ." The name leaves his mouth, as if it were a question, as if it were a devotion, a desire. A request.

Heat roars in my cheeks. I feel his heart racing beneath my palm, and the divide between us evaporates, as if the particles of air couldn't possibly exist between us. As if nothing would dare separate us. As if fate were a force stronger than any fear coiled tight in my chest.

His lips hover over mine. Barely touching all the hurt I hold, both of us scared to death. Both of us unable to pull away. Both of us . . . lost in a future we can never have.

And maybe this is why.

We have nothing more to lose. . . .

I breathe, unable to hold myself steady another second more. I press my mouth to his, deep and angry and broken. I let my lips sink in; I let myself forget every moment before this one. I don't care if I shouldn't. If it'll only make the goodbye harder. I kiss him. I kiss the only boy I've ever dared to press my mouth against, and I feel his warm, dangerous fingertip slide carefully along my jaw, behind my ear, into my hair at the base of my neck.

I kiss him for every minute we lost with each other.

I kiss him for every night I lay awake, wishing I could touch him again.

I kiss him for every line of his face I drew with my pencil, etching him into memory.

And he kisses me back, ferociously, like he knows I'm going to slip from his grasp. Eventually. Always. Like he knows what he feels for me is long gone. And this is the last goodbye.

Because it's my heart that feels shredded, that feels tangled up in the sway of his mouth, his hands as they slide up the back of my shirt, soaked with rain, against my skin. I feel dizzy and drunk and like I'd trade everything to be with him. Sacrifice every plan I've made. I'd give it all up, *all of it*, just to hold on to this feeling, just to be here with him in the warmth of his truck, the rain falling down, and forget about the life waiting for me beyond this town.

I am a stupid girl, I think again. But I don't care.

His mouth finds my throat, and I hope he never lets go. I hope time stalls on this moment, refuses to click forward. I hope this isn't a dream. I hope I never wake. Why do his hands feel like relief against my skin, like the only thing I need?

My eyelids flutter open; I need to remind myself to breathe. . . .

I blink and stare at the paperback on the dash. *Atonement.* A story of loss and heartache and passion. I think of how he's touched its pages like he touches me now. I think of the stories resting beneath his skin. I think of how we are a story that keeps weaving together.

Fated.

Predestined.

Doomed.

I think how impossible it is to forget him. His hands trace my rib bones, and I think of the first time I saw him, standing in the parking lot, shoulder pressed to a tree, a book in his hand. I remember how he looked walking away.

And I hated it. Even then. Before I knew his name.

I hated seeing him striding away from me, not knowing whether

The Beautiful Maddening

I'd ever see him again, whether his eyes would ever peer into mine. I knew I needed to be closer to him, even then. Even when I tried to push the thought away.

He was always there, beneath my skin, as if he were stronger than the curse.

As if he might be the only thing to save me.

But he wasn't. It was all a lie.

His mouth strays over mine, and I feel myself unraveling again beneath his hands, forgetting about the train, about leaving, about the house carried away into the trees. But I can't pull my eyes from the book, something about it . . . something keeps me glued to its wrinkled pages, still damp from the flood. They fan open slightly, the pages beginning to dry, heat pouring from the vents, and there is something there. Pressed flat.

Innocent and delicate—tucked between the pages.

Hidden.

Safe.

I narrow my gaze, trying to see. . . .

A cruel, treacherous *red* against the white of the paper.

Bloodred.

Angry red.

Lying red.

Oak's mouth stalls against mine. "What's wrong?"

I reach out—Oak's hands pressed against my ribs—and I grasp the silky petals. It's flattened from the book, dried a little, lost its weight and moisture. But it's still intact, verdant—ready for its next victim.

Time squeezes against me, and the air falls from my lungs.

"Lark . . . ," he begins, his dark eyebrows pinched, his full lips still hovering so close to me, I could sink into them again.

But no, *no, no, no.*

I push back from him, across the wide truck seat, until my back hits the cold door. "How long have you had this?"

"Lark, I just . . . It's not what—"

"How long have you had it?" I demand, feeling like my voice is going to cave in. My throat a desert.

He tries to reach for me again, but I shake my head. "Oak, where did you get this?"

I can see the breath held in his throat, see his mouth slacken. "It was just on the road. . . . It was there and I picked it up. I didn't think anything of it."

"When?" I sputter, the word tangled against my teeth.

"I—I don't know. A month ago, in the spring."

My vision shifts out of focus, then snaps back. "Where on the road?"

"In front of your house. I was walking by." His eyes are pleading, I can see he wants to move closer to me, but he resists. "I heard voices, girls whispering, it was late, and I saw them leaving from your house. They were carrying flowers, and they dropped one."

Clementine, I think, *and her friends.* It was probably the first night they raided the garden and stole the tulips. "You were walking by my house that night?"

He nods, breathing through his nostrils.

I try to imagine it, Oak striding up Swamp Wells Road that same night—maybe he'd been walking by every night for weeks, curious about the Goodes, about the family who broke his—until one night

The Beautiful Maddening

he saw a group of girls squealing and laughing as they sprinted away from the garden, dropping tulips behind them as they ran up the road toward town.

"I told you someone broke into the garden," I press. "I told you that someone stole the flowers, but you never said anything?"

"I didn't know who they were." He shakes his head. "And I didn't think it mattered, they were just flowers, I didn't know . . . I didn't realize it was so important to you back then."

My hand is trembling, my lungs are heaving in and out. "But you kept it," I say. "You found this tulip and you kept it in each new book you read. . . . Why?"

"I . . ." His eyes slope down. "I held on to it because I thought, I don't know, it reminded me of you. That's all. It wasn't . . . I didn't know . . ." He's grasping at his own thoughts, unable to pinpoint it exactly. But I know why: he kept it because of how it made him feel. Just like everyone else who's possessed a tulip—he couldn't part with it, couldn't let it go.

But this isn't the worst of it.

This isn't what makes my head start to whirl and crack.

If he's possessed a tulip—hidden in a book, tucked in his back pocket—this whole time, since the night Clementine and the others stole our flowers . . . If he's had it since the day he saved me from the mob in front of the school, since we lay on our backs on the train, since he held my hand while thousands of lightning bugs swarmed around us . . .

Then maybe . . .

It's not his heart I should have been worried about.

Maybe he never felt entranced, charmed, bewitched by Lark

Shea Ernshaw

Goode. Maybe he wasn't lured closer to me by a family curse that grew behind our house.

Because *he* possessed a Goode tulip from the start. Instead, I was lured closer to *him*.

Maybe . . . it's my heart I can't trust.

We've never known what would happen if a tulip was stolen, held, *hidden*, by someone who wasn't a Goode. We've never known what would happen to *us* if we fell in love with someone who kept a tulip secreted away.

And now.

I was afraid that whatever Oak felt for me . . . was a lie.

But . . . what if my heart is the one in danger?

My heart is the one that felt what it shouldn't.

Love is a mistress who will clench her fist around your heart until you bleed.

Mom warned us. But she never told us what might happen if someone else kept a tulip pressed inside the pages of a book and we let our hearts spill into theirs.

I'm starting to doubt everything.

My eyes begin to water, and the inside of the truck feels too hot. Too suffocating.

This thing I feel for Oak, this need, this longing I've felt for him from the start—a feeling I couldn't quite pinpoint—was never real at all. It was a feeling that came on much too fast, burrowing under my skin, making it impossible to forget him.

I felt fascinated by him. Hypnotized. Entranced. Obsessed with finishing the sketch. With seeing him again.

I shake my head, the realization slamming against my skull.

The Beautiful Maddening

It was the tulip—the one he kept hidden. Safe and preserved.

I never really loved him.

Ever.

I exhale, and it feels like a storm, a hurricane across a sea that will destroy everything in its path, and I snap my gaze away from him.

My heart was a lie, everything I felt . . . was a lie.

I clench down on the tulip, crushing it in my fist.

"Lark," he says again. But I shrink away.

There's nothing he can say. No words to put this right. Everything I've felt wasn't real. Whether he meant to keep this from me or not. It doesn't matter.

Everything he stirred up inside me only moments ago, with his mouth on mine, *wasn't real.*

It was the tulip.

I reach for the door handle.

"Wait . . . ," he says. "Please . . . I didn't know. It's just a flower. It doesn't mean anything."

I can see the guilt, the regret, behind his eyes. While the sting of tears rises in mine. "It means everything."

Our entire lives, others have been drawn to Archer and me like insects to lamplight. Dizzy and delirious. But I never considered what would happen if someone else possessed a tulip and I fell under the same spell.

I shake my head, the tulip still in my fist. "Like you said before. It was only a summer thing. And we can't be sure if any of it was real. If you and I . . . were ever real." I open the truck door and slide down to the pavement, the rain falling gently. I let myself look back at him. "Will you tell my brother that I'm okay? Tell him I left on the train."

Shea Ernshaw

Oak nods, and we stare at each other one last time.

Nothing more to say.

Nothing that can put these broken pieces back together.

So I slam the door closed, forcing myself to walk away.

I walk through the rain to the office of the train station, leaving Oak sitting in his truck, a boy marred by desire and deceit. Two things so knotted together, I'll never be able to pick them apart.

FIFTEEN

I throw the flattened tulip into the large trash bin outside the train station, among rancid food wrappers and coffee cups—a place I'm certain no one will try to unearth it.

I purchase my ticket from the tired-looking woman at the window, who tells me that the train is a half hour delayed due to the storm. But I don't care, I'll wait as long as it takes. I sit on one of the benches outside, beneath the awning, puddles at my feet. I'm still wearing Oak's sweatshirt, the one he put over my shoulders when he saved me from the storm. I want to throw it away too, leave it behind—it smells like him, like heartache—but it's the only dry thing I have. So I zip it up and promise myself that I'll burn it when I reach my new home. Other passengers stand around me with looks of desperation in their eyes, waiting for the evening train to arrive.

Oak's truck is gone. And my heart is in pieces.

Archer and I believed we had collected all the stolen tulips—we thought we'd set everything right. But we were wrong. One remained in the hands of the last person I thought possessed one. The person I needed, the person I could never shake from my thoughts.

Shea Ernshaw

And now I know why.

My mind carries me back to every moment I spent with him, trying to unravel the way he made me feel, looking for the truth. But the deeper I go, the more I understand: It was only because of the tulip. It was the reason I couldn't shake him from my thoughts.

The reason I stayed in Cutwater longer than I should have.

Our summer together was a riddle that had only one answer: a tulip he saved inside a book.

The drizzling rain has begun to let up, the sky cracking apart to reveal a ceiling of stars.

I thought Oak would be the one to alter the course of my life. But I broke myself against the fortress of his heart again and again. Overcome by a madness that was so terrible, so beautiful, I might be foolish enough to do it all over again.

I cannot be trusted.

Someone laughs, the sound echoing through the dark, and I lift my eyes to see a group of shadows striding down the road in front of the station. As they step into the overhead lamplight, I see Dale Dawson and Chloe Perez. They're making their way toward town, and Chloe sways a little like she might be drunk. Maybe they're on their way to someone's house or meandering home after the storm. But I see someone else trailing behind: Jude.

The paper chatterbox moves swiftly in his hands as he walks, giving a fortune to a girl who I think is Lulu Yen—it's hard to tell as they move in and out of the shadows. He peels back a paper corner and reads the words to Lulu. She laughs, throwing her head back, the stud in her nose glinting against the light from the streetlamp, then she hands Jude something small I can't see—payment for the

264

The Beautiful Maddening

fortune—before jogging to catch up to Chloe, her eyes shimmering from the secret fortune only she knows.

I haven't seen Jude since the day at the drive-in, when he touched my palm and told me: "Tears and rain . . . it's all the same. Forsaken Creek is the only way to leave."

I draw in a breath, understanding now—he was right.

Earlier tonight I cried, slumped over in the garden, and my tears bled in with the rain, flooding the banks of Forsaken Creek. Maybe this is only the story I want to believe: where fate has known all along how this tale would end. Maybe it was only a storm, maybe the rain filled the swamp, and it finally took away the house that's been threatening to collapse for decades.

Or maybe . . . the Goodes really are witches, sorcerers, conjurors of ill magic. Maybe I am descended from those who carried alchemy across the Atlantic, hidden in our cells. Maybe there is enchantment in Forsaken Creek. Maybe Fern Goode cast a spell into the tulip bulbs that made us weavers of fate, of destiny. Maybe I had the power to destroy the garden all along. I just didn't believe it.

Whatever the cause, Jude saw what would happen.

The future he told me that day came true.

But he also told me something else. He pointed to my heart and said, "This must break. This must weep, and then you will finally be free."

This part I wish he had been wrong about.

Across the road, the group is nearly out of sight, but I stand up from the bench and cross the sidewalk. Jude looks up, seeing me—blond hair curling around his small ears, freckles along his cheekbones—and he takes a step back, startled.

"I need another fortune," I say quickly. "I can pay you." I need to know that my future has changed; I need to know what comes next.

Jude's eyes flick to his friends, who have stopped walking and watch us with obvious nervousness. "I don't take money," he answers quickly, his eyes now looking anywhere but at me. "Only trades."

"I'll trade whatever you want."

But he shakes his head, looking down at his white Converse high-tops. "I don't want anything from you."

He's thinking of the tulips—the only thing of value I really have—the tulips that swept through town and broke the minds of everyone who possessed one. He wants nothing to do with them. Or me. He doesn't know that the tulips are long gone anyway.

"Please," I beg, stepping closer. "I need to know . . ." I hesitate, unsure what I really want. "I need to know that there's something better waiting for me outside of this town. I need to know that my past won't follow me wherever I go, that the curse is broken, that the tulips are really gone."

Jude's pale eyes soften, and he looks at me with a flicker of sadness. But he pushes the paper origami into the front pocket of his slacks, out of sight. "Fate is like a river . . . ," he breathes, cheeks hollowed. "Always pushing us toward something we can't escape." He tilts his chin to his shoes again, yet watches me through the length of his blond eyelashes. "Whatever fortune I give you won't alter what's to come. Maybe it's better not to know. Maybe you need to stop looking for fate to show you the way. You make your own way, Lark Goode."

The Beautiful Maddening

He doesn't smile, but there is a softness in his eyes, a gentleness that can't be conveyed in words. He turns away from me before I can ask anything else.

Behind me, a bell rings, and someone yells that the ten p.m. train is now arriving. Jude and his friends have already made their way up the sidewalk, laughing, safe and buoyant, like their lives haven't been twisted and bent by a curse since the day they were born. As if they have nothing to fear.

I board the train and settle into a seat by myself, peering out at the town I've only ever wanted to escape. I'm leaving behind the carcass of the girl I used to be. My home is gone. The garden destroyed. And if I'm lucky, the curse was carried away with it.

"You make your own way, Lark Goode," Jude said.

And maybe he's right. I've spent most of my life trying to run from who I am. Maybe now I need to run toward something.

The girl I'm supposed to be.

I make my own fate now.

Because I have nothing more to lose.

The train lurches into motion, clattering forward over the tracks, and I know—*I know*—I'll never see this town again. Once I leave, there's no going back.

A "summer thing."

A thing we couldn't trust from the start.

The train picks up speed, vibrating, a metal monster thundering through the dense evergreens, and I think of Oak, sitting in his truck when I said goodbye, the vacant look in his eyes. The hurt that rose inside me, and the pain I could see in him.

Both of us damaged.

I think of the cold water that rose beneath the floorboards of my house.

Maybe it was just a force of nature, violent enough to finally break the house free from the dirt, to upend the tulips. Or maybe it was something else.

The end of a story written long ago by Fern Goode.

My tears swelling the banks of the creek, the blood in my veins possessed by a sorcery passed from one Goode to the next. My heartache capturing the storm and thrusting it down to destroy the source of all my pain.

Whatever the cause, I'm leaving it all behind.

This is the fate I make for myself.

I want the history of the tulips, of our name, to be lost with time . . . and forgotten. Until no one remembers the Goodes or the madness that overtook the town one summer.

I tip my head against the window, the soft spray of rain covering the glass. I've spent so many nights atop the abandoned train car in the woods, dreaming of this, the sway and motion of a train carrying me, mile by mile, away from this wretched place.

This is the feeling I couldn't name when I sat in Oak's truck and stared at the empty land where my house and the garden once sat:

Freedom.

SIXTEEN

The sea is darker than I imagined, waves thundering against the rocky shoreline.

I walk along the stormy waterfront, past cafés and taffy shops and bed-and-breakfasts, the rain soaking my hair. I feel adrift, with nothing more than the clothes I'm wearing and the hope of starting over.

I couldn't sleep on the train—my thoughts were too heavy—but I crave rest now, and at the end of town, I rent a room at a tiny motel—a cheap, one-bed room with a view of the rain-soaked parking lot. I fall into bed, and I sleep for a full day and night. A deep, unending slumber that feels absolute, the kind I might not wake from.

But the next morning, my eyes peel open, the room smelling of the sea, and an aching hunger clawing at my stomach.

I leave the motel and walk back down the waterfront to a small coffee shop facing the Pacific. Only a handful of customers are seated inside, and no one notices me when I walk to the counter. No one looks up from their lattes or cell phones. I am a nameless girl. Without a past—at least not one they know.

I smile a little to myself, unsure how to feel.

After ordering a lavender scone from a young girl who smiles politely, without fear or disgust or hunger in her eyes, I scan the cork bulletin board near the door. I read through paper notices for lost cats and waitresses wanted and lawn mowers for sale. Until I spot a handwritten note: *Single-room cottage for rent. Must like dogs.*

I ask the girl behind the counter if I can use the shop phone, and I dial the number. A woman answers. She tells me that the cottage is small, located behind her house, but it faces the sea—I just have to be willing to endure her two large dogs that often roam over to the cottage, and a baby grand piano that she likes to play late at night.

I tell her I don't mind at all. And I can pay two months up front.

It's nearly everything I've got. But at least I'll have a place to stay until I find work.

Following her instructions, I leave the edge of town while nibbling on the scone and walk until I reach a driveway overgrown with blackberry bushes that leads me along a small bluff. At last it comes into view: a two-story, gray-shingled house that looks like a layered cake, overlooking the ocean.

Margo, the owner, meets me in the gravel driveway with a warm smile and a cup of hot cocoa. I nearly sink into her arms with relief—this stranger. But she feels like a momentary safe harbor, and her smile is full-cheeked and easy. She is a short woman, with cropped gray hair and hands that are always moving: fussing and fixing. Her two dogs, Palo and Lox, follow us around the side of her cake house, down a short dirt path through the windblown trees, to where the small cottage sits atop the bluff, facing the gray sea.

"I've never rented it before," she tells me, the soft corners of her

The Beautiful Maddening

eyes wrinkling. She smells of cloves and rose water and sea salt. "We kept it for friends and family when they came to visit. But when Lonnie passed last year, I thought . . ." She stalls on the words, glancing out to the ocean, her cheeks flushed in the damp air. "It just made sense to make a little money each month. And I figured it might be nice to have some company." She flashes her hazel eyes at me, kind but strong. "I worried I wouldn't find the right person, but when you called, I just had a sense about you."

I cringe. If she knew who I was, she might think twice about renting to me. But as she unlocks the front door of the cottage, she makes a comment about superstition and folklore, and she hopes I don't mind a town filled with "legends and a few unshakable curses," because apparently I've just wandered into such a town.

I tell her I'm used to these kinds of things, and she nods gravely, like she's seen her fair share of heartache in this town.

"Looks like you could use a few belongings," she says, nodding at my lack of a suitcase or anything to unpack. "I think I can find you some clothes I've kept boxed in the attic. Probably not your style, but enough to get you by."

"Thank you." I feel like I could cry, but I hold it back, not wanting to collapse in front of this woman I just met.

She leaves me alone in the cottage, and I walk to the front windows overlooking the crashing sea. In the distance I can see an island and a lighthouse at its center, a beam of light circling steadily around, warning ships of its rocky shores.

This place feels steeped in something new, something I don't yet understand, but already, strangely, it feels like it could be home.

Two days pass, rain falling against the cottage each morning, a

271

grayness in the air I've never known before. But I light a fire in the small fireplace and curl up on the tiny checkered couch, trying not to think of him.

My insides feel rusted and corroded, like a juniper tree with heartrot—an awful decay inside the trunk, so that when you cut it open, there's nothing inside. Only a hollowed-out center.

If you cut me in half, would you find the same?

At night, before bed, I bathe in the old claw-foot tub, the medicine cabinet stocked with handmade soap and honey-mint shampoo. And I try *not to think of him*. The memory of his hands like an apocalypse on my skin that will never be scrubbed away.

Thankfully, when I stand at the bedroom window, there are no tulips swaying out back, no family history haunting the corridors of this cottage, no risk of uninvited love.

Sometimes I sit beside the fire, notebook folded open in my lap, my pencil trying to recall the likeness of Mom: the sad arch of her blue-green eyes; the distinct wave of her hair, the way it sometimes coiled at the ends; the soft shape of her lips—the same curve as mine. But I find it harder and harder to draw her to mind, the memory of her sliding away, just like the tide.

She is a woman I'm losing bit by bit every day.

In the evenings I follow the narrow path that meanders down to the beach, finding bits of broken shells and sea glass buried in the sand. I walk barefoot from one end of the beach to the other, through tide pools and rocky inlets, each step an effort to push him away.

I beg the sea to take him from me, to draw out the memory of his hands, his eyes, and bury it out in the deep. I beg for some relief.

The Beautiful Maddening

I watch the waves skim across the beach, the sun settling against the sea, copper and shades of apricot, until stars tiptoe out from the carpet of black—a night sky that somehow seems different from the one back in Cutwater. I find the brightest star, then swing my gaze to the right, finding the nearest one, just like in *Peter and Wendy*: "Second to the right, and straight on till morning."

I fled the real world and came to Neverland.

So why do I still hurt?

Why does every part of me still ache in a way I'm certain will never heal?

Tonight, with the sky smeared in colors of lavender, I start back toward the cottage—wanting only to touch him one last time, slide my fingers along his collarbone, up into his dark hair. But I know *once more* would never be enough. A hundred times isn't enough. I crush my eyes closed, but I see only him, *green eyes*, so I peel them open and blink out at the sea. "Please," I whisper to the ocean—an incantation, a plea from a girl who's so desperate, she's hoping for a bit of real magic, the kind that lives only in the sea, that exists only in a place like this. The night wind coils over me, smelling of lost loves and faraway wishes tucked in glass bottles, then set adrift.

I wanted this town to heal me. I thought it would feel different by now.

I ran away, but he's still here.

After sunset Margo insists I eat dinner with her on the deck just off her kitchen. She's given me two full boxes of clothes, which I take gratefully. Oversized sweaters, cotton shirts, and linen pants that she must have worn in her younger years.

She tells me stories about the town: a history that is riddled with myth and death and the unknown. And I start to wonder if most towns have their own legends. "Heartbreak is a powerful thing," she says. "It casts spells and conjures up dangerous magic—I've seen it happen. Never stand in the way of someone with a broken heart," she warns. "It can curse a whole town. Never underestimate what heartbreak can do."

Heartbreak can destroy a whole family, I think.

I ask her about finding a job in town, but she tells me that most locals are wary of outsiders, and it'll take some time to earn their trust before they'll give me work. But Margo offers to pay me to help her in the garden—where she grows produce in a square plot of land, as well as inside a small greenhouse, then sells what she harvests at a weekly farmers market in town. The labor of gardening has gotten harder on her aging joints, so in the morning I work beside her, pulling up weeds, watering, and thinning out the dead leaves until it's ready to be harvested. One afternoon she eyes me from across an overgrown lavender bush and asks if I have experience tending a garden, because I seem so familiar with the plants. I tell her we grew only flowers back home.

A cursed, awful variety.

On a rainy Friday afternoon Margo knocks on my door and hands me a small package. At first I'm certain she's mistaken—it can't be for me—but then I see my brother's small, abrupt handwriting on the box. I wrote to him after I arrived, mailing the letter to the guitar shop, to tell him where I was. It was a simple letter, not much more than a note letting him know that his twin was still alive, because the betrayal was still heavy inside me.

I've tried to imagine Archer returning to our house . . . to find

The Beautiful Maddening

it gone. Only a muddy scar in the ground where it once sat. The garden flattened. Our lives carried away with the storm. But he is strong, resilient.

Now I carry the box to the kitchen counter and cut it open.

Inside I find a folded piece of paper.

> I kept these buried beneath the pine tree
> where we used to have the rope swing.
> I'm sorry I hid them from you.
> −Archer

Below the note, held together by a rubber band, is a stack of envelopes and postcards.

All from Mom.

He lied when he said he'd thrown them away, when he said he'd never read them . . . because every envelope has been opened, every letter pulled out and read in secret. Because even if he hates her, he couldn't destroy them, couldn't sever the only connection to her.

He kept them buried in the ground, maybe in a coffee tin or box, because they're undamaged. Not eaten through by beetles or damp from the rain. They even survived the storm and the flood. Buried beneath the pine in the far east corner of our property, on higher ground, where Dad built us a rope swing when we were five or six.

Staring down at the letters, I wait for the anger to stir up inside me again, but it doesn't come.

I understand why he did it, and my heart aches, knowing the guilt he's surely carried—the burden of keeping these a secret—all because he wanted to protect me.

Shea Ernshaw

I forgive him before I've even climbed into bed and opened the first letter.

With the window pushed up in its frame, listening to the Pacific crash against the sand far below—instead of the awful shushing of tulip stalks swirling in the wind—I start from the beginning, from the oldest letter Mom sent, right after she first left. Slowly I fill in the last three years of her life.

At first, she apologizes often, writing to tell us that she made a mistake, that she shouldn't have left without a word. That she'll return home soon.

But then her letters begin recounting her travels—sailing across the Atlantic, perhaps the same route that Fern Goode took all those years ago. She describes eating in small patisseries and wandering cobblestone streets through ancient seaside towns. Sometimes she mentions how much *we* would love it where she is, or that she hopes to return to Cutwater in the following season for a visit, for our birthday perhaps. But then her letters will stray, postcards sent from towns like Marseille and Valencia, or describing the month she spent on the island of Sardinia, and she forgets about her promise to return home. Sometimes she mentions *him*. The man she says she loves, who rescued her.

Oak's father.

But she never says his name. Never reveals the truth about who he is—that he left behind a son who would find himself drawn to the Goodes, just like his father.

She is a woman who got as far away from her old life as she could. She ran from it.

And maybe, in some ways, Oak's father saved her from a fate even worse if she'd stayed.

The Beautiful Maddening

Because I think her life in Cutwater was slowly destroying her. Just like it was destroying me.

Still, I swing between bitterness and envy as I read her words, touching the photos of sun-bleached coastlines. I've never wanted to be like her, and yet everything about her life is what I've craved.

Freedom, untethered by a single thing.

Maybe I'm more like her than I've ever wanted to admit.

In one of her more recent letters, sent only a month ago, she describes watching a sunset over the Mediterranean, how a dog was barking nearby, and a woman was laughing, and how she felt completely alive. She ended the letter with: *If you don't risk getting hurt, then you'll never feel a thing. If you don't risk breaking your own heart, how will you ever know what's real or not? I was wrong when I used to tell you to avoid love. I was afraid. Because if there's one thing worth fighting for in this life . . . it's the person you can't live without.*

I fall asleep with the late-afternoon sun still suspended in the sky, and I dream of him, while my mother's words spin back and forth inside my mind. I dream he comes to the cottage, and we wade out into the sea, the sun winking off our salty skin, his lips pressed to mine.

I wake and throw back the bedsheets—hating the torment of my dreams.

Hating the days I can't get back.

Time is cruel. It does nothing to wipe clean what I want to forget.

Days inch by, the hours coated in mud. Slow and merciless.

I tuck Mom's letters back into the box, folded away, because her words won't leave me.

I was wrong when I used to tell you to avoid love.

I don't know what to feel. What to trust.

The evening is calm, the tide low. But my heart is a violent storm. So I dress quickly, needing to be free of the cottage, and I walk outside in my bare feet.

I could make my way down to the beach, stroll along the shoreline, but I don't want to hear the sea. I'm craving something else. Silence. A place to curl up and hide.

The sky is overcast, heavy and gray, and a few drops of rain begin to soak the ground. I walk to the small greenhouse and slip inside, breathing in the wet, mossy scent. I stand among the plants, and the tears start to fall.

I want to shout, I want to scream until there's no air left in my lungs, but I don't have the strength. And there is no one to hear my pain. No one to mend me back together. I wipe at my eyes, angry for all the hurt still tangled up inside me, and through the blur of my tears I see someone walking up the stone path, toward the greenhouse. I quickly draw in a breath, not wanting Margo to see the tears in my eyes.

She pauses outside the door, and I think she's going to turn away, head back to her house, but then the door pushes open, and my heart stops beating.

It's not Margo.

The outline is too tall, too familiar.

He looks like the boy who ripped my heart in two. A boy from a town far away from here.

I must still be asleep in bed, letters scattered across the quilt.

He lifts his head, eyes as dark and paralyzing as I remember them.

The Beautiful Maddening

Steady and sure, green and painful.

My mind has cracked, split in half, because he can't be real—he's a hundred miles away. The salt air is unkind and unfair. Maybe this town is haunted after all, crowded with legends and lore and cruel ghostly memories, just as Margo said.

But he takes a step into the greenhouse, the door closing softly behind him, soft droplets of rain scattering from his shoulders, his eyelashes. And every cell in my body knows that it's him.

All my thoughts drain out of me.

He looks just as I remember: Dark jeans, a little rumpled, like he's been traveling for a whole day. Hair damp from the rain, mouth trembling with all the words he wants to say.

My ears begin to ring.

"Lark." Four little letters fall from his lips. Four letters that turn my beating heart in on itself. My body sways, and I reach for one of the planter boxes to keep me upright.

Four letters I never thought I'd hear him say again.

"Archer told me where to find you." He breathes, and every exhale is like the wind. "I knocked on the cottage door, but when no one answered, I started to leave. Then I saw someone standing out here."

There is a hum in the air, a numbing silence, as if the sound of the ocean fades from my periphery, fades from the world, and we are standing in a glass house, soft rain against the roof, the sea roaring silently behind us.

"I'm sorry," he begins. "I shouldn't have let you get out of my truck that day. I shouldn't have watched you go. I never should have said goodbye."

He shakes his head, and every part of my skin is vibrating. Every inch of my mind is crumbling.

"I didn't mean to keep that tulip—I mean, I wasn't trying to . . . I didn't believe in it, I didn't know what any of it really meant. I just knew I wanted to be near you."

He risks a step closer to me. But I hold up my hand.

"Stop, Oak," I say, because I'm afraid of what will happen if he touches of me. I'm afraid of everything that happens next.

His mouth looks unsteady, and I wonder if there's a paperback book in his pocket, I wonder if he drove here or took the train, I wonder about all the little details, because I want to hold on to this moment before it's all ripped away. "We can't trust this," I tell him, my voice broken and blistered.

"But the garden is gone."

I nod, agreeing. "But I don't know if it fixed anything."

His eyes sway over me, like they're lost at sea. A sailor searching for a harbor. "I don't understand most of this—the history of your family, those tulips—but I know why I came to find you. I know that I lost something once, and maybe it's too late, maybe there's no second chances. But I had to try."

I look to the windows, watching the rain streak the glass, trying to catch my breath. Trying to catch the past. Make sense of everything that's happened. "How can we ever know if what we feel is real?" I shake my head. "How can we be sure that our thoughts are our own? How can we trust anything?" The air feels heavy in my chest. "I'm afraid we'll just keep losing each other again and again. That we'll keep making the same mistakes. That fate will always push us apart. And we'll keep hurting each other, until there's nothing left of us."

The Beautiful Maddening

He nods, sinking his hands into his jean pockets. "I'm afraid too," he admits. "But I'm more afraid of what it will feel like if I walk away. I'm afraid that if I go back home, every second in that cold house will feel like a lifetime spent wondering what would have happened if I'd risked something with you." His eyes fall to the floor, and he looks uncertain of his own words, his own thoughts. "But I'll go. I'll turn around and never come looking for you again, if that's what you want." Tears well at the edges of his eyes, and I swear I can almost see the pulse of his heartbeat thumping at his throat. "Tell me what you want, Lark. And I'll do it. I'll do whatever you ask me to."

The rain falls harder, thundering against the greenhouse, blurring out the sky. Blurring my memory of the past. My eyes flick to the door, the path back to the cottage. *My escape.* I could tell him to leave; I could stuff my heart back down deep. I could pretend I don't think of him every day. I could lie and tell myself I'm better off without him—better off not knowing if it was tulips all along, or if the curse was broken the instant the flood carried the garden away. Convince myself that what we had is over, gone with the shifting seasons. That we both hurt each other too much to ever go back.

"Lark," he says softly—and each time he says my name, it rips me open a little more. It wedges itself between my ribs and reminds me how much I've missed hearing his voice against my skin.

He pulls his hands from his pockets, shoulders dropping, like he wants nothing more than to reach for me, to sever the space between us. "It wasn't a summer thing for me. . . ." His eyes are shivering, hands trembling at his sides. His mouth a broken line. "It never was. I didn't mean that when I said it, in the truck. I was just trying to convince myself. Make it true. And it wasn't the tulips; it wasn't because you're a Goode. It was none of those things. We were like Peter and Wendy, tangled up in a fairy tale—in a town with too many lies. But we're not in Cutwater anymore." He glances around us, at the rain, the walls of the greenhouse, the sea beyond. "There are no cursed tulips growing nearby, no rumors about your family. We're just two people . . . without a past. Without parents to warn us of *their* mistakes. We can make our own. . . ."

He swallows, and I allow my eyes to tip into his.

"We could take a risk, Lark." He smiles a little, the tiniest shift of his mouth. "We could start over. From the beginning. No more secrets, no more tulips, no more curses. No memory of who we used to be. Only this . . . right now. We get to decide what we believe, what we want to leave behind. I don't care about anything before this moment." I can see the tears breaking against his eyelids. "I don't want anything from that old life, that town, that past. It's meaningless. We write our own story, not what anyone else tells us it should be. *You and me*, Lark . . . this is all I want. All I've ever wanted. And I let it slip away, I let you walk away, and I've regretted it every hour, every minute, since. You're the only thing I've ever really cared about. The only thing I want to protect." He wipes at his eyes. "I'd do anything to take back everything that happened. To do it differently. I know I screwed up so many times. I kept things from you, I lied, I was an idiot. But I'll gladly spend the rest of my life apologizing. I'll spend the rest of my life telling you that I'm sorry and that you are the only thing that matters. The only thing I don't want to lose. You, Lark . . . you're all I want."

My chest barely draws in a breath, tears dripping from my chin.

The Beautiful Maddening

I've spent too many nights awake, pretending I would eventually forget him—my heart drowning in every memory.

I've betrayed myself, fooled myself into thinking I could start again, in a new town, and leave him behind.

Curse or not, I can't shake him from my mind, my flesh, my lungs with every inhale, and now he's so close, I could touch him. All the words choke in my throat, all the fear breaking apart inside me, leaving only one thing, only one thought: *I love him.* Undeniably. Stupidly.

The wind changes direction outside, blowing open the door behind Oak, swelling against my thoughts, pulling me free of myself—a girl shedding her old, useless flesh. Scales and curses and all.

Only one word finds its way to my tongue.

"Oak." I step forward, the wind gusting through the greenhouse, and I slide my fingers through his, touching his palm, which feels like the river behind his house, like it belongs to a boy who I've spent too many nights, too many hours, trying to forget.

But I don't kiss him.

I lead him through the open door, closing it behind us, and we step out into the rain.

We follow the stone path up to the cottage and duck inside.

Rain falls against the roof; the moon rises over the sea. And I let myself forget who I used to be.

In the tiny, square living room, Oak's eyes don't sweep around the cottage, they don't survey the place I've made my home, they are settled roughly on me. Like he'll never look away again.

I pull my sweater over my head and let it fall to the floor. A puddle of rain at my feet.

He is still, and I am still. But I am no longer afraid.

Of anything.

Especially not him. Not love.

Oak watches me with lightning in his eyes, a shuddering crack of relief and hope and love all twisted together. I lift up onto my tiptoes and I press my lips to his, careful at first, like I will break him. I trace the shape of his mouth, slowly, and his hands find my waist. I sink into his arms, fingers through his dark hair, the scent of the river laced across his flesh. His hands scrape over my skin, but the *need* is different this time; this is desire that takes a lifetime to unravel. A thousand years will never be enough. We will need longer to etch each other's bodies and bones to memory. Lips like paintbrushes, fingertips the only way to chart a course.

Flames snap and hiss in the fireplace, heating our pinked skin, and I kiss the soft place beside his ear, drawing him to me, closer, *closer*, but it's never enough.

I want this moment to last.

Today and every day after. Until there are no days left.

He moans against my flesh, his hands pressing me to the floor beside the fireplace, as if we could sink into the soil beneath the cottage, until I am a girl made of dirt. Until we are both tangled up in the earth and the crashing sea.

I love him.

And I say it against his ear. I confess it, and I'll never take it back.

The night is starry and rain-soaked, and we lie awake, my head against the slope of his chest.

The Beautiful Maddening

"I won't say goodbye to you ever again," he whispers into the night, a promise, an incantation made of the truest kind of magic. His arm stirs, and he pulls me closer, eyes fluttering closed. I breathe him in, listening to his heart.

But after the night has deepened around us, I rise from the floor, slowly, gently, so I won't wake him. I wait for the old kettle on the stove to heat, then place tea leaves into a mug, and I watch him sleep. My insides hum.

I pull my sweater back over my head and step into my shorts. I want to walk out into the rain, I want to feel the cold drops against my burning flesh, I want to make sure it's real: Oak, the storm, all of it.

But I feel something in the pocket of my shorts.

A thing I forgot about.

It was so long ago now, the start of tulip season. Oak pulled me away from the mob at school, then plucked a tulip petal from my hair. I pressed it into the pocket of my favorite shorts, forgotten, folded away.

But now I extract the single tulip petal.

It's flattened and dried, preserved. Kept safe and untouched. It didn't die with the others in the garden when the flood carried them away. A petal that's been tucked in my pocket all this time.

My eyes flash to Oak, his skin coppery in the firelight, breathing softly while he sleeps. I hold the petal in my palm, the last of a destroyed crop. Perhaps the last of the Goode family magic.

I cross the small living room to the fireplace and look down at the flames, considering.

With the garden gone, I started to believe, to hope, that the curse had been carried away too. But I've had a tulip all along. Hidden.

Even when Oak stood before me in the greenhouse and spoke about love and fear and forgetting the past.

I should burn it, drop it into the fire and watch it turn to ash.

But . . . *I don't.*

Because I love him so much that it hurts. And now I wonder, I fear . . . that this single tulip might be the only thing keeping him here.

I didn't want love this way—*like this*—a lie. But maybe it's all I will ever have.

All I deserve.

I'm bound to these tulips, whether I like it or not.

Because the pain I'd feel if I lost him again is more than I can bear.

So, with the rain pattering against the roof, I slide the tulip petal back into my pocket, and I sink to the floor, curling myself up against his chest, pressing my mouth to his sleeping lips. This boy I won't lose again.

"I love you," he whispers, half-asleep, half-mad with love.

I tuck my face against his neck, knowing a dried tulip takes up a small, imperceptible space between us. "I love you," I say back.

Because I do, more than anything.

And maybe it's wrong—keeping the tulip. But I don't care anymore. I've always believed I might be the villain of my own story: Lark Goode, a girl you shouldn't get too close to, or you'll tumble into a love you won't be able to find your way out of.

I was dangerous from the start, from the moment I was born into that house, wailing and shrieking, my twin brother beside me, the tulips blooming in the garden out back.

Love has always held more meaning for the Goodes: Love cursed us and spit us back out; it bit down on our bones and broke us into

The Beautiful Maddening

splinters. It made fools of us, lovers of us, filled us with regret and superstition and a thousand moments in the arms of those who loved us for reasons they didn't understand.

But maybe this is true of everyone—even those without the Goode last name. Perhaps this is just what love is: a thing meant for fools. For anyone brave enough to slip into its madness.

But now I choose love *and* madness. I drink it down.

Because what other choice do I have?

This thing between us is a perilous kind of love. The kind that should have broken us—defying all logic and reason. And this is why I won't lose it. Because it's mine. Messy and tangled, like the roots of a garden left to grow wild and untended.

This love was one I tried to resist. But it found me all the same.

I don't know if the tulips were ever truly to blame, or if they were simply a legend spun over the years until it became truth. Maybe the dried tulip petal in my pocket has no power, no meaning, but I won't take the risk.

Like Mom said in her letter: *If there's one thing worth fighting for in this life . . . it's the person you can't live without.*

EPILOGUE

There would never be a house built on that swampy stretch of land again. No tulip would sprout from the soil. The creek broke its banks and made jagged, fractured paths through the place where the garden once stood.

But from time to time, the spring air still chilled and sharp, someone wandering the shoreline of Rabbit Cross River will happen upon a single rare tulip sprouting from the dirt. If they're smart, if they've heard the rumors, they will leave the tulip right where it grows. But if curiosity nags at their thoughts, they will pluck it from the ground, bring it to their lips, and breathe in its sweet, intoxicating scent.

Before they've staggered back from the river's edge, their heart will begin unraveling from the safety of their chest.

The Goode family curse, like many fables, is something that cannot simply be washed away by a strong rain. It changes. Becomes something new and strange. More mercurial. More dangerous.

It is the way of all things.

So if you happen upon a tulip growing where none should be, petals white, streaked with red . . . walk the other way.

ACKNOWLEDGMENTS

A garden takes time, patience, and good weather to grow. This book took all of those things. Partway through the drafting process, I shelved this book so I could focus on my healing, and for a time, I wasn't sure if it would ever find its way onto bookstore shelves. But clearly it, too, needed time to breathe and bloom into the story it would become.

Infinite gratitude to my editor, Nicole Ellul, for your enthusiasm and patience. There aren't enough words to express what they mean to me. Jess Regel, thank you for supporting me and this book every step of the way.

To my publishing team, thank you for all the unseen magic you weave behind the scenes. Special thanks to Jessica Egan, Alyza Liu, Krista Vitola, Amanda Brenner, Erica Stahler, Sophia Lee, Sarah Creech, Hilary Zarycky, and Sara Berko. Thank you, Mitch Thorpe, Alissa Rashid, and Caitlin Sweeny for making sure people know my books exist. And thank you, Justin Chanda and Kendra Levin, for giving my stories a home.

Thank you, Jenny Meyer and Heidi Gall, for ensuring my books are read in languages far and wide. Leo Teti, your tireless support of my stories has meant everything to me. Thank you, Heidi Spear, for your serendipitous timing, and for sending me photos from afar of tulip festivals. Thank you, Darcy Woods, for your endless encouragement. Thank you, Eileen Lock, for your support and friendship. Thank you, Mona Mensing, Dimitria Cross, and Traci Benjamin.

Acknowledgments

Big thanks to Nichole for loving my stories from the beginning. Thanks to Wendy L. McKee for your kindness. Hello to Jenn, Robin Holmes, and Sydney Bodenstaff.

To Haunani Sullivan, you are an inspiration. On days when I didn't feel like writing, I thought of you and kept going.

Lastly, Sky, I'd stuff a thousand tulips in my pocket just to keep you around.

ABOUT THE AUTHOR

Shea Ernshaw is a #1 *New York Times*, *USA Today*, and Indie best-selling author. Her books have been published in over twenty countries, repeatedly chosen as Indie Next Picks, and she is a winner of the Oregon Book Award. She lives in a small mountain town in Oregon and is happiest when lost in a good book, lost in the woods, or writing her next novel.